HERO'S NATURE

Hero Academy Series Book 3

P.E. PADILLA

PARTIAL MAP OF DIZHELIM

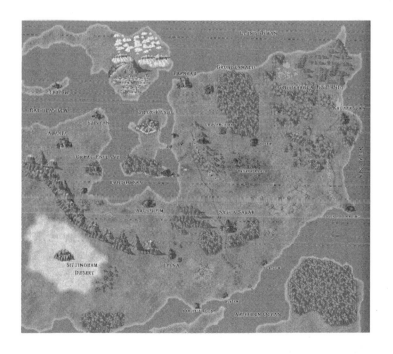

The arba, as a race, were fascinating, fantastical, and especially magical. Of course those of greedy disposition would destroy the humble naturists.

The War of Magic: How We Lost Our Way, and Our Power by Ahred Chimlain

PROLOGUE

Aquilius Gavros was the most powerful mage in the world. Sadly, not everyone knew it.

A glance at one of the mirrors in the chamber revealed that a few stray strands of white had found their way into his dark hair. He admired his reflection for a moment. Dark hair, nearly as black as the fur of an obsidian burrower —aside from the few offending white—and trimmed perfectly, not too long and not too short. He tilted his head to the side and lifted his chin. There were one or two grey spots in his facial hair as well, but that was fine. They highlighted the deep ebon of the rest of his hair. His beard, cut neatly into a point, was the height of fashion. A fashion he himself had started, he didn't mind saying.

The War of Magic raged, though there were whisperings of it drawing to a close. He hoped not. There were always some who believed it was ending. The War was good for business, good for his family. There were riches and power yet to be claimed. Pity if these things were ruined by peace.

"Quil?" the man who shared the room with him said. "Did you hear me?"

Vadim Plesca was an associate, a trusted companion from before Aquilius had gained his power and influence. One might call him a friend, though the term meant little to the mage.

Vadim was shorter than Aquilius by a few inches and his hair a touch lighter, a very dark brown instead of black. He looked the quintessential scholar or mage in his robe of subdued reds.

"Of course I heard you, Vadim. You are right next to me."

"Well, what do you think?"

Aquilius tapped his beard with a finger. "What do I think? I actually prefer not to think of him, if you must know."

"But, the news, the rumors. No, not rumors. The fact. It has been confirmed by several sources."

The darker-haired mage sighed. "Why? Why must everything be about him? I don't understand the world's fascination with the charlatan."

"He is the most renowned mage in the world," Vadim said. His eyes went wide at the end, and he stumbled to push more words on top of what he said. "I mean, he's well-known and...uh, people talk. About him."

There it was: that heat, the burning inside of him. Aquilius clenched his fists and closed his eyes. He breathed, counted to ten. Then to twenty.

"I shall talk to the emperor," Aquilius said. "He must be able to issue a commandment to prohibit the very mention of that name in the empire."

Vadim wisely chose to stay silent. He was a clever sort, usually. Aquilius knew how to be subtle and hide his emotions, but his companion was adept at teasing out Aquilius's feelings, usually accidentally. At least after he had done so, he was wise enough not to aggravate the matter.

"Regardless, this nonsense about building a school—"

"Academy," Vadim said.

Another sigh. "Yes, yes. Academy. This nonsense about building an Academy to prepare for the one he prophesied would come, it makes no sense. Why would he trade all his possessions, his resources, even favors owed to him, to fund such a thing? He is not a smart man, but he hasn't shown himself to be completely witless. Before now."

"Maybe, but he has obtained land, a great deal of it. Nearly the entirety of Munsahtiz."

"Munsahtiz?" Aquilius laughed. "That floating rock? It is of no importance. What will he do, while away his time secluded from society? Maybe he is building a secret base to continue in his traitorous activities, perhaps training assassins or insurgents there to fight against the empire.

"He pretends to champion nature. Anyone with a pinch of intelligence knows that nature is there only for exploitation. Have not the gods given us the abilities to use the natural world to make ourselves more powerful? He mewls about the nature goddess Mellaine and her realm, but we know that Migae, the God of Magic, is the more powerful and important."

Vadim looked at his feet, his face flushing. "And the prophecy? What of that?"

"Bah. Prophecy. I have the talent as well. Have I not proved myself a more capable foreteller than he?"

"Of course, but...but your prophecy seems to confirm parts of his."

"Yes," Aquilius said in a hiss. "Yes, it does. Perhaps he chanced upon a few tidbits of truth in his rambling. Purely by chance. No matter. I have thought it over and have decided what to do."

Vadim finally smiled. "Ah, I knew you would. May I know your plans?"

Aquilius met his associate's smile with a more predatory one. "Know them? My dear Vadim, you are part of them. You and I will begin a project at least as grand as his. We will form a council, one that will exist in perpetuity, long after you and I are gone. You, me, and eleven others we will select from the finest and most capable people in Dizhelim."

"Its purpose?"

"The council will monitor the state of the world and, more importantly, the progress of prophecy. My prophecy. It will find ways to interfere with the building of this academy and when the time of fulfillment of prophecy comes, it will snatch victory from any who elevate themselves to savior of the world. When the darkness comes, the council will be its champion and will maneuver circumstances to its favor. In the end, all will know that I, Aquilius Gavros, was the most powerful, most intelligent, and most deserving of acclaim. When the Dark Council rules what is left of Dizhelim, all will know who is responsible.

"No one will remember the name of the so-called great prophet and his silly structure that will have been destroyed, either by the darkness itself or by the Dark Council. The name of Tsosin Ruus will, if anything, be spat upon. My brother will fade into ignominy and only I will be remembered as the savior of the world."

⁂ I ⁂

Urun Chinowa, nature priest of the goddess Osulin, gasped and, by reflex, brought up his life shield. The magic shimmered around him in roughly a spherical shape as dark figures sped around him.

Right at his friends.

"Enemies," he shouted, then immediately felt stupid. The others had already spun to engage the attackers, their reflexes better than his could ever be. Which led to the question: *how did the assailants sneak up on them?*

No time for questions, though. Two of the dark creatures hammered on his shield, magic flashing as it mitigated the damage. He grunted and mentally threw more magic into his protective shell. It could easily withstand the attack of two enemies, but he had to focus to keep the shield strong in case more joined in.

Those of his friends who could create their own shields didn't have time, it seemed. Besides, Aeden had told him that their protective shells—at least his—worked better when missiles were being fired at them, not during face-to-face combat. It blocked from both sides, so the protected could not attack through it.

Arrows sprouted from the monsters attacking his shield, both placed perfectly in the eyes of the beasts. Urun nodded toward Tere Chizzit, who was already targeting and shooting other shadows rushing to have their chance at the humans.

It was twilight, not so dark as to prevent seeing the attackers, but definitely confusing the swirling black shapes and shadows around Urun. How many were there? It seemed like dozens, maybe hundreds.

Another flood of them splashed onto the party like a dark wave, this group coming from the south, where Tere Chizzit and Lily Fisher—formerly a Falxen assassin named Phoenixarrow—were firing arrows as fast as they could, trying to thin the numbers rushing to engulf the others. Tere cursed, slamming his bow stave into one of the attackers, and then let it go to draw his long knives. Lily, only a few feet from the man who was once called Erent Caahs, did likewise. The two of them moved with the same grace and strength, almost shadows of one another.

But the true shadows were several feet away. Jia Toun and Raki Sinde seemed to disappear and appear again, dancing through the dark patches of the battlefield, slashing at enemies and striking vital areas before disappearing from sight again. Occasionally, one or the other would throw some shape of sharp metal and end another attacker's ability to do damage.

But there were so many.

Aeden Tannoch cursed in some other language—Urun thought it might be the animaru Alaqotim the highland warrior had been learning from Khrazhti—and spun in between a dozen of the attackers, cutting down two at a time and opening up a little space. There were more, though, a seemingly endless supply of monsters. Teeth and claws enough for a hundred times the humans' number.

The battlefield was chaos. Dark twisted shapes flowed in like a fell wave and swept through the spaces between Urun's friends, attacking whichever of them was closest. Aeden motioned with his hands, like he was pushing something down toward the ground. Urun had seen that movement before, the last of a series for one of Aeden's spells. The priest was too far away to hear Aeden speak the words of power, but the effects were unmistakable. At least, they should have been.

Light flared out from Aeden, but unlike when Urun had seen the spell Dawn's Warning before, the dark shapes around the warrior were not thrown back. They didn't seem to be affected much at all. This time, Urun heard Aeden's curse clearly.

"*Cuir aet biodh!*"

Ah, that one Urun recognized as Chorain, the historical language of the Croagh aet Brech highlanders. Aeden's people, or at least the people he was born into before he was cast out. The priest didn't know what the phrase meant, though. Aeden was evasive when asked about his various curses.

Evon Desconse and Aila Ven cooperated with the Gypta woman, Fahtin Achaya, to watch each other's backs. It was for Fahtin's benefit, mostly, since Aila and Evon could take care of themselves more fully than Fahtin. Evon used a shield and arming sword, while Aila skillfully wielded her unusual weapons that consisted of chains with daggers attached. She called them vinci and used them to savagely slash the enemies.

Another group of the dark monsters passed by Urun, coming from behind. Only two stopped to pound against his shield, but didn't do enough damage to weaken it too much.

He pushed more magic into it anyway. The other creatures spread out, joining their fellows in attacking Urun's friends.

I'm useless, he thought bitterly. *I can't do anything but hold my shield and observe. The others are losing ground and getting injured, and I'm milling around like a rock that has lost its momentum.*

The two new attackers scratched at his shield with their claws but got nowhere. Reaching an equilibrium of sorts with his magic and the shield, Urun channeled a little of his magic into something else. Something that would maybe help the others.

With a flexing of his mind and a wave of his hand, he cast Life Blast. Magic exploded out from him and rushed at the enemies trying to bring down his shield. He was disappointed at the results.

One of the creatures was forced back half a step. The other leaned as if pushed by a strong wind, but lost not even a step. Urun muttered under his breath. Apparently he couldn't do anything but stay behind his shield and hope he wasn't important enough for more of the monsters to attack him.

While Urun looked for a way to help, Khrazhti spun and lashed out with her twin swords. The weapons were curved, almost like scimitars, in sharp contrast to Aeden's pair of blades shaped like the famous swords of Teroshi, single edged with the barest of bends.

The blue woman, once the leader of the animaru on Dizhelim, was a dynamo of blurring swords, fighting two of the more skilled opponents who had attacked. Both of them had weapons, unlike most of the attackers, who used only tooth and claw.

As Urun watched, Khrazhti dodged a slash from a large, two-handed sword and parried an overhead strike from a smaller sword wielded by the other attacker. In doing so, the blue woman stepped to the side, nearly bumping into Aeden, who had been spinning to block a sword and an axe from two other enemies while he lunged at a third with the sword in his left hand. A look of irritation flashed across his face before his normal intense battle expression smoothed it away.

The dark figure before Aeden batted the human's sword away with one of its blades and immediately counterattacked with quick combinations of stabs and slashes. The Croagh parried while slipping around another of his attackers, blocking the double-sword wielder from getting to him. While the enemy he held as a shield tried to get out of the way, Aeden ran it through with his blade and then danced back, out of range of the more dangerous opponent.

The creature with the two swords barked out commands to the other dark monsters and they immediately turned toward Aeden, one of them backstepping away from the battle with Khrazhti to do so.

Aeden valiantly attempted to withstand four of the more skilled, weapon-wielding monsters, but only lasted a moment. While he frantically dodged and counterattacked, the attacker with the two swords slipped an attack through Aeden's guard. It slashed the Croagh's left arm so seriously, the sword dropped from his hand.

There wasn't even time for a curse. Aeden whirled his single sword with a desperate ferocity, but the combined force of the most skilled combatants steadily pushed him back.

Urun's middle turned icy when Aeden got injured. He couldn't remember anything that had been serious enough to disarm the young man, even only one of his two weapons. The priest pushed toward his friend, intending to heal the injury before it made him pass out from blood loss or receive a fatal blow.

The two dark enemies were still banging on Urun's shield, though they seemed to be doing it out of habit more than a belief they could actually get through to him. He tried to push past them, but they stood their ground and he failed to move toward Aeden. His healing spells had a very short range. He had to nearly touch the one he tried to heal.

Urun tried to spin around the enemies, to use other combatants as obstacles to get through to do his healing, but the entire battle area was congested and his shield only made him larger than his normal size. He couldn't make it.

Off to Urun's left, a rush of dark figures swarmed Aila and Evon. The two fought skillfully, but there were too many—one of the attackers got past Aila and slashed at Fahtin with its claws. The Gypta woman barely blocked, but as she did so, another enemy came from the other side and slashed Fahtin's side with its talons. Fahtin screamed as blood splashed out, and she dropped to her knees, as if she were instantly weak.

No! Urun screamed in his head, but before he could voice his despair, the most skilled of the enemies—Urun thought the double sword wielder must be the leader—attacked Aeden with half a dozen strikes in the blink of an eye. Aeden, boxed in by other weapon-wielders, couldn't mitigate all of the attacks.

As Khrazhti cut down one of the creatures attacking Aeden, the Croagh himself was punctured by the leader's sword. The other followed and tore out Aeden's throat.

No, no, no, no, no. Urun's thoughts boiled down to disbelief. He had to do something, get to his friend. The priest lowered his shoulder and charged toward Aeden, intending to bowl the enemies over.

He pushed one aside before his momentum was spent. He had gone all of six feet.

"Aeden!" Marla Shrike screamed. Her sword and dagger blurred even more as she cut down several of the regular claw-and-tooth enemies. She had almost reached her twin brother when the monsters' leader shifted its attention to her and attacked.

Aeden's body had stilled, pulling Urun's eyes toward it, so he missed what happened next. By the time he looked back toward Marla, the red-haired woman was bleeding from at least three serious wounds. The leader, plus three more weapon-wielders, rushed her. She blocked two blades as two more punched through her chest.

She dropped to her knees and, when the enemies drew their swords from her, collapsed near her brother.

Things moved more quickly after that. Khrazhti, then Jia, then Evon all fell like wheat to a scythe. The enemies had turned themselves into an efficient killing machine, the core of it six of the more skilled attackers wielding weapons. They systematically targeted members of the party and killed them.

All in front of Urun, who they left completely alone.

Like a broken tool. A worthless figure doing nothing but taking up space.

"Enough!" a voice boomed. All combat ceased immediately.

2

Urun's shoulders slumped as he dropped his shield. Around him, the dead climbed to their feet, both the priest's friends and the dark, twisted creatures that had attacked them.

"Masters Yralissa and Yezras, if you please," Headmaster Qydus Okvius said as he stepped onto the battlefield, moving closer to where Urun and the heaviest part of the battle had been.

The animaru shimmered and transformed into humans or disappeared completely.

Aeden put a hand on Urun's shoulder. "That was a rough one. When they killed me, I almost believed it had actually happened."

"I know," Lily, the beautiful, red-haired archer said. "I didn't know things like that could be done with magic. It all seemed so real."

"Yeah," Marla said. Her hair was flame-red also, though not quite as bright as Lily's. The fact that he was surrounded by beautiful women raced through Urun's mind for the thousandth time, but he cast it out. There were other, more important, things to think about. "The Masters of the School of Illusion and the School of Conjuration and Invocation have worked together for so long to make simulations for student testing, even knowing it's magic doesn't keep me from believing it's real."

Master Yralissa Zinphinal and Master Yezras Farlingiam joined those gathered on the field. The blood that had splashed all over the battlefield and covered many of the combatants disappeared eerily as they joined the combatants.

The two masters couldn't have been more different from each other. Master Yralissa, the head of the School of Illusion, was a pretty, round-faced woman with huge pale-lavender eyes and black hair that revealed purple highlights as it shifted. Urun would swear it glowed. It always appeared to have sparkles in it, though whether that was simply a trick of the light or magic, he didn't know.

Master Yezras, the Master of the School of Conjuration and Invocation, stood several inches shorter than the tall Master of Illusion, was completely hairless, and had softly glowing runes of power adorning his bald head. From his pointed ears to his yellow eyes, he looked to be something other than human. Just what, the nature priest didn't know. Though the master carried himself with a politely reserved demeanor, Urun wasn't sure if he'd ever trust someone who specialized in bringing things into being where they weren't before and summoning creatures of power through magical means. Didn't that type of thing bring the animaru to their world?

The priest of Osulin blinked when the leader of the animaru attackers melted, as did its swords, leaving in its place a short woman with grey hair pulled back into a tail. Her face, a stoic mask of unemotion, was much too smooth and pretty for her hair color. Urun recognized her, though he'd never spoken directly to her.

Yxna Hagunai was the Master of Edged Weapons at Sitor-Kanda, the Hero Academy. Urun hadn't seen her fight before today, but Aeden and Marla were free with their praise of the woman. If anyone could have bested the twins in a sword fight, it would have been Master Yxna. The master shared a small smile with Marla, and the red-haired Academy graduate beamed. Not the expression Urun would have worn had *he* just been killed by her.

"It was a good exercise," the headmaster said. His perpetual scowl and the thin, pointed shape of his head seemed menacing, even when giving his approval. His pointed beard and mustache dipped as his lips formed a frown and the furrows in his forehead deepened. "What went wrong?"

Marla bit her lip and Aeden sighed. "We were outclassed. When they started ganging up on us, focusing on one person and throwing all their most skilled fighters at him or her, any mistake at all was instant death."

"It didn't help that the life-based magic didn't affect the attackers like it would with real animaru," Marla said. "I've seen Aeden's spell Dawn's Warning instantly destroy a dozen animaru around him and throw another couple dozen back head over heels. It didn't do anything at all when he cast it."

"Still," Aeden said, "if we are basing any victory on just one spell, we have some things to work on."

Master Qydus nodded, as did Master Yxna.

"I am sorry," Master Yezras said. "Between Master Yralissa and myself, we can reasonably simulate combat with a number of foes, the effects of weapons, and even injuries or death, but it is very difficult to refine the magic so specifically to react in certain ways to individual spells."

"No, Master Yezras." Tere bowed slightly to the man. "What you created was marvelous, more complex than I had ever imagined possible. Aeden's right. If we pin all our hopes on one type of attack or defense, we're asking for trouble. As we've seen recently, magic changes. Sometimes we can even lose it, as I know personally. We thank you for allowing us to practice safely. We'll need to analyze our performance and use the information to improve."

"I would like to take part in the analysis meeting, if possible," Master Yxna said.

"As would I," the headmaster added.

"Good," Marla said. "Should we move out of the sun and to a meeting room somewhere? I don't know about the rest of you, but being killed makes me hungry."

Several of Urun's friends agreed with the sentiment, but he couldn't even think of food at the moment. Marla was comfortable with the masters and with what had just happened, but he was not. In fact, the thought of the whole thing made him feel like his stomach would empty itself.

The Masters of the School of Illusion and the School of Conjuration begged leave to go and prepare for classes, while the headmaster and Master Yxna accompanied Marla and the others after they thanked and dismissed the Academy students who had played the part of some of the animaru.

It wasn't long until everyone took seats in a meeting room around a large table. A messenger had been sent to ask the kitchen to bring food and drinks, as Marla had wanted.

For a group of people who had been slaughtered by dark monsters, Urun's friends chatted comfortably and amiably.

"I'm sorry I failed everyone," Urun blurted out before the meeting could truly start. His lip threatened to quiver and his eyes felt full. "I couldn't get to anyone to heal them."

All conversation stopped.

"Urun?" Aila said. "We all failed. The enemy's numbers and the skill of their"—she waved toward Master Yxna—"leader and elite forces were too much for us. It's no one person's fault."

Urun chewed on his lip, wanting to say something, but

also not wanting to get into an argument. Instead, he shrugged and turned his eyes down toward his hands resting on the table.

The food arrived soon, and in between eating and drinking the entire group took part in the discussion about their failed battle. Even Raki, so shy he typically avoided speaking at all, managed a few sentences. He eyed Urun, one eyebrow arched, but didn't make eye contact. The priest would have averted his eyes anyway.

He wasn't really paying attention to the analysis of their performance. He couldn't seem to focus. No matter what they said, he knew it was his fault they failed. If he could have healed Aeden's injury—or taken the attention of some of those attacking him—things may have turned out differently. They *would* have turned out differently.

Healing was the very least he could do. He'd prefer something a little more...active, but even simple healing seemed beyond him.

He wondered about the future. With the animaru flooding into their world to try to destroy all life, what happened when Urun's friends repeated the day's failure? What would he feel like watching all his friends die while he cowered behind his shield, protected from harm for the most part? What would the world suffer if he failed his friends again?

THE ANIMARU HIGH LORD KIRRALOTH STARED UNBLINKING at the semhominus in front of him. He had found in his thousands of years in S'ru's service that such a look intimidated the recipient. Fear was a useful thing.

Kirraloth finally spoke after what was assuredly an interminable period to the other animaru. A mage, as it happened.

"You have sensed some magic?"

"Yes, High Lord," the mage said. "A very strong emanation."

"Where was this emanation?"

"Near the area we had been searching for the Gneisprumay, by the large body of this water that seems to be everywhere."

"Go on," Kirraloth prompted.

"It is unlike anything I have ever sensed. The type of magic is unfamiliar, as is the magnitude of it, yet I would not have felt it at all if I hadn't been close to the area with one of the search groups. It seems to...contain its effects in some way I do not understand."

"I see. What is it that you want...?"

"Zhadril, High Lord."

"Zhadril." Kirraloth knew the mage's name. He knew the names of thousands of animaru, definitely all the ones of sufficient power to merit his remembrance such as this former High Priest of S'ru. He preferred to withhold knowledge of his talents, be it magical or intellectual. Even after so many thousands of years, he would be underestimated if he were to be attacked. "What is it you want, Zhadril?"

"I would ask leave to go and study the source of the magic. If it is something we can capture and harness, it would mean another weapon against the fessani."

"And you would be the one to wield this weapon?"

"No, of course not. I wish to study it, to bring it to our side. I would present it to you, of course. You are S'ru's surrogate on this world. You would be able to decide better than me what should be done with it."

Kirraloth fixed Zhadril with another stony gaze. The mage fidgeted under the attention. "Very well, go and perform your study. Do not allow the fessani to know what you are doing or where the power is centered. The Gneisprumay has proved to be both clever and powerful. We do not need him to become more powerful."

"Yes, of course, High Lord."

"If it comes to it, Zhadril, you will accept permanent destruction rather than to let the fessani gain the power. Is that clear?"

"Yes, High Lord. Very clear. Thank you."

"Go," Kirraloth said. "Find this magic and make it ours, to S'ru's glory."

The mage bowed, rose, and quickly left the chamber, leaving Kirraloth alone with his thoughts.

He tapped a finger—more like a fessani digit than the claws of many of the types of animaru—against his chin. He wondered what type of magic Zhadril had found and if it indeed could be captured. S'ru knew they needed more weapons. None had predicted those from Aruzhelim would have so much trouble purging the world of the hated Gneisprumay.

On the one hand, the fessani were weak, easily killed. They could not even harm the animaru, for the most part. The Gneisprumay, however, the First Enemy of the animaru, could not only harm but permanently destroy the creatures of the dark. He had already lessened their troops by thousands, and it seemed he had shared the secret of harming the animaru with others. It would not do to fight large groups of enemies wielding the damaging magic.

Sometimes he felt as if he should hunt the creature down and end his life himself, but no. S'ru had told him not to expose himself. He was to command, to organize the troops and prepare for the bigger war.

He would do as instructed, though he couldn't help but to think that it would all be easier if he were given free rein to attack their primary enemy. Or the traitor Khrazhti. He growled, low in his throat, at the thought of S'ru's former High Priestess.

Both of the enemies would die, though, given time. Casting aside thoughts of the enemies and the mage who had just left him, Kirraloth walked over to his map table. This light-contaminated world was large and full of parasites. It would take time to conquer it all. He would organize the forces and fulfill his mission. Not only the Gneisprumay and Khrazhti would be destroyed, but the entire world, even if he had to personally kill every living thing in this new world himself. He might have to do just that, and he would do so with pleasure.

✻ 3 ✻

"**U**run, are you listening to me?" Aila Ven said, stretching her neck to look the priest in the face as she leaned against the table in the meeting room.

Urun Chinowa sighed. "Yes, Aila."

"Stop beating yourself up over the combat drill the other day. It's not your fault."

"Yes, Aila."

The woman glared at him. He swallowed. She was marvelously effective at glaring, for all that she was two-thirds his height. He immediately felt guilty for his tone.

"I'm sorry," he said. "I know you're trying to help, but it's a fact that I'm nearly worthless in a fight. And I was completely worthless in that particular battle."

"Just because you couldn't reach anyone to heal them doesn't make you worthless," she said.

"Fine, then tell me one thing I did that helped."

The dark-haired woman took her bottom lip in her teeth as her brow furrowed. "I...uh..." A moment later, she snapped her fingers. "Aha. You occupied several of the enemies so they couldn't attack others. They beat on your shield and so weren't part of the main fight."

He shook his head. "That's all you've got? I was a decoy? You just made my point for me."

"No," Aila said. "I didn't—"

"Stop, Urun," Aeden said, walking around the table they had been sitting at for another meeting with the headmaster and some of the other masters of the Academy. "Even if positioning made it difficult for you to do much in that fight, you are *not* worthless. You are an important part of the team, and not only because of your healing."

Urun turned to his friend and it struck him that yes, Aeden *was* his friend. When exactly had that happened? He had joined the group because the goddess Osulin had told her priest to stay with Aeden, that the fate of the world depended upon it. He was usually the voice of reason, the one who tried to keep the others out of danger. The priest did like Aeden and all the others. That made it so much harder.

"I know I have value outside of combat, especially after combat when I can heal injuries. All I'm saying is that I'm not worth much at all when we're in battle. I don't have the necessary skills and I'm a coward."

The young Croagh barked a laugh. "Coward? Come on, Urun. You're no coward. I would have to say you're actually brave."

"No."

"Hmmm," Aeden said. "I seem to recall a fight on the edge of a cliff over a river. I think I remember a priest—a priest of Osulin, in fact—who was told to flee with the rest of the group. It seems to me that the priest disagreed and planted himself in front of hundreds of dark monsters to help his friend, and by so doing saved his life. Does any of this sound familiar to you?"

Urun sighed again. "Okay, I have my moments, but lately, I haven't contributed when we've been faced with enemies."

"I can teach you to use a blade," Master Yxna said, stepping up to the group. "I am the Master of the School of Edged Combat, after all."

"Or I could teach you unarmed combat," another master said as she joined them.

Urun knew her name and her place at the Academy, but not much else. She was Shanaera Eilren, the Master of the School of Unarmed Combat, and she looked it. Her distinctly monk-like clothes were sleeveless padded leather with bits of fur in places that seemed odd to Urun. Her hair, white but not from age, was cut short with a stylish wave on the top. From her laced, soft leather boots to her leather wristbands, her appearance screamed formidability. He'd never seen her fight, but she was fit and moved like a stalking tiger.

"Thank you, Masters," Urun said, "but no. I'm a priest, not a soldier." He raised his hand to stave off whatever Aeden had opened his mouth to say. "I know, it sounds contradictory, but let me explain. I do want to help, but I don't want to spend time training in some discipline that does not bring me closer to Osulin or the nature that is her domain. I just want to do a better job of helping while still doing her will."

"Magic?" Master Isegrith Palus asked. She was the Master of the School of Fundamental Magic. "We can teach you offensive spells."

"Thank you also, Master Isegrith, but my magic has its origin from my goddess. I don't want to—and probably shouldn't—learn other types of magic. It seems almost sacrilegious to me."

"Yes, I understand."

"Listen, everyone," Urun said. "I do appreciate you trying to help me, but I'm not looking for help or advice. I may have to suffer through this on my own. I will talk with Osulin and hope she is in a position to speak with me. Communication has been strained lately, which doesn't help. She is facing challenges she refused to explain to me." His voice cracked, a dagger of sorrow lancing through him. He wasn't sure if it was because it felt like a slight or if it was solely his concern for Osulin.

When he had met his goddess last and she gave him a bit of extra power, there had been some underlying issue he couldn't identify. The goddess almost looked...tired. Was that even possible?

Fahtin nudged Aeden out of the way and pulled Urun into a hug. "I'm sure it's not your fault. With how everything is changing, I could see even a goddess having trouble right now. Maybe she isn't allowed to explain or she didn't want you to worry about something you can't help with."

Urun nodded, closing his eyes and allowing himself to sink into the embrace. When he first saw Fahtin, he thought she was the most beautiful mortal he had ever seen. He still thought so. He had grown very fond of her, but not in a romantic way. He couldn't explain why not. She seemed to be like a sister to him, as close as Aeden, almost a brother.

"Thank you, Fahtin. It's probably true, but that doesn't lessen my worry in any way. Like I said, though, this is something I'll have to work out. Don't worry about me. I'll be fine."

The beautiful Gypta woman released him and looked him in the eyes. "We're here. You know, if you want to talk or anything."

He smiled at her.

The silence seemed to stretch for some time before the headmaster, who Urun hadn't known remained in the room, cleared his throat.

"Speaking of training, I believe someone has recently said they were going to focus a little more on the healing arts." He pointedly looked at Marla, off in a corner of the room watching everyone but not taking part in the conversation.

"I have already spoken with Master Videric and will be working on a schedule for instruction and practicing on my own to improve on what I learn. I've been convinced that magical healing is valuable and of utmost importance." She flashed a smile at Urun and he got the not-so-subtle hint.

"Good, good," Qydus Okvius said. "And what of you others? Will you be availing yourselves of what the Academy has to offer? We are in special circumstances, and I have decided that any of Aeden's and Marla's allies may receive instruction as if they were officially accepted students of Sitor-Kanda. Our primary purpose is to aid those two; increasing the skills and knowledge of their closest associates is part of that responsibility."

Urun felt a pang of something. Was that guilt? Head-master Qydus was making an exception for Urun and all his friends, freely offering the opportunity to study at the prestigious Academy. For a moment, he second-guessed himself, wondering if maybe there was something he could—or should —learn. The feeling passed quickly. As he had told them: his focus needed to be on Osulin and the natural world. It was no time for him to be looking elsewhere for help, not when the answer should be evident within himself.

People started breaking off in little groups, no doubt discussing what they'd like to study. Urun was a little irritated by that. The world was ending, monsters from another world invading and trying to destroy them, and they were talking school? Didn't they care that the recent changes in the world, maybe to magic itself, were powerful enough to affect the one deity who had remained with the mortals of Dizhelim when all others left?

The priest forced down the sick feeling in his stomach. No, that was too harsh. They were good people, his friends, trying to equip themselves with the weapons they'd need to succeed. Osulin knew they'd need it.

He suddenly felt a strong need to go somewhere to pray. Several excellent park areas on the Academy grounds and the forest outside the walls where the vegetation was heavy made excellent places to commune with nature. Human interaction wouldn't solve his problem, but maybe some time alone in his goddess's realm would.

With a final look at the others, all engaged in conversation with their little groups, he opened the door and stepped out in search of a place for meditation.

❧ 4 ❧

"**M**arla Shrike," Master Videric Dewitte said as the red-haired Academy graduate stepped into the master's office.

"Master Videric. Thank you for seeing me."

"Of course. I was wondering when you'd eventually stop by my school."

"Yes, well, I've had a pretty full schedule."

"I imagine you did. And still do."

"True. I've been meaning to learn magical healing for some time now, but I always seem to procrastinate on it."

Master Videric sat at his desk, back ramrod straight, eyes turned to her. He was a thin, tall man, his narrow face friendly but dignified. He wore spectacles, and a patch of hair on the top back of his head always stuck out at odd angles. He looked like a harsh schoolmaster who had just begun to soften as he got older. Grey flecked his black hair. He didn't look old, maybe in his mid-fifties, but she knew he was actually older than that. He sighed.

"I understand. I can't blame you for it, I suppose. Most reach for the sword first and only think of the bandage after they get injured. You, however, have mastered the School of Mundane Healing."

Marla's face heated. "I've always been something of a loner, and with the structure of the Academy, I never thought of injury much. The medica was always here, and with no companions to watch out for, healing didn't seem a high priority, because magical healing can't be done on oneself. Just between you and me, I mastered mundane healing because the way the body works has always fascinated me."

"Yes," he said. "Many feel similarly about not needing healing. Without being able to heal oneself, magical healing may not seem worthwhile."

"I don't mean it that way. It's—"

"Peace, Marla. I take no offense. I fathom the opinion. Some people want only to help, to heal, but for those who may be called on to fight, I can certainly understand wanting to spend as much time training to not get hurt in the first place. My question to you is, what has changed?"

"I had always planned—"

"Yes, I know. You, with your unique opportunity to possibly master every school in the Academy, I have always known you would make it here eventually. But why now? What caused you to change priorities?"

This wasn't going well at all. Marla felt like she'd insulted the master, or hurt his feelings. Well, there wasn't anything she could do other than soldier on.

"I have been traveling with others, including my twin brother. It's not only me anymore. It would do me no good to survive because of my combat training if I can't help the others to survive, too. I need to be able to help them if they get injured, to heal them. Mundane healing is...too slow."

The master cracked a smile for the first time in the conversation. "Ah. Good. Very good. I am glad you have arrived at that realization. I'm assuming you will proceed as is your custom with other schools, taking private instruction and practicing to develop your talents on your own?"

"It seems the most efficient way. I can't commit the time necessary to attend the normal lectures with other students, even if I wanted to."

"I agree," he said. "If you took classes in the standard way, you'd never have enough time to master all of the schools. I have a long-standing bet with Master Goren that you will indeed eventually master all forty-nine schools. I do not doubt you will do so before I die."

"I, uh...thank you. I'd prefer it if I did so before *I* die, as well, which in a way, is why I'm here." She grinned at him.

He smiled back. "Of course. There are few better ways to ensure that you do not fall than to make sure your friends are still standing around you, able to fight as well. So then, we will discuss what you know and then I will supplement that knowledge. Do not be misled; I will require you to attain the same proficiency all other students must attain before they move on to more complex subjects and spells."

"Of course," Marla said. "I'm not asking for favors, just the opportunity to learn in the most efficient way possible."

"Very well. Incidentally, as I'm sure you realize, your knowledge gained from the School of Mundane Healing overlaps with my school. That should shorten the learning curve significantly. Let us review anatomy—human first—before moving onto instruction." He checked a clock on a shelf near his desk. "We should have enough time to get through a general survey of anatomy, physiology, and healing theory. Perhaps I can teach you the first introductory spell as well. All of that depends upon my accuracy in predicting what knowledge you currently possess, of course. Are you ready?"

"Yes, Master. Thank you."

"No, my dear. I thank you. You—and your brother—are the reason for this institution. There is no greater receptacle of my healing knowledge than you. Let us begin. There is much to learn."

Three and a half hours later, Marla left Master Videric's office, head full to bursting with information he had deluged her with after she demonstrated her knowledge of anatomy. Specifics of their conversation swirled in her head as she bounced toward her room. She didn't even pay attention to the path she was on, leading from the Medica to her quarters, her body guiding her subconsciously on the familiar route.

She didn't mention to the master that the reason she had been so interested in anatomy originally was to increase the damage she inflicted in battle. She hadn't shared that bit of information with him because he tended to be sensitive about people trying to undo his work and end others' lives.

But he'd been satisfied with her knowledge, and so he may have gotten a bit carried away in the sheer amount of information he threw at her. She'd need to go somewhere quiet later and chew on it for a while, figure out how it fit into what she already knew. That habit helped make her such a quick learner, though with the whole savior of prophecy thing, she supposed she had to admit part of her skill in learning new things may have something to do with magic and the need for her to be the best she could be.

The entire world was relying on her, after all. Her and Aeden. She smiled thinking of her newly found twin. It still didn't seem real, but it was definitely a source of happiness.

Marla forced her mind back to what the master had taught her, not only background information and theory, but her first healing spell. She couldn't wait to practice it. She would impress the master even more the next time she had a session with him. She would cast the spell for him, something he'd never expect in such a short amount of time. It would only take—

"Get out of the way, *girl!*" a voice said from what seemed inches away.

Her eyes snapped up toward the origin of the sound and then widened. Aeden was standing in front of her, looking an awful lot like a brick wall in his stability. He had a wry smile on his face.

"Ass," she said, returning the smile.

"You almost ran right into me. Again. This time, though, you were the one with your head in the clouds. Are we going to have to fight again?"

She laughed. "Not today, *boy*. I don't want to dirty my knuckles with your blood."

"Fair enough," he said, putting an arm around her shoulder and starting them walking again. "What has you not paying attention to where you're going? Anything wrong?"

"No, nothing like that. I just had my first session with Master Videric, the head of the School of Magical Healing. I'm going through what he taught me so I can start practicing my first spell. What are you doing?"

"Ach. I did some work with Master Yxna earlier, and just now I had a long talk with Master Isegrith."

"You're working on edged weapons combat and general magic?" she asked.

"Yes. Master Yxna said that with my ability and experience, I could probably test to master the School of Edged Weapons within a month or two. There are a few things she'll need to teach me, but she seems impressed with what I already know and can do."

"Of course she is. I know firsthand how good you are with those swords." She gestured to the weapons sheathed on his back. She'd rarely seen him without them. "That's exciting. Mastering your first school. Many of the students will be jealous. They're envious every time I master a school, and I've been here most of my life."

"It's not a big thing for me," he said. "Some piece of paper that says I mastered something is not going to impress the animaru armies, nor will it make me more capable of fighting them. I do like to learn new things, though, and Master Yxna is amazing."

"She is. What about the magic?"

"Master Isegrith, like other masters I've talked to, is confused as to how I can actually cast the spells of the Raibrech. Apparently, the magic of the Song isn't well understood. Even though the Raibrech is known, and some of the masters thought they understood it, they can't reconcile what I can do, especially enhancing some of the spells and making them more powerful, even creating different effects from the normal spells. Master Isegrith did say I seem to have an affinity for using magic, though. She muttered something about family traits."

Marla chuckled at that. "Some of the masters are annoyed I learn so quickly, too. They feel like it's cheating or something. I've had to put up with that for years."

"She liked it that I knew a little bit about the qozhel and how magic generally works. Thank you for that, by the way. Everything I know about it came from you and Evon."

Marla dipped into the mockery of a curtsy as they walked. It almost made her trip.

"I guess we have some work to do," he said, face going serious.

"We do. Anything and everything we can do to become better at killing those dark monsters and interrupting their schemes is valuable. I'll not let them take our world."

"Aye. I'm with you on that. I wish we knew what we're supposed to be doing, though. Training is fine, but we don't have any plans. It's like we're waiting, biding our time, until the monsters take the next step, and then we'll react to it. I'm not fond of fighting defensively. If I'm going to engage, I attack, not wait for the enemy to do so, because then he's dictating the battle."

Marla reached over and patted Aeden's arm. "I feel the same way. We'll figure out something. We have the greatest minds in Dizhelim here at the Academy. Any time now, someone will get an idea and we'll wish we'd had more of this down time to train and prepare."

"You may be right," Aeden said.

"Oh," she said. "Don't forget that I need to introduce you to my parents tomorrow. They're excited to see you, a link to my past. You'll love them. Everything I've learned about being a hero has its start with how they raised me."

Aeden smiled at her. "I wouldn't miss it. I'm so glad you had a good upbringing, even after being torn from the clan and essentially left for dead."

She smirked at him. "As if you're one to talk."

They walked in silence for a time. When they got to a split in the path, Marla headed left as Aeden continued on straight for a few steps. When he realized she was no longer beside him, he stopped.

"You're not going to *Batido*?"

"To where?"

"Batido, the dorm building where we're staying. Evon named it when Fahtin made some offhand comment that it's like an inn but it didn't have a proper name. It's Dantogyptain for *second home*."

"Ooh," she cooed. "I bet that got Evon a few points in Fahtin's book."

Aeden laughed. "I suppose. I've known her for six years, but I've never seen her respond to anyone like him. The boys in the caravan were at once protective and possessive of her. They all wanted to marry her."

"Of course they did. She's fantastic, and gorgeous, too. Anyway, I was going to go back to my room so I can think about what I learned today and to practice the healing spell Master Videric taught me."

"Oh." His smile slipped a little.

Marla looked toward the building her room was in and then back at her brother. She sighed. "I guess I could go and chat for a little while, maybe eat a meal with the rest of you."

Aeden's smile widened as she joined him.

The common area of the dorm buzzed with energy, as normal, when the twins came through the door. Marla did need to work on her spell, but a warm feeling filled her when she saw her friends. It was funny, how comfortable she felt with the others. She had never been social. In all her time at the Academy, the only real friends she'd had were Skril Tossin and Evon Desconse.

As she thought of her fellow Academy student, the blond-haired young man waved her over to where he was sitting and chatting with Fahtin. Of course. He was rarely far from the beautiful Gypta woman if he had a choice in it.

Aeden followed his sister and sat down next to Fahtin while Marla took a seat next to Evon.

"Hey," she said. "What are you two up to?"

Evon blushed for some reason, but Fahtin's face lit up and she bounced in her seat.

"The masters are going to study my visions and see if they can help me figure them out," Fahtin said.

"Really?" Aeden said. "That's great."

"Which masters?" Marla asked.

"Well..."

"Master. Singular," Evon interrupted. He wore a small frown, but it disappeared in a moment.

"Oh, stop," Fahtin said, swatting him lightly with her hand. "The headmaster suggested I speak with the Master of Prophecy—"

"A waste of time," Marla muttered.

"—and Master Marn said he's 'much too busy with important things to deal with someone's delusions.' Instead, he assigned Evon to study them in his place. So, Master Jusha and Master Evon will be helping me understand my powers."

"Don't call me that," Evon said. "You'll get me in trouble with Master Marn."

Fahtin winked at Marla, and the red-haired woman felt her attachment to the darker haired beauty strengthen.

"If you had been even a little assertive, you would be Master of Prophecy right now," Marla said, "and we'd probably all be better off."

"Let's not talk about that again," Evon begged. "Besides, even if it did happen, then I wouldn't be able to travel with the rest of you to do what's necessary to save the world. I'd be stuck here teaching students. I probably wouldn't even get any research done."

"A valid point," Marla agreed. "Still, it's fantastic that you can study her." She realized after she'd already said it that her phrasing probably wasn't the best. "Her visions. Yeah, study her powers and see if it's real prophecy. But Master Jusha is the Master of Psionics and Meditation. What does he have to do with visions of the future?"

"He says I might actually be transferring my mind to other locations or even times. There isn't a whole school for things like that, he told me, so he volunteered to help me out. Evon and I talked to him today, and he's already helped me."

Khrazhti, who had been sitting in a corner of the room, stepped up to them, waiting patiently for them to finish talking. She was extremely polite that way. Who'd have known an animaru would have such manners?

"Khrazhti," Aeden said, then threw a few phrases at her in the animaru Alaqotim. The blue woman smiled and answered. Something about what she had been up to and how she was. For the convenience of the others, the animaru switched to Ruthrin.

"I have spoken with the Master of Language and he wants to speak with me about the true—I mean, the version of—Alaqotim I speak. He rightly believes that it may be very close to the pure Alaqotim as spoken at the beginning of the Age of Magic, possibly during the Age of Creation."

"It seems we've all found things to do here while we wait for the next thing to happen," Aeden said. "Marla and I were talking about that earlier. It's good for us to try to improve as much as we can, or to help the Academy in their understanding. As long as we're ready when it's time to attack the animaru forces, it seems a good use of our time."

Marla picked up motion from the corner of her eye and, keeping her head pointing in the direction of the others, moved her eyeballs to determine what the motion was. She saw Aeden doing the same thing.

Lucas Stewart, the young Academy student who the masters liked to use as a messenger, looked around the room, his face nervous and tense. That wasn't too strange, though. The young man always seemed to have an anxious expression. He ran his fingers through his short, sandy-blond hair and his grey eyes scanned the people present, no doubt looking for the one for whom he had a message. When he caught sight of Marla, he seemed to take a deep breath and calm himself, then walked over.

"Hey Lucas," she said. "Are you here to visit or do you have a message for someone?"

"Visit?" His face went blank like he was being tested.

"It was a joke," she said, "though if you want to grab something to eat or drink, help yourself."

"Oh, uh, thank you. Actually, I do have a message. Everyone is to gather in the amphitheater in two hours, when the Headmaster and other masters will be making an announcement and discussing important things."

The message had the sound of a blanket announcement to be delivered to everyone in the Academy, meant to be repeated verbatim.

"Everyone?" Aeden said.

The young man turned toward Aeden and backed up a step. Marla didn't blame him. Aeden was impressive with his armor and the two swords he always carried. Plus, his resting expression was stern, almost a scowl, though not nearly as harsh as Master Qydus's. You had to know her brother to understand it didn't mean anything. She'd never seen him act unkind or even impolite, even when confronted with a rage-filled woman looking for a fight.

"Yes," Lucas answered. "All students, masters, and long-term guests are required to be there." He swallowed and couldn't seem to meet Aeden's eyes.

"We'll be there," Marla said. "Don't be scared of Aeden. He always looks like he ate rocks for breakfast."

"What?" Aeden said.

"Okay," Lucas said. "I need to go...to tell the others about the meeting."

"Great. Thanks, Lucas. We'll see you there."

The young man threaded his way between the people and slipped out the door.

"He's still got a crush on you," Evon said. "And he's still in awe of you."

"Please," Marla said. "All the younger students are a bit in awe of anyone who has mastered a school."

"Like I said, he's in awe of you. The crush is real, too."

Marla snorted. "He's a good kid. I think he'll be an asset to the Academy once he pushes past his bashful stage." She turned toward Aeden and the others. "I need to do some things before the meeting. I'll meet you all there, okay?"

She didn't wait for them to answer. She crossed the room and went through the door. Less than two hours. Well, some meditation on what she had learned and some practice with her spell would be better than none at all. She wondered what the big announcement was about, but then pushed the thought from her mind. She'd know soon enough.

Hopefully it was good news. But then, she knew better than to have such hopes.

5

Aeden hadn't been to the amphitheater before. It looked to have been scooped out of the base of a hill by a giant spoon. A crooked, broken spoon. At the bottom, terraces and seats stretched upward from the stage, forming a bowl made of rock and soil. It was more than large enough to hold the four hundred or so people there.

A student at the entrance told Aeden that the headmaster wanted him and his friends down on the stage. As he walked down the aisle toward the stage, he winced at what sounded like someone talking right next to his ear, then realized it was actually people at the bottom speaking. It mixed with the chatting of people on other levels, but still, it was a strange phenomenon. He made a mental note to keep his voice low when he was down there so he wouldn't be heard by everyone else in the entire amphitheater.

They didn't have to wait long. In a surprisingly short period of time, everyone was seated. Even Marla, who had shown up later than the others, had taken her seat near Aeden. As Master Qydus stepped out onto the stage, the noise died down to almost nothing. The headmaster hadn't even raised a hand or given a signal.

"Thank you for coming," Qydus Okvius said. "This gathering will be short, but there are important things to announce and it is best done with everyone together."

The audience had gone completely silent. Aeden had no doubt that those even at the top of the rows of benches heard the headmaster's voice. Even without the acoustics he had noticed earlier, the headmaster's voice always seemed to carry easily.

"Many are concerned," the headmaster started, "by the things happening in the world, and those with knowledge and rare abilities no less so than the common man or woman. Sitor Kanda was created for one purpose: to retain knowledge and skills that could be passed to the Malatirsay at the end times in order to give our world the best chance to survive.

"As each of us is aware, the Bhavisyaganant, the Song of Prophecy, has always been our guide to determining when our purpose is to be fulfilled, when we have reached the end times described in the Prophecy. Students in the School of Prophecy know how keenly the masters have been examining happenings in the world.

"I tell you now, the official determination by the masters of the Sitor-Kanda Academy is that we are in those end times. Now is the time of the great darkness, and now is the time—more than any other—the world needs the promised heroes."

Whispered conversation broke out among the audience. The masters, gathered in front of the stage and to the headmaster's right, were largely silent, though a few leaned in to quietly say something to the master next to them.

The headmaster raised his hand and utter silence returned.

"That is not all."

Aeden had been watching the reactions of some of the

students, but shifted his attention to the masters instead. He thought he knew where this was going.

"I am pleased to announce that the consensus of the masters supports what I am to say next." He scanned the audience, picking out individuals and meeting their eyes. His head swung to Aeden and Marla—who were standing next to him—and he gave a tiny nod.

Here it comes, Aeden thought.

"The masters of the Academy declare Marla Shrike and her twin brother Aeden Tannoch to be the long-awaited Malatirsay. A new understanding of the prophecy reveals that they *together* are the promised savior."

Master Marn frowned deeply before realizing he was so visible, and then schooled his face into the normal look of mild displeasure or disinterest. The headmaster had said consensus. It was by no means unanimous. *I wonder how many masters don't support what Master Qydus just said?*

"As such," he continued, "they are afforded all aid and resources necessary to carry out their task in protecting Dizhelim from the dark tide threatening to overwhelm it. That includes the cooperation of each of you. It is our purpose for being, I remind you.

"Furthermore, I know many of you have sensed the erratic nature of the world's magic of late. Let it be known that a task force of several masters, as well as some students, will carry out research into these changes with the aim of identifying exactly what is happening. Some interesting information has already been gathered. When we have arrived at a conclusion about what is occurring, we will share our findings."

The headmaster looked out over the audience again, silently observing them. Time dragged on uncomfortably, and people began fidgeting. The headmaster finally broke the silence.

"That is all for now. I would remind each of you of the reason for this school's existence, as well as your obligations as students. If you have questions, please see one of the masters. Take pride in our roles now, at what could be the end of all things. We have the Prophet's words to guide us, but it will not be an easy task. Already the forces of dark creatures are arrayed against us. We will need every person to do their part in protecting Dizhelim, standing behind and supporting the Malatirsay.

"You may now return to your previous activities."

Master Qydus stepped down from the stage and walked toward the administration building. The students sat for a time as if confused about what they were to do. The masters shooed them away from the amphitheater until only Aeden and his friends remained.

"What does all this mean for us?" Raki asked.

"Well," Marla said, "for all of you who aren't Aeden or myself, it only means that you'll get some extra attention, besides the obvious benefits of being able to study with some of the masters. For Aeden and me, it means we won't have a moment's rest. We're celebrities now."

"To be fair," Evon said, "you've always been a celebrity. Mastering schools like they come in bundles of five isn't really a way to keep a low profile."

"Yeah, but if the jealousy with some of them was bad before, it's going to be worse now."

"Did you see Master Marn's face?" Aeden asked.

"Oh, you mean like this?" Marla put on a frown so exaggerated, it made her look like her face was made of rubber and had been pulled down by handfuls of skin.

Aeden couldn't help but to laugh so hard, it came out in a snort.

"That one will cause you trouble, if he can," Tere said,

though his mouth appeared to be twitching into a smile against his will.

"Let him join the crowd," Marla said. "Trying to impress Marn Tiscomb is the last thing on my list. Just below cutting off my left leg. I'm hoping I get a two-for-one with those two tasks if I ever reach the end of my list."

"Anyway," Aeden said, "we shouldn't worry about what others think. We have a responsibility, so we should focus on that. Once we find out what we need to do next, we won't have time to worry about whether people like us or not."

Fahtin stiffened and Aeden thought back to what he had said. Had he said something that hurt her feelings?

The color drained out of the Gypta woman's face and she gave a little gasp. Then she closed her eyes and swayed on her feet a little.

Aeden caught one of her arms and Evon caught the other. "Fahtin," they both said together.

She groaned a little and put her hand to her forehead. "Ugh. I think it's passing. I should go lie down, or at least sit down. I'm dizzy."

"Is it a vision?" Evon asked.

"Yes, I think so, though I haven't seen anything yet. Soon, though. I feel it coming on."

Aeden swung his arm under her legs and swept her up. He headed toward the dorm. "Come on. Let's get her settled. A cool drink and a rest should help."

❦ 6 ❦

As Fahtin rested in her room, Aeden and everyone else retreated to the common room to discuss the day's announcements. Evon began pacing.

"Evon," Marla said, "would you sit down? She's fine. You know as well as I that when someone comes into their magic, they have a difficult time of it."

"I know. I do. But it seems whatever magical talent she has, it's pretty strong. I think she's having more than mild discomfort. What if it harms her?"

Aeden laughed, prompting a look on Evon's face that made him want to laugh harder. "Don't look so shocked, Evon. I'm only laughing because Fahtin is much tougher than most people think. She is a pretty flower, but she's a flower made of good steel. She'll be fine. You've been studying her talents. You should know better than anyone. Have some faith."

Evon chuckled nervously. "Yeah, I suppose you're right."

"Now sit down and relax or I'll tell her you're doubting her strength and ability to endure discomfort."

Evon plopped down on a seat so quickly, Aeden blinked. He refrained from laughing again, but only just.

Marla did laugh, a snorting guffaw. "She'll get through the uncomfortable part and then she'll have a vision to tell us about. Maybe she'll be able to tell us what we need to do next. I wouldn't be surprised if—"

The door swung open, flooding the entry with sunlight that seemed brighter than the light coming through the windows. A man stepped in, followed by a woman and a mixed group of half a dozen other men and women.

The man was familiar to Aeden, though he couldn't help but to see the boy the man had been when they were best friends. Now, he was a proper highland warrior, a hair taller than Aeden himself with probably ten or fifteen pounds more muscle on him. His chestnut hair was worn long, in the fashion of the Croagh, and though he didn't have a full beard, his chin and lips did have a fair amount of hair on them, giving him a wild look.

"Greimich," Aeden said, rising to his feet and heading toward his friend.

The two men grasped forearms, smiles springing up on both their faces.

"Cat." Aeden nodded toward Greimich's wife behind her husband. She smiled and waved. "I thought you were going to try to gather the clans," Aeden said to Greimich.

"Aye, that was my mission. I did what I could."

"That doesn't sound promising."

"No. Let me introduce you to the Croagh I've brought back with me. There is Dubhghall and Naomhan of the Trebhin clan, and Niall of the Ailgid clan, Conall and Grier Corcan, and Cora and Tamhas of the Seachaid clan."

As Aeden opened his mouth to greet the newcomers, one of the men from the Trebhin clan—Dubhghall, Greimich called him—pushed his way to the front of the group. He was a big man, larger than Aeden, almost of a size with Tere.

"What have we here?" he said with the deep accent of the highlands, his eyes drilling into Marla. "Is this the evening's entertainment, now?

Aeden's sword was halfway out of the scabbard on his back before Marla caught his arm. She shook her head at him and he dropped his sword back down in place.

"What's your name, pretty lady?" the man continued. "Turn around and give us a look. Mmmm, and do it slowly so I can take it all in. Then come over here for a kiss and you'll see how we grow men in the highlands."

"Dubhghall," Greimich growled, but again, Marla put up a hand.

"You want a good look and a kiss?" Marla cooed toward the Trebhin.

"Aye, and maybe more, but we can talk about that in private."

"Oooh, *private*," she said. Aeden had never heard her use that purring voice. He had to blink twice to make sure it was really his sister who spoke.

He didn't know what she was doing, but he trusted she knew the situation. He squirmed at what he was witnessing, but he would let her handle the pig. If things got worse, he'd gut the bastard, even if she didn't.

Marla slinked over to Dubhghall, moving so provocatively that Aeden wondered if Fahtin had been training her...or if all women knew instinctually how to move in alluring ways.

"I'll tell you what," she said, turning in a slow circle while she somehow still moved toward him without a break in her rhythm. "Let's play a little game."

"I like games," he said, licking his lips. The other member of the Trebhin clan, standing next to him, tapped on the man's shoulder and whispered something, but he elbowed the other man's hand away, his attention focused completely on Marla.

"Goooood," Marla whispered, sending vibrations through the air that seemed to be magic. "It's very simple, so even someone like you can understand it."

"What?" Dubhghall said, seeming to snap out of the trance he had been in from watching Marla's sinuous movements.

"You," she said, then exploded into motion. "Are." She struck the man three times in the abdomen with straight, lightning-fast punches, followed by an elbow to the jaw as she stepped through the strike, meeting his head, which had gone forward from the lower hits. "A pig-buggering." Before he could react, she snaked her lead leg behind him and kicked backward so forcefully that both his legs flew out from under him and, for the briefest moment, he was completely horizontal in the air several feet off the ground. "Bastard."

Then he crashed down on his back on the wood plank floor of the common room with a grunt and a whoosh of air. When he was able to drag his eyelids open, they widened. Marla knelt alongside him, her dueling dagger dimpling the skin of his throat. A pinprick droplet of blood formed and trickled down his neck.

"If you ever say anything remotely like what you just said, not only to me, but to any other person in my hearing," she said in a cold, hard voice that sent an icy finger up Aeden's back, "I will kill you so fast you won't even know you're dying. Do you understand me?"

Dubhghall tried to swallow, but only got halfway through before his Adam's apple pushing against the knife caused him to abort the action. "Yes," he croaked.

"Good," Marla said cheerfully. She wiped the tip of the dagger on the man's tunic and straightened up. Then she put out a hand to him to help him to his feet.

The Trebhin looked at her, then toward Greimich and Aeden, then finally toward his clan member. The other Trebhin shrugged in an *I told you so* kind of way. Dubhghall cautiously took the proffered hand and allowed Marla to pull him to his feet. The look on his face showed his shock that she managed it. She was strong, Aeden's sister was.

"Anyone else want to act inappropriately?" Marla asked innocently.

Greimich's wife, Catriona, smiled at the red-haired Academy graduate, as did the other Croagh woman. Cat took that opportunity to hug Marla and whisper, "Good to see you again."

The entire room was silent for a moment. Until Lily, the other red-haired beauty in the room, burst out in laughter. She said something to Tere, who was standing next to her, but Aeden only caught "teach him, sister."

Greimich cleared his throat. "Please let me introduce Aeden Tannoch, son of Sartan, clan chief of the Tannoch clan, and his twin sister, Marla." As he continued the introductions of the others, Aeden felt the eyes of the other Croagh settling on him.

It was not going to be a comfortable conversation, he thought.

"Uh," Aeden said. "Are you hungry, or would you like something to drink? We can have the kitchen make us some food."

"Ale," the Ailgid said. The others nodded vigorously.

"We have some here." He pointed toward a cask on a stand in the corner of the room. "As well as water and some wine. We can get more sent over. I'll get us some food, too, in case anyone else is hungry. It's near enough lunch time." It struck him as odd that it was so early despite all that had happened already.

The silence settled over them like a wet woolen blanket.

Everyone got the drink they chose, and not only the newcomers, but Aeden's friends who were chatting amiably a few minutes ago stared at each other and at the walls and floor.

"Okay," Aeden said. "Why are you here, Greimich? Or, more importantly, why aren't there more with you?"

Greimich met eyes with his wife and then he shifted his attention back to Aeden. "We ran into a bit of a snag."

"What kind of snag?"

The other man wrapped his hand around the back of his neck. "The clans aren't convinced they should be leaving their homes right now."

"I can understand that, but unless we all unite, they'll be overrun with animaru. Even with the same numbers on either side, it would be disastrous. It's hard to kill those monsters."

"I did tell everyone I met about the magic. Hopefully we can put up a better fight now than before. Still, the clan chieftains and the clan elders aren't convinced coming here to join some army is the way to go."

Aeden sighed. His people were stubborn, but couldn't they see they faced complete destruction?

The silence returned. Aeden couldn't think of anything else to say.

Cat spoke up. "Marla, would it be too much to ask for us to see some of the Hero Academy? I've heard they have the best combat training facilities in the world here."

Marla grinned. "We do, and it's not too much to ask at all. I'll show you the large training field where we sometimes carry out mock battles with armies. The School of Combat is something to see."

"That sounds like a great idea," Cat said. "All right, highlanders, let's go see what we can make of their combat training. We'll see if it stacks up to our traditional clan training." She winked at Greimich and herded the other clans' representatives out the door, Marla at her side.

"I love that woman," Greimich said, looking to relax for the first time since he arrived. "I'm not sure how much time we'll have, Aeden, so let's try to get through all of this.

"The clans all knew your father. Even the Trebhin clan, who usually hate Tannochs, respected Sartan, or at least his strength and ability. We were able to talk our way in, offering to give them information on how to hurt the animaru, but there is still no love lost between our clans."

"I know it's difficult," Aeden said, "but can't they see it's a necessity?"

"Maybe they do, but like I said, they respected your father. However, they don't know you. They're not willing to take drastic measures—either leaving the Cridheargla or joining forces with the other clans officially—until they know more about you. Like it or not, you are now the chief of the Tannoch clan."

"I didn't ask for the title. Don't want it. Until this animaru threat is taken care of, I'll not spend any time on figuring out what to do with our clan. A clan, I'll add, that consists only of two people, or three if you count Cat."

"Four," Greimich said. "Marla is your sister and so is part of the Tannoch clan as well."

"Four then. I've much better things to do than to play politics with the other clans."

"But that's just it, Aeden. You have to do it. If you don't appease the other clans, satisfy their curiosity, they won't band together. They won't follow you."

"I don't want them to follow me!" Aeden shouted. "Codaghan damned hard-headed...*Daeann daedos ist!* We all need to unite—*all* the people of Dizhelim—to fight this threat. If we don't, we and everything we know will not survive."

"You need to tell them that."

"I sent you to tell them that."

Greimich smirked at him. "Aeden, I'm not a clan chief. And don't say you're not, either. You were raised knowing the job would be yours someday. At least until you were cast out of the clan. Still, you *are* the clan chief, and it's going to take a clan chief to convince the other clans to go along with what we're proposing."

"Aruna recipia dui."

Greimich smiled. "You've learned some new ones since we were children."

Aeden responded with a flat look.

"Aeden," Tere said. The archer had been sitting off to the side throughout all the discussions. "He's right. Men need something to believe in, a symbol to follow. The clans are facing what could be the end of clan life as they know it."

"What they—what *we*—are facing is the end of *all* life, known or not. We've no time for these games."

"Yet we have to play them. You have to show them the importance of uniting with others. But before they'll even listen to your argument, you have to show them you're worthy of their consideration."

Greimich nodded, but Aeden only felt the hot prickle of irritation increase. "How can I do that? What if I'm *not* worthy of consideration?"

"Then we are truly lost," Tere said.

Aeden scanned the others. Lily had a firm set to her jaw, standing like a statue of some warrior goddess. Jia and Raki were next to each other, as was typically the case since the former assassin began training the Gypta boy in the art of stealth. Evon, Aila, Urun, all of them were focused on Aeden.

Khrazhti's eyes drilled into his. She had the shadow of a smile on her face, her chin raised as if in pride.

The Croagh slumped. "Fine. What should I do?"

"Go," Tere said. "Go back with Greimich and the members of the other clans. Let them get to know you on the journey and when you get to the Cridheargla, show them what a true clan chief is like, what the Malatirsay is like."

Aeden huffed. "How do you know so much about how the clans think?"

Tere's smile was a little sad. "You don't spend years traveling with Raisor Tannoch without information about the clans being pounded into your brain."

Greimich started.

"Oh, right," Aeden said. "You don't know. Tere is Erent Caahs. It's a long story, but yeah, he spent a lot of time with Raisor."

Greimich blinked. "What?"

"Later." He sighed. "Fine, I'll go, as much as I hate to leave before we figure out what our next move is."

"Maybe this is our next move," Aila muttered. It carried loud and clear enough for the others to hear, though, and it made Aeden think. The dark-haired beauty was probably right.

A noise from upstairs made Aeden's ears perk up. It sounded like a muffled moan or at least a sound of exclamation. There was only one person in the building who wasn't in the common room.

Fahtin.

7

Evon was already halfway up the stairs, but Aeden closed the gap, taking three steps at a time. They arrived at Fahtin's door at almost the same time. The blond-haired Academy graduate stopped abruptly, looking at the door as if it were a city wall. He knocked on the door.

"Fahtin? Are you all right?"

Aeden didn't wait for an answer. He opened the door and charged in.

Fahtin was sitting on her bed, mouth open to speak. When Aeden intruded, she squeaked and closed her mouth.

"What happened?" Aeden asked, scanning the small room for enemies. "It sounded like you were struck or fell down."

Fahtin's hair swayed as she shook her head. "No. It was just me reacting to what I saw. I'm sorry to have worried you."

There didn't appear to be any danger, but Fahtin did look pale.

"Are you okay? Here, have some water." Aeden filled a cup

from the pitcher he had left on her table earlier and handed it to her.

"Ugh," Fahtin grunted, sitting up straighter and taking a sip of the water. "Thank you. I'm fine."

Evon hovered near the door, moving his foot to step inside, but then bringing it back, and repeating. Aeden waved the man into the room.

"Was it a vision?" Aeden asked.

Fahtin nodded and took another drink. "Give me a minute and we can go down to the common room so I can tell everyone at once. I'm too tired to repeat it to everyone individually."

A few minutes later, the three descended the stairs, Aeden leading in case Fahtin fell and Evon bringing up the rear, watching her carefully so he could catch her if she did slip. When Aeden looked back, he caught her rolling her eyes. Her independent nature clashed with being protected and babied. He smiled at her and winked, causing her to laugh.

Once they got her settled in a seat at the table, she took another sip of water and cleared her throat.

"I've had another vision," she said, looking around the table at her friends. "I'm not sure what each specific part of it means, but I do have a sense of what its purpose is.

"First, I saw a landscape made up of mountains and a valley, much of it heavily forested. There was also a vast expanse of blue water next to part of it. I saw a city, but not like Ebenrau. It was more spread out, and many of the buildings had sharply curved roofs.

"People scurried about. Their clothing was mostly black, long jackets or robes that stretched almost all the way to the ground.

"In the middle of the city was a stone castle, itself with a curved roof with huge wooden beams supporting it, though the surface was covered with clay tiles. Sculptures lined the castle walls, some in stone and others in lacquered wood. They depicted serpents, some with wings, and beasts that looked something like lions, but more stylized.

"There was a man, older but still vital, dressed in fine clothes. Silk, I think. I'm not sure how I knew, but he was a king, or some other kind of ruler. Maybe it was his demeanor. He stood, eyes focused on nothing, as he held a ball of shadow. He passed it from hand to hand as if playing with it. His mouth twisted into the semblance of a grin, but more sinister.

"I saw another man, this one in clothing that was less fine, though still better than a common citizen. He sat on a thin reed mat with his legs crossed and his hands cupped together directly in front of him. His eyes were closed and he breathed rhythmically, intentionally. In his cradled hands a faint light shone, but it pulsed, like it was trying to flash, but didn't have the strength to combat the shadows surrounding it.

"Something...something about the second man calmed me, made me feel more comfortable. I sensed that he was a good man. To him, his actions and words were the most important thing in his life. That sounds silly as I say it, but I don't know a better way to explain it. If the first man made me fear for the future, the second gave me hope.

"I also saw some flashes of brightly painted wagons," she said, her lip quivering. "I'm not sure what that means, but it's obvious they were Gypta homes.

"That's all." Fahtin took another drink. Her eyes seemed to stick to Jia when they passed over the black-haired former Falxen assassin.

Almost as if Fahtin's attention was a cue, Jia stood up. "It sounds like you're describing Shinyan."

"I thought so, too," Fahtin said. "We haven't visited the cities there often—they don't like Gypta—but the little exposure I got to them seemed to indicate that was where my vision was centered."

"Is that it, then?" Aeden asked. "We're to go to Shinyan next?"

"I think so."

"Then we have our next move," he said. "We'll just need to tell the masters that—"

Urun burst through the door from the outside. Aeden hadn't even realized the nature priest had left the room before.

"Osulin is in trouble," Urun gasped. "She's...I'm...I need to go. Right now." He ran for the stairs, but Aeden caught the priest's arm and stopped him.

The anger that flashed in Urun's eyes made Aeden rear back in surprise. He loosed the other man's arm and barely kept himself from putting his hand on the hilt of his sword.

Urun's eyes flicked from Aeden to the stairs and back again. He closed them and shook his head, then took a breath. "Sorry. I need to go."

"So you said," Aila said, crossing her arms across her chest. "You need to calm down for just a minute and tell us what's going on, Urun. You're obviously frantic. Take a few breaths and tell us. Maybe we can help."

For a reason Aeden didn't know, Aila's clipped words did seem to calm the priest. He almost looked embarrassed. It sometimes seemed their experiences in the prison in Praesturi had created a bond between them.

"Okay. Osulin contacted me, sent a message directly to my mind. I felt something, which is why I went outside earlier, so I could try to concentrate on it. She sent me feelings of danger and harm. And hopelessness. The communication wasn't good, almost as if her voice was breaking apart. I only got one real word out of it: Mellafond."

Tere groaned when Urun said the word *Mellafond*. Aeden

felt briefly like he was falling from a high place. He wasn't sure what any of it meant, but if Tere—a hero long before the Croagh was even born—groaned over just one word, it couldn't mean good things for them.

"Mellafond?" Aila said. "You mean that swamp on the mainland side by Praesturi? The place we thought about going into but that you and Tere were too scared to actually visit? *That* Mellafond?"

"Yes," Urun said. "My goddess is in trouble, and it has something to do with the Mellafond. I'm going there to try to help her."

"Urun," Aeden said. "If she's in trouble, what do you think you can do? She's a goddess."

"I don't know," the priest said. He was trembling. "I don't know, but I have to go. Even if it means my death, that's fine if there's a chance to help her. You can't talk me out of it, and discussing it will only waste time. I'm getting my gear and leaving. Please don't try to stop me. I don't want to use my powers against you."

He sped up the stairs. His stomping footsteps echoed from the floor above, soon joined by sounds of items being banged around and then a door slamming. He raced down the stairs so quickly, he almost lost his balance and tripped.

"Wait, Urun," Tere said. "I know you're in a hurry, but just wait a small moment. Please."

Urun danced from foot to foot, but he waited for Tere to speak.

"I know how it is to want to rush to the aid of someone you care about or are committed to, or both. Believe me, I know. You have to stop and think, though, or you could make things worse than they already are. Charging in and getting yourself captured or killed will not help the goddess. You have to be smart."

"Tere, I appreciate your counsel and I would love to talk

about it, but I don't have a lot of experience in planning something like this. I'll do what I can, in whatever way I can do it."

"You're right, you don't have experience in this. That's why I'm going with you."

Urun stared at Tere, his face blank. "You what?"

"I'm going with you. You're our friend, Urun, and you have saved us many times over. If I can help you to aid your goddess, I'll do it. I still have a few skills left that could help, especially since I got my full sight back."

"I..."

"I'm going, too," Lily said. "You have always sacrificed for your friends. Hells, you even helped me when you didn't know me from a common assassin. Tere and I can both be useful."

"I..." Urun said again.

"I'm going, too," Marla said, walking through the door Urun had left open. "I didn't hear all of it, but you could probably use someone else who can do magic."

Urun didn't try to speak again, only nodded, his eyes going liquid.

"Give us enough time to gather some supplies and we can head off," Marla said, squeezing the priest's shoulder. "No one messes with your goddess, not unless they want to feel our wrath."

Evon headed for the door. "I'll get some supplies for you. You should use the time to figure out exactly what you'll do. I'll be back in a little while."

As Evon headed outside, Aeden caught Fahtin looking at the young man's retreating form and smiling.

It occurred to Aeden that Marla had come back alone. "Marla, where are the other clan members?"

"They went back to their rooms in Dartford. I asked if

they wanted me to try to find them rooms here and they declined."

"There were a few things that maybe you didn't hear. Fahtin had a vision and it seems to indicate that our next step is to go to Shinyan. We were trying to figure out what to do when Urun burst in and told us about Osulin."

"Oh." Marla looked around the room. "I guess we'll be splitting up, then."

"It seems so," he said. "I'll go with Greimich to try to talk to the clans. I'll take Khrazhti with me." He half expected an argument, or at least questions, but none came.

"I already told Urun I'd go with him," she said, "so I'll be going to the Mellafond, apparently."

"So, it's you, Urun, Tere, and Lily going to the swamp; Khrazhti and I are going to the highlands, and the rest will go with Fahtin to Shinyan. I hate to split up again. I was always worried about Tere's group when we split up last time."

Marla smirked at him. "It's something we have to do. Who knows which of the tasks is more important overall? They could all be crucial to saving the world. I have a feeling they are. We have to do what's required of us. We're the world's best hope, after all."

"So everyone keeps saying," Aeden said. "I'm still not sure I believe them most of the time."

"Oh," Marla said. "I have an idea. I'll be right back. Don't go away. I think this will solve some problems."

Marla got back before Evon did, three small tablets in her hands. She handed one to Aeden and the other to Tere, keeping one herself. Both of the men looked at her like she was crazy.

"What?" Tere asked. "You want us to take notes of what we're doing?"

Lily playfully swatted at his shoulder. "Don't you know what those are? They're magic. Each brace had at least one to keep in communication with either Vatheca, our headquarters, or the person who hired us."

"Really?" Marla said. "These things are wickedly expensive and very hard to make."

"Assassination pays good money," Lily deadpanned.

"Right." Marla picked up her tablet and wrote a few lines on it. "Watch your tablets," she told them.

Aeden stared at his for a moment before writing magically appeared on it. It was a beautiful, flowing script, which read:

IF YOU CAN READ THIS, GAPE AT IT LIKE YOU'RE SOME KIND OF MORON...OR A FISH.

LILY CHUCKLED. TERE GAPED.

"I linked these three with each other, so whatever is written on one will appear on the others. I don't really have time to show you how to change how they're paired—or tripled?—but this should work in a pinch. I don't think it's necessary to check in with each other every day, but a comment now and then will help to ease our minds about how the others are doing. I'll give this one to Evon, since I'll be traveling with Tere."

"These are fantastic, Marla," Aeden said. "I didn't know anything like this existed."

"Yeah. We're the only ones who can make them. Like I said, they're really hard to produce. It takes at least five different types of magic at a very high level, with a large chance of failure during the process. Please keep them safe. I still can't believe I got three. Use the little stylus in the holder on the side and write whenever you want, or use whatever else you want to write with. You can even use your fingers, but please don't. I don't want to have to translate ugly, blocky letters written by a finger."

"Being able to communicate will make me feel a lot better," Aeden admitted. "I have a feeling we're not going to simply be traveling without being in danger constantly."

8

Heedless of the demonstration of the magical writing tablets, Urun danced from foot to foot, waiting for Evon to come back with the supplies they needed. The priest tried to be patient, but his goddess was in trouble. Could gods and goddesses be killed? The heat left his body at that thought. What if she could? What if his delay kept him from helping her in time?

He almost tore off through the door, leaving the supplies and the others behind. Part of him knew that he wouldn't even make it through a day's travel without supplies, but he was very close to leaving anyway.

Think, you idiot, he said to himself. *Stop panicking, and make a plan.* What would have happened if he had rushed off without the others and tried to help Osulin on his own? He would have failed spectacularly. Hadn't he been moping about for the last few days because he felt worthless in battles with enemies? What did he think he could do without his friends?

He looked to Marla and shook his head at himself. She was half of the prophesied warrior, foretold to be the only one who could save the world. She didn't know Urun well, but still, she volunteered to go with him. He was not worthy of his friends, just as he was not worthy of his goddess.

The old sayings said you never know a person's worth until they're put in a tough spot. Well, he'd been in plenty since Tere had showed up with Aeden and the others on Urun's doorstep more than half a year ago. It was true, and he had learned that he was no hero. Fortunately, his friends were.

Evon finally showed up with several full packs. He had commandeered a few young men—they looked like students —to carry the supplies.

"Thank you, Evon," Urun said, snatching a pack from the younger man. It was fairly heavy, though if it contained food, it would become lighter soon enough. Urun slipped his arms through the straps, ready to go.

Tere, Lily, and Marla took packs and hitched them up. Tere fiddled with his for an interminably long time before dropping it to the floor and heading upstairs. Urun wanted to shout at the man, but he focused on his breath and tried to stay calm.

The archer came back down the stairs with two packs in his hands. One was his and the other was Lily's. The woman smiled at him and accepted it. Both of them transferred the supplies from the pack Evon brought into their own containers.

Evon's face reddened.

"Thank you, Evon," Tere said. "But our packs are specially designed to be worn over our quivers and to allow us to still take arrows out of them easily. We appreciate you getting the supplies, but we'll be more efficient using our own packs." He handed back the empty satchel Evon had brought for him and Lily did the same with hers a moment later.

Urun stood in the middle of the common room to the building where he had lived for the past several weeks. His impatience fled as he faced his friends. The place had started feeling sort of like a home, and these people around him like family.

"I..." His words faltered as Fahtin rushed to him and enfolded him in a hug.

"I'm so sorry I haven't seen anything that can help you, Urun. I would go with you—I hope you know that—but the vision I was granted gives me the sense that grave consequences will arise if we don't go to Shinyan."

The priest patted the gorgeous Gypta woman on the back, a lump in his throat. He squeaked through it, "It's fine. We all seem to have our tasks. I have to go to Osulin, or I would join you and the others."

"I know." She released him and stepped over to hug Lily, then Tere, then Marla.

Aeden put his hand out and clasped wrists with Urun when the priest reached his out. The warrior pulled Urun into a quick hug. "You take care of yourself, and of each other," he said, nodding toward Tere and Lily, then toward his sister. "I've no doubt your mission is no less critical to all of Dizhelim than ours are. I'd join you as well if I weren't needed elsewhere."

"I understand," Urun said. "I feel fortunate anyone can go with me. Or will. I don't need to tell you how many things are in motion right now. You and Khrazhti take care of yourselves, too. We'll all meet back here when we've completed what we set out to do. Maybe save some animaru for the rest of us to fight?"

Aeden laughed. "There will be more than enough to go around."

The Croagh left to speak with his sister and Raki approached, Jia next to him.

The young Gypta's eyes momentarily met Urun's, but then went back to the ground, then darted around to scan the room. "Be safe, Urun," Raki said. "We'll miss your presence. You go and save your goddess and come back. We have a lot more stuff to do after this, I think."

Urun smiled at the boy. "I think you're right, Raki. Just when we all get back together, it seems we have to split up again. Make sure you take care of Fahtin and the others. Don't go risking yourself needlessly. We all know you're brave; no need to prove it unnecessarily."

Raki's eyes widened, and his face reddened. "I'll do my best."

Urun winked at Jia, who seemed amused at Raki's shyness. "You too, Jia. Be careful. I hear Shinyan is a little unstable right now."

The former assassin laughed and tossed her blue-tinted hair. Her smile nearly made Urun forget to breathe. Like so many of the women he seemed to be around lately, she was beautiful enough to twist his mind in knots. If it weren't so full of other worries.

"I have some...uh, special talents that are suited to dangerous and unstable places. In fact, often places are dangerous and unstable *because* of me. Or do you forget my past?"

"How could I?" he said. "Be safe. I'll see you when we all meet back here. Or wherever we end up gathering together again."

"It's a deal," she said, putting a hand out. Like Aeden, she pulled him into a brief hug when they clasped wrists. This time, her smile was more mischievous.

No sooner had he released Jia than a similarly sized body slammed into him, crushing the breath out of him.

"Ugh. Aila?"

Aila Ven squeezed him hard one more time and then let go. "Don't go getting all brain-dead again, Urun, okay? Keep your mind sharp, don't zone out, and whatever it is that's giving your goddess trouble, make sure you smack it with your staff a couple of times for me, okay?"

After taking a breath, he chuckled. "Will do."

Aila seemed unsure of what else to say, something Urun had never seen before. "Don't get yourself killed, either. That would make me very sad. Even sadder than having to spend all that time in a cell with you and your filthy stench."

"Hey, you smelled just as bad as I did."

"Not true. I'm a pretty flower. I could never smell as bad as a dirty man."

"Oh, you must be right. What was I thinking?"

"I don't know. As usual, you'll need a woman to watch over you. Or two. Lily and Marla are good candidates. Listen to them. And to Tere."

"I'll try," he said, smiling down at her. The expression slipped from his face as thoughts invaded his mind. Thoughts of Osulin being in peril.

She seemed to notice. "Stop dawdling. Get going already. I'll see you when you get back."

Urun nodded, then turned toward Tere. He and Lily were standing by the door. Marla was finishing up a conversation with Fahtin and Evon. She caught the priest's eye and headed toward the archers. Warmth suffused Urun again at the thought of his friends and their willingness to take action on his behalf.

He joined the three and took one long, last look at the friends who wouldn't join him.

"Ready?" Tere asked.

"I am."

"Then let's get going," Marla said. "The Mellafond isn't going to come to us."

❧ 9 ❧

U run stepped through the dorm building's door and out into the sunlight, and almost ran into a black-speckled grey horse standing there.

"Rainstorm?" He had used the animal on their previous trip, the mount the Academy had loaned him. "What are you doing here?" The priest realized after the words left his mouth that he appeared to be having a conversation with a horse, waiting for the animal to speak an answer.

Marla walked past and patted the nose of her own horse, Surefoot. "When Evon got our supplies, he brought our horses over, too."

"But," Urun said, "we're going to the Mellafond. It's a swamp, and there is obviously danger there or Osulin wouldn't need my help. I don't want to take them to their deaths."

"You were the one ready to leave without telling anyone and without getting supplies. The horses will make the trip faster."

"They're smart and well trained," Tere said. "If it comes to it, we could turn them loose and they would probably head back here. We won't take them into the dangerous parts of the swamp with us, but if you don't want to delay, then we should ride, Urun."

Urun saw the reasoning, but he still wasn't sure. He was a nature priest, after all. Killing helpless animals for the sake of speed wasn't something he felt comfortable with, but weighed against his goddess's life, he was sad to realize he would be willing to do it. He looked to Marla, torn.

"He's right. They're trained to come back home if something happens to their riders, if they're free to do so. My girl, Surefoot is very smart and she'd probably lead the others to return. You don't have to worry. By horseback it's only about a two-day trip. Without anyone on them, they could probably make it back in half that. They'd be fine. No chance they would die of starvation or anything."

"Okay," he said. "That eases my mind. We *are* in a hurry."

"You don't act like it," Lily said, swinging into her saddle. She had apparently already tied her pack to the saddlebags. "Let's go."

The other three mounted and they were on their way, Urun's queasy stomach giving him a jolt with each of Rainstorm's footsteps.

Within a few hours, they clopped southward on the River Road.

"Which part of the Mellafond will we be going to?" Lily asked. "I've seen it off in the distance from the road, but I never went any closer."

"We did," Tere said. "When we were trying to get to Dartford to meet Aeden, when you and the other Falxen were chasing us, we tried to go around it and straight north to Dartford. There were a lot of animaru in the area, even on the road. They were looking for something and were out in force, so we had to turn back and go to Praesturi. We thought for about a second of going through part of the swamp, but wisely decided not to try it."

"Really?" the red-haired archer said. "Is it all those stories about dangerous monsters? Do you believe that stuff?"

"It wasn't like that," Urun said. "I felt the ill intent of the entire area. It was like something immense and alive. Something that wanted to kill us and could do so almost without thought."

"And you want to go there now?" Lily asked.

"I have to. My goddess is in trouble. I can do no less than to try to help. You three don't have to, though. I appreciate you volunteering, but you're not obliged to—"

"Stop trying to talk us out of helping, Urun," Tere said. "We're going and that's that. Focus more on what we'll do when we get there. Like what Lily asked a moment ago. What are your plans? Where will we go?"

"I...uh...I was hoping that when I got closer I would sense where I needed to go. If I can't, I suppose I'll have to think of something else."

Tere huffed. "That's your plan? The Mellafond is twenty-five or thirty miles across and possibly that much wide. Do you expect to wander around until something comes to you?"

"I don't know, Tere. I don't know. I'm confused and upset and don't know what to do. My goddess is in trouble. She used the last of her strength to send me a message. I don't know if a goddess can die, but all I can think about is her trapped in that place with that rot and evil. I'll do what I have to do. That's all I can tell you for sure."

"Okay, okay," Marla said. "We'll see how you sensing the direction works out. We understand that you're distressed. Let's get there, and then you can lead us where you think we need to go. Does that sound all right?"

"I guess." He didn't like to think about it, but Tere was probably right. What was he doing? He was charging in without a thought, like an idiot. Maybe he deserved to die in his attempt. But his friends didn't, nor did Osulin. He simply had to do better.

"I'll try to think of something more practical," he continued. "I'm sorry my mind is not right at the moment. I'll try to focus more."

"We're here for you, Urun," Lily said. "We'll get through this and rescue your goddess. But we have to be careful doing it. It's no time for recklessness."

"I know."

The four travelers were silent for a time. The ominous feeling of the Mellafond growing closer amplified in Urun. It was a relief when something else appeared besides the empty road and the trees and grasses alongside it.

The priest spotted shapes on the road up ahead and he squinted to try to identify them. Closer, they resolved into wagons, white boxes pulled by four horses each.

"Great," Marla said. "Just what we need."

The wagons had stopped, and several figures in white robes scurried around them. They weren't blocking the road precisely, but their presence did constrict things.

"Damn Vandals," Tere spat. "What are they up to now?"

The small group stopped their horses in front of three robed men when the one in the center raised his hand in a gesture intended to halt them. Urun's eye twitched and he had an urge to gallop his horse between the three.

"Good afternoon, travelers," the center man said. "Where are you headed?"

"Our destination is our own business, priest," Marla said.

"All things are the business of the One most high."

"Not Academy business. Now move or we will run you down."

"Ah, students are you?" He seemed to notice Tere. "And perhaps graduates as well? How is fine Master Aubron, the

Master of Religious Studies? I have worked with him often, discussing the intricacies of our God Vanda's words."

"He's fine," she said. But to the others she whispered, "It's the School of History and Literature. Religious studies are only a small part of it."

"Good, good," the priest said. "We are spreading the news that the end times are nigh. Darkness threatens to take over the world, and now is the time for all right-hearted people to unite under one banner: that of Vanda's holy church."

"What makes you say the end times are here?" Tere asked.

"Look around you, traveler. Have you not seen or heard of dark monsters invading many kingdoms, tearing people apart and spreading their shadow? Some have said that several of the pagan religions are being revived, even that a powerful leader in barbaric nature worship has reared his ugly head. Nature priest, indeed. This one is a minion of the darkness and must be eradicated from Dizhelim so that he may not distract those of pure heart from the wholesome worship of Vanda."

Urun bristled and his lip raised on the left side of his face. He was about to say something, but Tere headed him off.

"It's your job to watch for things like that, I suppose. They make no difference to us. We have a long trip ahead of us and can't spend the time talking. We'll ask you one more time to move, or you will be moved."

"It is not wise to act in cross-purpose to the church," the priest warned. "You would do well to—"

Tere kicked his horse and clicked his tongue to start the beast forward. The priest squawked and jumped out of the way in such an exaggerated fashion, Urun almost laughed. The horse was walking, not sprinting. Even so, the three robed men in front of them split up and moved to the side of the road, acting for all the world like they were in danger of being trampled.

Urun met eyes with the priest who had been speaking. He passed by, not saying a word, struggling to keep his face emotionless. Barbarian was he? Pagan? He was sorely tempted to cast some unpleasant magic at the Vandals, but let the thought go. He wouldn't be petty. He had much more important things to do.

"We will unite all good people under Vanda and fight the minions of darkness, whether monster or human. The time of choice is at hand. Do not become an enemy simply by not choosing to join us. You have been warned."

Marla stopped in front of the priest as she passed him. "Don't try to block the roads near the Academy, or you might find there is more power in Dizhelim than you realize. *You* have been warned."

❧ 10 ❧

Cara Moore activated her meeting stone in the room in her house she had set aside for Council business. The familiar momentary disorientation caused the world to spin before righting itself, depositing her in a large chamber with a round table and chairs arranged along its edges. Four people were already there. Well, not there physically. It was the illusory magic of the stone.

Alloria Yurgen, the Vituma of the Council, sat in a chair that was larger and more elaborate than the others, as befitting her station. Compared to Cara's black hair and olive skin, the leader looked washed out. A ghostly pale imitation of a person.

Two seats down slouched Thritur Nyhus, a massive man with enough beard for two men. He scowled at Cara and grunted. His way of greeting her. Cara wasn't sure if he was really that weary of the world and all those in it or if his gruffness was an act. She wiggled a few fingers at him and smiled.

He stared at her like she was something he'd never seen before.

Amatia, the beautiful dark-haired and dark-skinned seer,

sat in her usual seat, inspecting Cara. When Cara met her eyes, both women smiled, the black-haired woman raising her chin in greeting. She liked Amatia. She was deliciously... uncanny. It wasn't only her mysterious seer ways, either. The woman at times didn't seem like she was even human. In a good way.

The fourth person was Isbal Deyne, who resembled what, no doubt, everyone pictured as the perfect grandmother. Round face, wrinkles where her skin creased every time she smiled—which she did all the time—and twinkling eyes that suggested the matronly woman was thinking of something mischievous that only a woman her age could get away with.

She gave Cara the creeps, her skin prickling at the predatory gaze beneath the friendly one.

No matter her looks, Isbal was the most ruthless, blood-thirsty, and vicious of them all. Some of the things Cara had seen her do—let alone things she had heard Isbal had done—made the younger woman uncomfortable, and *she* was a killer through and through.

Though she wasn't squeamish and had performed more assassinations than she could count, Cara would never think of crossing Isbal Deyne. The woman had legions of followers supremely devoted to her. No, Cara did not underestimate how dangerous Isbal was.

The others sat silently, waiting for the rest of the Dark Council. Not half an hour ago, the flashing and buzzing of the meeting stone—which Council members were required to keep on their person at all times—had called them to attend a meeting.

"What was the big rush?" Cara asked.

"We will wait for the others to arrive," Alloria said. "There is no use in repeating myself."

Figures. Cara extracted a dagger from one of the sheaths strapped to her thigh and picked at a fingernail with its point.

She should have known not to answer the summons right away. Now she had to wait. It would be unseemly to manipulate the stone to cut the connection, fade from the others' views, and return later.

One by one, the others arrived. Ren Kenata, with his handsome face and short but well-styled black hair, appeared in his chair with his fingers steepled, patiently waiting. Sure, it was easy for him to be patient. He'd just arrived. People had been waiting on him!

Thalia Fendove materialized. The woman looked a lot like Cara, as far as having dark hair and a body fit and toned from training and battle. Their facial structure was even similar, though Thalia's was a bit rounder than Cara's. And that smirk, the one Thalia always seemed to wear. It screamed that she knew more than everyone else and that they weren't privy to whatever joke she was about to play on them.

Evindia Elkien and Yoniko Takesi arrived at the same time, the women almost as opposite in their looks as Cara and Alloria. Evindia was a drop-dead gorgeous woman with pale blonde hair, and Yoniko's beauty was defined by her dark hair and eyes angled more sharply than Evindia's, typical features of those from Teroshi. Her black hair was also shorter, framing her face and emphasizing her cheekbones, while Evindia's long locks flowed down her shoulders and back like they were made of water.

Gareth Briggs's handsome face coalesced at Cara's side. Pity, that. If he were seated across from her, she could appreciate him without turning her whole body and advertising that she was staring. He grinned at her as if he guessed her thoughts. He probably had; most women he met probably did the same thing.

Hane Bryce appeared, and then Thomlyn Byrch did so a moment later. Hane's brown hair lay on his head like a sleeping cat, and Thomlyn's hair and bushy beard seemed to explode out from him in a white corona suitable for any constellation.

"Good," Alloria said. "Ren, please explain what you told me earlier. It is the reason we are meeting on such short notice."

"Yes, Vituma. Well, as you know, I cannot spy at the Academy myself, not since the debacle with Quentin and the murder of Master Aeid. I do still have operatives in place at Sitor-Kanda, though. Those operatives just tipped me off to what is happening."

"Yes, yes," Thalia said. "We know all that. Tell us what's going on."

Ren's chin raised fractionally and he huffed. "Fine. Some of the group consisting of the friends of Marla Shrike have left the Academy in a hurry. No one but the rest of their group was around, so we can't be sure where they went or why."

"You called us here to tell us you *don't* know what's happening?" Thritur bellowed.

"No, not at all, Thritur. Please allow me to finish."

The bearded barbarian grumbled, but said no more.

Ren cleared his throat. "As I said, no one seems to know where the group went. Marla herself was with them, as well as the two archers and the nature priest." He had obtained information about Marla's companions from his sources at the Academy and described them to the Council. He had previously given their names, but in this case, simple descriptions would work best.

"As for the rest of them, it appears that they are also planning to travel. I am working on getting information on their destination and goals. I should have that information before we finish this meeting."

"That is good information, if sparse, Ren," Gareth Briggs said. "But what does it mean for us?" He turned toward Alloria. "Are we to act on it in some way? Does it change our plans?"

Alloria nodded. "Good questions. We are at something of a loss right now. Our path forward is unclear. I wanted the opportunity to discuss these happenings." She turned toward Amatia. "And to give Amatia a chance for her visions to trigger as we talk about circumstances."

"I have seen no visions of this, but I am leaving my senses open," Amatia said. "Perhaps, as you say, something in our conversation will trigger my sight."

"One of the companions of the so-called Malatirsay is a Gypta woman," Alloria said. "She has apparently had visions as well. We must pay attention to what these others are doing. If she has seen something, we must take their cue and see if we can mitigate their plans."

Cara refrained from shaking her head, but did so mentally. She would have hoped the Dark Council would be smarter than this. Were they really basing their entire strategy on reacting to others' actions? Sometimes she wondered what her ancestors had been thinking, the ones who originally dedicated themselves to serving on the Council.

"Of course," Alloria continued, "we cannot rely upon being able to react to what others do. We must have plans of our own. Ones which must be flexible, but not simply a response dictated by the events in the world. We are the Dark Council. *We* must force the world to proceed down the path we designate."

Okay, that was good. Perhaps the Council wasn't as incompetent as it had appeared. Cara was glad for that, or she might have to be the first one in centuries to quit her position, though things would not turn out well if she did. There were stories...

"First," Alloria said, "there will need to be someone to oversee tracking and—if possible—foiling the efforts of those at the Academy, especially this Malatirsay. Cara, you will take on this task."

Cara had only been half listening, thinking ahead to what she would do to place herself most rewardingly. She blinked. Did she hear what she thought she did?

"Excuse me," Cara said. "Could you please repeat that last part? I'm not sure I heard you correctly."

Alloria's pale face drew into a smirk. "Of course. I said that you will handle keeping track of the group coming from the Academy. Not the one that left already. It will require more effort than it is worth to track them down. The remaining ones, though. These, you will follow to find out what they are up to. Speak with Ren for more information."

"I...okay. Why do I have this honor?"

"You are skilled and smart and can easily handle surveillance activities, as well as other situations that may require a more forceful action on your part. Also, you are closest to the Academy geographically and so may more easily follow them when they leave."

The Vituma seemed to have thought it through. Cara had to give the woman more credit than she had previously. It was a good move, though still reactive. She rued telling the council of her home in the Molars, and that she spent most of her time there when she wasn't out on a mission.

"I'll get on it right after we finish this meeting," Cara said.

"Thank you. Now, as to what we must do to force others to react to our actions, we can't simply roam the world in search of some hidden magic to aid us. Though the Council maintains an extensive network of spies, assassins, and fighters, we are vastly outnumbered by the other important factions in this race to control all of Dizhelim.

"Instead of trying to increase our own numbers or to concoct brilliant military strategies to decrease the numbers of our enemies"—she nodded toward Yoniko, their strategy specialist—"the logical thing to do is to give them other enemies to fret over.

"We will begin immediately to foment conflict between the nations of the world. Not only will they fight these dark creatures, the animaru, but they will fight amongst themselves. Our goal is for our enemies to deplete each other's resources and to leave everyone but us weakened. Then we will be able to strike. Until then, we must all cooperate to sow discord."

Regrettably, Cara elevated her opinion of the Vituma yet again. Until recently, she had not worked much with the other woman; the Council had largely bided their time until the prophesied end times. Things had seemed much easier when she considered the Council's leader an imbecile. She had been wrong. Perhaps the pale woman did have some planning abilities, maybe even some leadership skills. That was to be seen. She still had a long way to go until Cara had the respect for her that a leader should garner.

"To that end, I would like to recognize Gareth's contribution to the cause. I am not sure how he managed it, but it is clear that the Church of Vanda is mobilizing for a holy war. They are even now searching for those they can inflict harm upon, for no other reason than that they are not of the church. Continue your work in aiming them where it will do the most good to our cause."

Gareth nodded and flashed a smile that caused Cara's heart to do a little flip. Gods, but the man was handsome. She wondered how he utilized his talents with the church. No matter, she supposed. The fact that he did it was enough for her.

"Now I would like to hear where each of you are at with your own plans so we can coordinate as best we can. We will take as long as it must. This is no time to scrimp on planning."

Urun looked out over the swampy area in front of him and swallowed. When he was last this near the Mellafond, he had felt a wrongness about it, something counter to the clean, natural feeling that nature normally gave him. It wasn't only that it was a wetland, with its requisite stagnation and mildew. He had felt the distinct energy of that type of climate before, an area with a damp, fetid environ. It wasn't pleasant, but it still had felt natural.

This didn't. Not at all.

"It feels so wrong," he whispered. "Scary wrong."

"Even I can feel there's something not right about the area," Marla said. "But that's just from a magical point of view. The magic seems...skewed."

"It looks hazy to me," Tere said. "The magical matrix seems unfocused somehow. Almost like I'm viewing it through a warped or scratched lens on a sightglass."

Lily shrugged.

The four stood on a small grassy hill at the edge of the Mellafond, their horses beside them. The area in front of them resembled a forest. One with twisted, stunted trees, but still a forest. Just within the boundaries—ones which seemed to be lined off with glowing white paint that attacked his senses—the ground would become softer, wetter. Urun could barely pick out where the water level rose above the ground level.

The priest didn't look forward to sloshing through endless miles of water, mud, and muck. They couldn't ride the horses in such a place. He patted Rainstorm and regretted riding her to the area. Now she and her equine comrades would be a hindrance. Maybe the humans should set them free now.

"Well," Tere said. "What are we going to do? Should we move around to another area on the edge of the swamp in hope of finding better footing or will we enter here? Either way, we'll be getting wet soon."

Urun sighed. Normally, he would have communicated—that probably was too grand a word for his way of communing with nature—with the plants in the swamp, but they turned a deaf ear toward him. He couldn't even detect their mood. Were they mad, or under stress, or waiting to attack them? It wasn't clear.

"We might as well go in here," Marla said, scanning the vast area in front of them. "There are over five hundred square miles of swamp in the Mellafond. We could waste days circling it, looking for a likely place to enter. Best to jump right in." She poked a finger at the ground directly in front of them. "So to speak."

Urun didn't feel strongly enough about it to disagree. "I sense Osulin, I think, far into the Mellafond that way." He pointed to the southwest, toward the area near the coast of the Kanton Sea where it separated the mainland and Munsahtiz. "It's not enough to lead us right to her, not at its current strength, but I'm hoping it'll get stronger the closer we get."

"It's settled then," Marla said. "Let's go."

She took three steps before her boots made a squishing

sound and she stopped. Lifting her boot with a *schlup*, the Academy graduate frowned and shook her head sadly. Her horse turned one huge eye to meet hers and nickered softly. With a sigh and some whispered words to the horse that sounded like an apology, she continued on, each step squelching. "What's the worst that can happen?"

"You do realize," Lily said, "that we're here because a goddess has been put in jeopardy and we're here to help her, right? A goddess."

Marla waved a hand in the air. "Yeah, yeah."

Urun felt like he had eaten bees and they were buzzing around in his stomach. And stinging him. He swallowed, but that only made him taste bile, so he stuck his tongue out and then spat. He wasn't going to do that again. His face was wet with perspiration all of a sudden, though a hand to his forehead told him that he was clammy.

"Are you all right, Urun?" It was Tere's voice. Urun blinked at the white eyes a few inches in front of him.

"Gah. Oh, sorry, Tere." Urun swallowed again despite his earlier resolution. "I'm not paying attention. I—"

Tere's brows drew down, a grotesque sight coupled with his white, dead eyes. "Breathe, man. Is it fear that has you, or is it something magical?"

Urun had known Tere for years. They were neighbors in the Grundenwald and had spoken many times. Since they both left their forest homes, the priest had spent every day with the archer. If anyone in Dizhelim could be called Urun's friend, it was Tere Chizzit, even if the man had hidden that he was actually Erent Caahs, the most famous hero in the world who had disappeared two decades ago. He could be honest with the archer.

Urun sighed. "Maybe a little of both. Mostly fear, I think, based on the feelings of dangerously corrupted magic."

Tere nodded. "I don't blame you. The place gives me bad

feelings, too, and I'm not sensitive to nature magic like you are. Are you sure this is what we're supposed to be doing?"

Urun searched his feelings, pausing before he answered. "Yes. Osulin's word was clear. Mellafond. Along with that, there's obviously something wrong with the place. I'm sorry for being a coward. The wrongness vibrates in me. I feel sick."

"I've felt that before," Tere said, though Urun didn't believe it for a minute. The archer was a legend, a great hero. Nothing in the world scared him. "It's not being fearless that makes a hero; it's meeting that fear and continuing on."

Sure, the old, tired platitude was easy for Tere to say. He wasn't the one who felt like his bladder would lose control at any moment.

"But you don't need to hear any wise old sayings. How about some conversation? Do you know how the Mellafond came to be?"

The priest thought on it for a moment. Osulin had told him many tales, but the one about the swamp's origin—did a swamp actually need an origin?—was not one of them. Aside from stories told to him by his goddess, Urun had always been ignorant of many things the average person would know. He hadn't paid much attention to tales when he was a boy, more interested in being out in nature and learning about how it worked.

"No, I don't think I do."

"Well, then, let me tell you. It's an interesting story."

Urun noticed Marla raising an eyebrow and casting a glance at Tere. She probably knew several stories about the Mellafond. Would she quietly listen or would she interrupt Tere and correct what he said? He hoped for all their sakes that she didn't. Nothing ruined a story like someone butting in and adding their thoughts.

"Okay. Maybe it will take my mind off things." Urun doubted it, but it couldn't hurt to listen.

"Good. I can tell it as we walk. Just pay attention to where you're putting your feet. If you get too caught up in the story, you might walk into a bog." The archer chuckled and, for a wonder, it did make Urun feel a little better. Maybe distraction *would* be good.

"Over eight thousand years ago, this entire area was like the rest of the coastline of the Kanton Sea. Trees, bushes, forest wildlife; all of it was like the land to the north and south of the now-swamp.

"There were fewer people then, and the wide world was open to exploration. This part of Dizhelim was populated, of course, because Surus had placed the thinking races nearly in the center of the world and they spread out from there. Still, there were no great cities and no population centers as there are now, especially in this area.

"Nevertheless, some people found their way here and began exploring. They chanced upon a cave opening and set about investigating the tunnels. Quickly, they found something that delighted them. Large orichalcum deposits littered the entire area. They began to mine.

"The ones who discovered the precious metal did their best to keep it from being known, but their secret didn't last long. Within a few years, many had heard about the riches and swarmed the area to try their own luck at mining. Soon, the place was crawling with would-be purveyors of the precious metal, scrambling all over each other like insects on a two-day old carcass.

"The tunnels they carved—widening the original small cave they had found—spread for miles, and their activities started to affect the delicate balance of the area.

"Collapses and sink holes from shoddy tunnels, trash and cast-off supplies and chemicals from their smelting and refining operations, and other effects of the trespassers violating the soil threw the area out of equilibrium. Some animals and plants died, creatures moved on to other areas, and generally all of nature for miles around was thrown into upheaval.

"Things got so bad, it came to the attention of Mellaine herself. The goddess of the natural world was not pleased when she inspected the area and found out what havoc the miners had wrought. Standing on a nearby hill, she peered into the magic of the area and scanned the dying land, and her heart burned with her fury.

"The goddess took action. With the permission of Aesculus, she brought water from the Kanton Sea as well as waters from nearby rivers and inundated the area. So quickly did the water flow onto the land, the people still there had no chance to escape. Like a bucket of water dumped onto an ant hill, the liquid flowed around and into the caverns that had been carved, destroying all those who were damaging the natural cycle.

"For a fortnight, the water stood several feet above the ground, but then it receded, but not all the way. Instead of the vast lake it had been, it was now a marsh, a mixture of water and land, never again to be the dry ground it had been before the mining.

"Mellaine let it be known that she was the cause of the change so others would take heed not to repeat the actions of the greedy miners. It wasn't long until humans began to call the place the Mellafond, because the water of Mellaine had created it. The name means *pit of Mellaine*.

"Until our day, the swamp has stood as it was after the floods had receded. It has always seemed a place of special magic, though not of a malignant kind. Maybe that's why the rare metal was so abundant here."

Tere finished his story. Urun had lost himself in thought

as the archer told the tale, but once Tere stopped talking, the priest looked toward him.

"Up until now, it may not have been malignant," Urun said, "but it certainly is now. If not evil, it's at least corrupted."

"Then I guess we're in the right place," Marla said.

12

Less than an hour later, the small group came to the edge of what looked like a pond—or even a lake, since it stretched out in either direction as far as Urun could see—except that within the water were anchored tall trees. Cypress trees. Their thick trunks narrowed sharply as they stretched away from the muddy soup, and curtains of moss draped down gently over the trees' branches like burial shrouds. The thin fingers of the trees' leaves had always struck the priest as looking elegant, almost too artistic for the real world.

Urun stopped and stared at the water. "I thought we would be walking on solid—if soft—ground, not splashing through the water."

Tere chuckled. "I'm afraid you thought wrong."

"Aren't you supposed to know about all this stuff?" Lily asked. "You're a nature priest, right?"

Was the woman joking with him? He couldn't see it in her expression, but maybe she was one of those people who liked to joke with a straight face to confuse people.

"I've never seen a swamp. There's a lot of nature out

there, and some I haven't had the opportunity to experience. Like a desert, and like a swamp."

Tere was busy fiddling with the cloth wrapping on his bow stave. He finally got the knots out of the string tying it all together and unwrapped the bundle. It wasn't just his bow within. There were...sticks? They were half as thick as Urun's wrist and nearly as long as he was tall.

"Here," the archer said. "We'll need these. If we get lucky, we'll find some relatively dry ground, or at least firm ground, to walk on, but mostly we'll be sloshing through the water. Use the sticks to probe the area in front of you."

"Probe?" Urun said. "Probe for what?"

"Mainly for holes. You don't want to find out the ground under the water drops three feet by pitching into the liquid face first as you fall. Also, if there are things under the water, your stick will most likely frighten them off."

"Things? Most likely frighten them off?"

"Exactly." Tere waggled one of the sticks in front of Urun until the priest took it from him. "I'll go first, but you should still probe with your stick."

"Wait. What *things* might I scare off with my stick?"

Tere sighed. "There are snakes and insects and...animals. You probably don't want to have close contact with anything in the swamp. In fact, try not to touch the trees or the moss and especially the plants I point out as poisonous. If you brush too close to a tree, a spider or insect may attack you."

"Attack?"

"Urun, you're a nature priest. I've seen you walk through a forest while the plants actually moved out of your way."

Urun wiped his forehead, where perspiration gathered. "Yes, but that was the forest. This place doesn't seem to want to listen to me. I've never sensed anything like it. It's as if it's ready to pounce and swallow us up. It especially seems to hate *me*."

Marla put a hand on Urun's shoulder and he jumped. "We understand it's probably a lot worse for you because of your connection to nature. Tere has been through swamps before. Listen to him and we'll get through this. It may take a while —we're not going to be breaking any speed records walking carefully through the water—but we'll find your goddess and we'll do what we can."

"I...yes, you're right," he said. "Thank you. I'm really not this much of a coward usually. It all seems so overwhelmingly hostile, specifically to me."

"We know you're brave, Urun," Lily said. "Maybe if we get moving, you'll feel better."

Urun nodded, but didn't get a chance to say that he appreciated her words.

"Yeah, about that," Tere said. "We need to figure out where to go. The swamp is huge. If our plan is to wander until we find something, we'll be here for weeks."

"I've already thought of that," Urun said. "I plan on using the swamp itself to help us. I will commune with it and use its own sensation of where the corruption is to lead us there like a beacon."

"A sound plan," Tere said. He regarded Urun as if waiting for something.

It didn't pass Urun's notice that the others seemed to be waiting on him also.

Understanding dawned. "Oh. I should probably do that now, huh? Very well. It shouldn't take but a few minutes."

The priest turned his senses more fully on the swamp with the purpose of locating the core of whatever it was that made the area feel so unnatural. He beckoned to it, pleading with the Mellafond to reveal what was causing the corruption.

"Uh," he said after trying for a full five minutes. "There's a problem."

"What problem?" Marla asked. She had mounted her horse, probably so she didn't have to sit on the wet ground.

"The swamp doesn't seem to think anything is wrong. I am trying to use its own sense of where the problem is affecting it most, but it's like the whole thing insists that things are as they should be. It seems to think that all this unnaturalness is...natural."

"Can you ask it where the source of its power is?" Marla asked.

"I can't really ask it anything. It doesn't truly *think*. I try to pick up the sensations that travel throughout the area and use those feelings to get information. As for power, I can't search for that, especially since it appears that the source of power for the swamp and the corruption is one and the same. Tere? Can you search for the power with your magical sight?"

"No. There is a lot of magic here. I can't see where the source is, at least not until we're close to it."

"Well, damn," Marla said. "Then what do we do?"

"Maybe we can go to the center?" Urun said. "I would think that if there was one source of power, it would spread out equally in all directions, so the center would be the most logical place to look."

Marla cocked her head at him. "That...almost seems logical, though it shouldn't. Not really. Magic follows its own rules."

"It's something, though," Tere said. "It'll give us a direction, for now. With my tracker's sense, I should be able to keep us headed toward the center. Good enough. Let's do it. Urun, keep your senses peeled. Let me know if you get any feelings about where to go."

"I will."

The group started off again, Tere in the lead. Much of the day was spent sloshing through water. Most of it was ankle deep, but at times it got to mid-thigh. The trip was slow going, with having to prod ahead with the walking sticks and trying to keep balance in the uneven muck.

They had to be especially careful with the horses because their narrow hooves punched into the mud and at times were difficult to pull out. All they needed was for a horse leg to get stuck and topple the horse, breaking a leg.

They found two small areas of relatively dry ground, but it was too early in the day to stop. Urun gave each a sorrowful look as he plunged back in the water with the others.

Finally, an hour before sunset, they found another raised section of soil that was firm enough to use as a campground. Though they could probably travel another two hours, they decided as a group to stop early and continue in the morning.

Their home for the night was barely above water level, populated by matted grass and a few sickly bushes. There was one tree on it, seeming no different from those whose trunks were surrounded by water. Urun paced out four and a half steps on one side and six on the other, the extent of their slightly-less wet domain.

None of the wood in the area was dry enough to burn. Warm, humid air pressed in on them, though, so there was no need for heat, but Urun, for one, could have gone for some hot food. He sat on the ground in some of the longer grass, staring at his pack.

"You okay, Urun?" Lily asked.

"Yeah. I'm wishing we could build a fire so we could eat some hot food."

"I hear you."

"I'm not sure I can help with building a fire," Marla said, patting her horse on its flank and walking around toward the others. "But hot food? I think I can do that." She lifted her hand and a small flame danced in her palm.

Urun had to admit Marla's ability with fire magic was handy to have. There was still nothing but waterlogged wood around, but she heated up some food for them, including four fat fish Tere had spotted near their little island and taken with his arrows.

While they all sat on the damp grass eating, Urun gazed toward the center of the swamp, seeing nothing in the unnatural darkness. Was Osulin there, surrounded by the corruption he felt but was unable to do anything about? Was his goddess suffering while he ate a dinner of broiled fish? He hadn't even realized he was on his feet and stepping toward the water when Tere spoke.

"Urun, you'll do no good trying to splash through the water at night. Besides you not being able to see, many predators are nocturnal. You won't accomplish anything by trying to travel farther tonight."

"Osulin..." the priest said.

"There's nothing you can do tonight. I know you're anxious, but you can't go wandering about in the middle of the night. It won't do any good and it'll probably cause harm."

"He's right," Marla said. "It's hard to sit and wait like this, I know, but we have to. If we got attacked by something while trying to move at night, it could end our mission. You said yourself this place was corrupted. Do you think your spells will keep you safe? Even if they do, you'll get lost and probably cost yourself more time. Sit down, eat. As soon as it's light, we'll head out again."

With one more glance out toward the darkness, he did as she asked. Maybe he ought to go to sleep so time would pass more quickly. Then a thought occurred to him.

"What are we going to do for a watch schedule?"

"Three watches," Tere said. "One of us will get a break tonight. We'll rotate each night to be fair. Who is going to be the lucky one tonight?"

"Let Urun have the night off," Marla said. "Time will go faster for him if he sleeps through the night."

.E. PADILLA

Lily nodded, but Tere simply waited for some sign Urun would accept the privilege.

"I can take a watch," he said. "I'm not sure I could sleep anyway."

After discussing it for a few minutes, the others convinced Urun to not take a watch that night. Was it because they thought he'd leave in the middle of the night, trying to find his own way? He wasn't even sure himself if he would take such a risk. Of course, it would mean leaving his friends without a guard, which he doubted he would do. Still, the temptation would be there.

"Okay," he said. "I'll take tonight off, but I expect to have a watch tomorrow. Maybe the middle shift, to make up for sleeping all night tonight."

"Deal," Tere said.

Urun wasn't ready to sleep, though. None of the others were turning in, even though they'd be getting less sleep than he. It was still early yet and none of the other three had even laid out their bedrolls. Marla sat on her saddle blanket while Tere and Lily sat in the grass, him with legs crossed and her with her legs underneath her. It was surreal how much like every other evening of camping it was.

"So," Marla said, "what do you think will happen with Sutania and Rhaltzheim?"

Urun blinked. Was she talking to him? "Sutania and Rhaltzheim?"

"Yeah. They're at each other's throats."

Tere snorted. "They're always at each other's throats. What is it this time?"

Marla tried to run her fingers through her hair, but they got caught in a tangle. With a sigh, she pulled it back and wrapped a small leather string around it. "Same stuff as always, I think. They're fighting over the land at their borders. The area along the River Road isn't being hotly contested, probably because there are always people on that road; people from many different kingdoms. I've heard there have been skirmishes near Lusnauqua and Tarshuk."

"Actual fighting?" Lily asked.

"Yeah, some, but they haven't declared war on each other. Yet. With this animaru thing, we really need to be gathering all the nations together, but some seem determined to be in conflict with their neighbors. We need to figure out how to bring everyone together to fight the animaru. If we're squabbling, we won't be able to save Dizhelim. There are way too many of the monsters. If we can't stop them from coming over, I don't know how we'll withstand their invasion."

"You have a point," Tere said. "We need to figure out how to get to all of them, maybe travel from one nation to the next, gathering support."

"But how?" Lily asked. "Normal people can't barge into a king's throne room and demand that the king hear them out."

Tere chuckled. "You're right about that. I've had some dealings with monarchs and city leaders. It's difficult dealing with the politics. People in authority by their nature look down on common people. We'd need the Academy to give us legitimacy."

"They're working on it," Marla said. "Once the announcement about the Malatirsay is spread around, we should be able to get more support."

"Do you think so?" Tere asked.

"I...I assumed. Why? Do you disagree?"

"I'm probably not one to answer that. I've been in the Grundenwald for twenty years, so I'm a little out of date with my knowledge of things, but back when I knew what was going on in the world, the Academy didn't have the respect it did centuries ago."

Urun didn't know anything more than Tere did about things happening in the world. He'd been in the forest for a fair amount of time, and even when he lived in the town he grew up in, he paid little attention to peoples' attitudes in general, let alone what they thought of the Hero Academy.

"He's right," Lily said, gracing Marla with a sympathetic look. "I've been traveling all of Dizhelim for years, and the Academy is sometimes talked about as a joke. I'm sure it's only because they don't know what goes on there."

Marla sighed. "No. There's probably a reason for it. It's been so long since the Prophecy was given and Sitor-Kanda was built. I think we lost sight of our true purpose to train the one—or ones—to come. The Academy settled into passing on knowledge, but it was trapped between wanting to train the Malatirsay and realizing what it meant to be a resource for the Malatirsay.

"It seems clear now that the masters should have been working with the governments of all of Dizhelim, aiding them with their knowledge and maintaining good relationships. After all, the purpose of the Academy, of the Malatirsay itself, is to unite the world behind them so everyone can fight the animaru. Over all the years, we lost sight of that important point. I think people believe the Malatirsay will just wave a hand and defeat the animaru.

"It's no wonder people don't take the Academy seriously. We've kept to ourselves like we were above everyone else. Like those rulers Tere just mentioned. Now we're paying the price of that arrogance."

"I don't know if it's that serious," Tere said, "but what you say has some truth. Do you think the masters feel the same way?"

"Some of them do, I'm sure. The headmaster and a few others. I don't know about the rest. I can only hope that they see the evidence and arrive at the same logical conclusion I did. We'll need to work hard to make up for lost time."

"Master Qydus seems competent," Tere said. "I'm sure he's already working on it."

"Yeah, probably."

The four travelers sat in silence, the only sounds the shuffling of the horses and the crickets and other insects that had started their evening symphony. It didn't feel awkward to Urun, only a momentary chance at reflection. It was comfortable, in a way, which surprised him.

He was going to say something, but the thought flew out of his head when a screech nearby shattered the mood, followed closely by a deep, angry growl.

❧ 13 ❧

"So what have you been doing besides finding a wife?" Aeden asked Greimich. They walked the North Road, the green splotch of the Grundenwald back behind their left shoulders. The grasses that populated the area between the massive forest and the Cridheargla allowed them to see for miles toward the north as they made their way east, back toward the highlands. Aeden had thought to borrow horses from the Academy, but Greimich told him they didn't need the animals. Many of the clan members that came with Aeden's friend couldn't ride, and it quickly became apparent there would be arguments if Aeden tried to push the issue.

"Let's see," Greimich said. "After you were ritually killed for failing the Trial of Magic, things were strange. Not only your parents and I were affected. It seemed to strike a blow at the entire class of trainees. The traditional celebration was subdued, almost like people didn't want to celebrate, even though they had passed their training and were clan warriors. No one could believe it, and the elders didn't hide what happens to those who fail the final trial.

"It was a month until things seemed to get back anywhere

near to normal, but maybe that was just my opinion. The elders and the training masters seemed to make a special exception for the situation. Whereas normally, a new warrior would be put to work or sent out with raiding or hunting parties right away, they allowed us time.

"I finally began to take part in battles with the other clans and in rotations for patrol duty. Slowly, life got back to normal. As normal as it could be, in any case.

"I started helping out Eimhir, the clan healer. I'd go and fetch herbs and roots she asked for and occasionally captured or killed animals or insects as well. It was on one of these foraging trips that I first saw Catriona, who was doing similar duty."

The man from the Trebhin clan, Dubhghall, sneered when he heard Greimich say it, as if someone had suggested sex with animals. It was clear the man was thoroughly convinced of his clan's superiority and that the other clans were lesser humans, if humans at all. Affection for a person of a different clan was typically frowned upon by all the clans.

Aeden figured he couldn't blame Dubhghall for having that attitude. Aeden himself was raised to believe his clan was the best. Didn't he still believe that? Still, he had no problem with Greimich and Catriona being married, even if he did feel at least a little superior to the Trebhin man. Attitudes like that would cause them problems in trying to unite the clans.

"We talked after a tense few moments," Greimich continued. "It wasn't like I was going to attack a woman."

Cat scoffed, expelling air in a hiss.

"Not because I don't see them as skilled warriors," he explained, "but because I was raised to be polite to women folk. Warrior or not, they're prettier than me, so I try to stay on their good side. It helps when they're deciding if they want to stab you for staring at them." He showed all his teeth to his wife and she laughed.

"The tension wasn't because I was deciding whether to start a fight. It was because she looked to be getting ready to attack me. Thankfully, she did not, and I was able to give a greeting with my hands in the air."

A disgusted sound from Dubhghall interrupted Greimich, but he only rolled his eyes and continued.

"Once we started talking, I found that my Cat was not only beautiful, but she was intelligent and clever as well. I'd interacted with women in our clan—though never in a romantic way; who had time for that during training?—but never felt a connection like with Cat. We saw each other a few more times after that. I tried to predict when she'd be out searching for herbs so I could talk with her. Soon, we were setting appointments to meet up.

"Her father hated Tannochs and would have killed me on sight had he known. Hells, he'd have killed me on sight even if he hadn't known, just for being Tannoch. He came around, finally, and with his authority as an Ailgid clan elder, he secretly married us, though we had to *keep* it secret.

"In the end, their clan was almost completely destroyed by the dark beasts. Marriage between the clans doesn't seem to bother those who are left. Even between us, we have a bare handful of Croagh from both clans."

"Aye," Aeden said. "Something we need to prevent from happening with the others. Tannoch, Ailgid, Trebhin, Corcan, Seachaid, all of the clans, we're still all Croagh. Unless we gather together to fight the animaru, there may not be even a handful of highlanders in all the world."

Aeden noticed that the other Croagh nodded at his statement, even Dubhghall. Maybe there was hope for them after all. If he could at least make the Trebhin see the necessity, it might be enough.

Aeden had already told Greimich about what happened to him, so he didn't need to explain in detail about how he had been adopted into the Gypta—something else Dubhghall sneered at—and the awakening of his magic. He did speak more specifically about his dealings with the animaru, and the other Croagh seemed to take an interest.

Finally, the representatives of the other clans explained their dealings with the animaru. There hadn't been much, not like with Aeden's clan and with Catriona's clan, but there had been skirmishes, all resulting in dead highlanders. The monsters had not attacked the clan villages, mainly because they didn't need to. Their top priority was to find and kill Aeden.

Now it was different, though. More animaru had come over, enough that they could spread their forces out and start attacking locations with small populations. Places like the highlands.

He was thinking about what that meant for the future when he caught sight of the first of the groups of people plodding down the road toward his party.

Aeden and Greimich stopped, and the others came to a halt behind them, waiting for the ragged figures in front of them to come close enough to speak. The people, nearly fifty as far as Aeden could see, trudged along, some of them carrying sacks or packs, others with only the threadbare clothes on their backs.

Many of the people wore roughspun cloth in a style that marked them as farmers. A few others wore tunics and pants or dresses that had once been fine, but were no longer so.

All the people had one thing in common, though: expressions of bone-weary fatigue etched on their faces. Fatigue and maybe hopelessness.

"Ho there," Aeden said to the older man at the front of the group. It was obvious the others were following him. He was in his middle years, ragged but not so old as to be frail. "From where do you come and where do you go?"

The man raised a hand and the procession came to a stop. "We are not harming anyone, nor are we causing problems. Let us be." He spoke with an accent, the clipped consonants of someone from Kruzekstan. It made sense, since the North Road ended in that nation.

"I'm not challenging you," Aeden said. "I am merely curious what would cause such a large group of people to travel where there are few settlements. Is there trouble to the east?"

The man gave a mirthless laugh. "Trouble, you say? Yes, there is trouble. The darkness has come and the world should be wary."

"Darkness?" Aeden said, glancing at Greimich and then at Khrazhti. The blue woman had pulled her cloak tight and brought her hood down further to cover her features. She slouched behind Greimich and Catriona, trying to remain unseen. That was good. In this case, anyway.

"Yes. Foul dark creatures have attacked some of the smaller settlements around Nanris. They destroy farms, slaughter livestock, and kill people. When they strike, they leave none living, but neither do they eat the dead, leaving them to rot."

"Have you seen these creatures?"

"Do I look dead to you?" the man asked bitterly. His face took on a pensive cast and he continued, "Completely dead, in any case? I am aware I and my fellows look at least half dead. But no, I have not seen them. There is one among us who spied them from a hiding place, however; the only survivor of Dmirgan. We took what we could and fled, for our village would have been next and none of us is fond of the thought of being torn to pieces and left to rot on the ground."

"I understand," Aeden said. "We have fought these creatures. They are called animaru. We go to gather the forces in the highlands to battle with the monsters."

"Then you go to your death," the man spat. "They cannot be killed. The entire city guard in Omri was slaughtered to a man by a less numerous force. No matter how many times the beasts were cut or impaled, they continued to kill the people."

"There's a trick to killing them," Greimich said. "Light or life magic is needed."

The man blinked at Greimich and then stared for a dozen seconds. "Magic? Who has magic these days but the heroes at the Academy?"

"We do," Aeden said, calling up a simple flame from the Academy spell he had been practicing. It wasn't much more than a flicker, but from the oohs coming from the crowd, it was enough.

The man dropped to his knees and, a few seconds later, so did the people behind him. "I'm sorry, great lord. Please, don't turn your magic on us. We're simple people trying to find somewhere safe, somewhere away from the monsters."

Aeden stepped forward and put his hand on the man's shoulder. "Please, get up. I only showed you the magic so that you would take heart that there are those who can harm the creatures. Continue to the west, as far as the Academy at Sitor Kanda if you can. There are fewer of the animaru there. If we're successful, we will hold them to the east, if not destroy them.

"It's true that there is darkness in the world, but there is light, too. Tell everyone you meet of what has happened in Kruzekstan. We will need everyone to unite to fight this threat."

The man got to his feet. "Thank you. I and my people will tell of our experiences. All we want to do is to live without fear, if that is even possible in these days."

"It is a time of fear," Aeden said, "but it is also a time of heroes. Erent Caahs has returned, and there are other mighty ones fighting for Dizhelim."

"You tell everyone the Malatirsay has arrived," Greimich added. Aeden threw the man a look, trying to keep him from speaking more, but his friend ignored it. "The time of darkness spoken of in the prophecy is at hand. We must all fight for our very world. Tell them, and maybe it will help."

"I will, sirs. Thank you. I will."

Aeden nodded at the man. "Safe travels, then. Have you any coin?"

"Very little," the man said.

Aeden reached into the purse at his side and pulled out a handful of gold coins. He still had two full purses from the gold they had found at Broken Reach, from the treasures some of the animaru had brought back from their raids, though he still couldn't figure out why because they used no currency.

The man's eyes went wide. He made no move to take the money.

"Take it," Aeden said. "Buy food and supplies. If the monsters win, money will be worthless anyway."

Finally, the man accepted the coins, bowing his head to Aeden. "You are too kind, sir. Thank you. May I ask your name so I will know to whom I am indebted?"

"I'm Aeden Tannoch, but there is no debt, unless it is to keep your people safe and fed."

After several more expressions of gratitude, the man finally chivvied his people into motion, lumbering west on the road. The ragtag appearance of the group, especially the children, tore at Aeden's heart.

"That was kind of you," Catriona said, though Dubhghall scoffed in the background. Of course.

"What good is money to us," Aeden asked, "especially compared with what they've experienced?"

"They're the lucky ones," Greimich noted. "How many others of their friends or kin are rotting in their villages to the east?"

"True. We need to get to the highlands. Uniting what's left of the clans will not only help the Croagh, but maybe it will help others as well."

"We aren't going to spill Croagh blood to protect the damn Kruzeks," Dubhghall said. "They can die for all it means to us."

Aeden shared a look with Greimich, but let it go. The Trebhin was generally disagreeable and it would do no good to enter into conflict with him. The elders of the clans would make the decision. Dubhghall was just a clan warrior.

"Let's go. We've got some distance to travel yet. Time is even shorter than I had thought."

❧ 14 ❧

The growls and screeches of a predator catching its prey stopped Urun from speaking. He scanned the darkness around him, trying to snatch a glimpse of what had produced the shriek and, maybe more importantly, what had snarled. Both creatures had gone silent.

It wasn't anything new to the nature priest, not really. He had lived in the wilds of nature for some time and had heard the evidence of the constant struggle to survive among the animals. He couldn't place the sounds, but that shouldn't have shaken him since this was an entirely new natural cycle for him. He really was out of sorts.

"The beasts are no concern of ours," Tere said to no one in particular. Urun couldn't help but to think the comment was directed at him.

There were no further noises, though Urun thought he heard tearing and chewing barely evident on the wind. He was probably imagining it. Lily set herself up to watch while the rest of the little party laid down wherever they could find relatively dry and flat ground on their little island, knobby with cypress roots. Urun worried he wouldn't sleep at all, but found himself drifting into slumber as soon as he lay down. The energy-sapping anxiety of the day seemed to have caught up to him.

In the morning, the group waded off again, heading toward the center of the swamp. Again, they spent most of the day splashing through the water, walking slowly and prodding the way ahead with every step. Snakes Urun didn't recognize swam through the water, their sinuous bodies sliding effortlessly as they made S shapes in the liquid. The priest saw few other creatures; because there were none or because they were wary, he didn't know.

In the early afternoon, Tere stiffened and put his hand up to halt the rest of the travelers. The archer cocked his head as if listening. Urun strained his own ears and heard faint sounds. Some splashing and...grunting?

Tere seemed to have determined where the sounds were coming from because he handed his walking stick to Lily, tied his horse to the nearest cypress tree, and took up his bow. Then he headed off to the left of their route. After similarly tying their horses, the archer woman followed close behind him, as did Marla and Urun. As they got closer to the source of the sound, it resolved into something familiar.

To Urun, it sounded like combat, but not combat with swords and knives, for there was no clanking of steel on steel. There were dull thumps and tearing sounds, almost like cloth ripping. Someone was fighting. Or some*thing*.

When Urun was positioned to peek around Tere and Lily, he blinked and rubbed his eyes. Nearly a dozen shapes moved around at the edge of an island of dry land, some in the water and some on the dirt. They were indeed fighting, and they were humanoid.

It was clear to which side each creature belonged. The majority of them were dark shapes, some black and some grey, while the few others were forest colors, greens and browns. They were all humanoid, but it seemed to be a battle of monster factions, the shadowy creatures versus the nature-hued figures.

Urun stepped to the side, hiding behind a nearby tree. The combatants hadn't seen the humans yet and the priest would prefer it if they didn't. The others seemed to have the same opinion because Tere and Lily ducked behind another tree while Marla crouched and found her own hiding place.

Tere motioned back the way they had come. Better to let the monsters kill each other than for the humans to risk themselves by interfering. Urun agreed, but cast one more look toward the creatures before leaving.

The dark creatures looked to have raised up from the swamp itself, tendrils of vegetation hanging from their bodies and what looked like moss or other fungus coating parts of their unclad forms. Their hands ended in sharp claws that they used, along with their teeth, to tear into their enemies. Already, three of the green creatures sprawled on the ground leaking—surprisingly—blood that looked like that running through human veins. There didn't appear to be any of the dark creatures down.

All of the combatants were misshapen, though in different ways. The dark creatures were tall and gangly, with long arms compared to humans of that size. The green and brown monsters had bulges and a strange asymmetry to their forms.

The green combatants seemed to be using tools or weapons, though crude ones. Small wooden cudgels, a metal knife or two, and that was about it. They couldn't seem to withstand the other monsters. It was clear which group would be the victors.

Urun whispered a prayer to Osulin that the green creatures, who were intelligent enough to use tools, wouldn't suffer long.

As he turned to leave—Tere was hissing at him to hurry—Urun glimpsed something at the edge of the dry mound, a tiny movement in a clump of bushes. He narrowed his eyes to focus and as he did, his mouth dropped open.

Raising his staff in both hands, he splashed through the water, running as fast as he could without tripping in the muck.

Right toward the battle.

Tere cursed and other splashing soon followed. Urun couldn't spare the breath to explain. He hoped the others would take his lead and go with him. What he had seen in those bushes changed everything. As he ran, he called on his power and began casting something he hoped would help.

Two of the dark swamp creatures on the edge of the fighting noticed Urun and turned their focus to him. He paid them no mind. Another two steps and his magic flared to life. It was the first time he had cast it in real combat, a spell called Life Spike he had received when Osulin had granted him more power. He hoped it did what he intended.

The magic flew from his staff in the form of a triangular mass of life energy and slammed into the dark monster that had been stealthily moving around the bushes he had seen move. The energy threw the beast to the side, puncturing the upper part of its chest and provoking a screech of anger and pain from it. The attack also flushed out the denizens of the foliage. Three small figures, green in color, scampered out of their hiding place and ran for the few larger green combatants.

"No!" one of the fighters screamed, its voice sounding definitely feminine. Now that he was closer, Urun realized that what he had thought was a malformed body was in actuality some type of camouflage clothing or armor covering a woman who looked—except for the color—to be human.

Another of the people, this one male and more brown

than green, threw a gaze Urun's way and yelled to him. "Flee. The monsters cannot be killed. Take our children and flee. Please. We will hold them off as long as we can."

The speech, perfect Ruthrin with only a little accent, stunned Urun for a moment, but not as much as the implication of what he said.

Urun whirled to see Tere, Lily, and Marla a few steps from him, racing toward the priest.

"They're animaru," Urun shouted. "Some type we haven't seen before."

Tere nodded and launched three arrows at the dark creatures attacking the green woman. Two of Lily's arrows were not far behind, one of them a special fire arrow Marla had given her. All of them struck true and four of the creatures dropped to the soggy ground, one hit by arrows from both archers and another blown half apart from the combination of the fire and the life energy within it. All of Urun's friends had for some time imbued all their weapons with life energy each day in case they encountered animaru. He was glad of the habit now.

Marla, not to be outdone, threw her hands out and jets of flame washed over the two monsters bearing down on Urun. They screamed, but did not die immediately.

Animaru were susceptible to fire but not nearly as much so as life magic. You could harm an animaru with fire magic, but not kill it. He cast Life Spike again and a jagged bolt of life magic tore through the two creatures.

One of the animaru—were they really the creatures from Aruzhelim, looking like swamp monsters?—abandoned its original target and sprinted toward the children, who had dropped to the ground in fear. Urun gritted his teeth and threw his magic out one more time. A pale shield engulfed the children. The dark creature launched itself at them, teeth bared as it swiped at them with both claws.

And bounced off the shield protecting the small ones.

Two arrows raced each other to take the monster in both sides of its head, twisting its body with their force and ending the attack.

As soon as the last of the monsters fell, the green woman ran to the young ones. She slowed when she approached, wary of the shield, but when it didn't prevent her passage—Urun had dropped the spell—she swept two of them up in her arms while putting a hand out to the other.

The green man, dressed mostly in brown, eyed the newcomers but splashed to one of his injured companions who had been slashed with one of the attacker's claws. He was bleeding profusely and wouldn't last long with the wound.

The nature priest joined the two. The uninjured man looked at him warily, but made no aggressive movements.

"I'm a priest of Osulin," Urun said. The man's eyes widened in such a way that left no doubt he knew who the goddess was. "Let me heal him before he loses too much blood."

The man nodded. "What would you have me do?"

"Comfort him with your presence. It won't take long, though with a wound such as this, I'll need to use herbs as well as magic." He took a few herbs from the pouch at his belt—feverbane, white fennel, and godshead—and began entreating Osulin for power. He knew the goddess was in no position to grant him extra magic, but regardless, he gave thanks to her as he used what power he had. As he prayed and drew on his power, he crushed the dry herbs and sprinkled them on the wounds.

If the green man's eyes had been wide before, they were impossibly big now. A very slight glow accompanied healing, but Urun didn't think that was what awed the man. It was almost as if he could sense the magic.

It took three castings of healing spells to mend the wound

and stabilize the injured man. When it was done, Urun sat back on his feet, breathing heavily. He hadn't paid attention to anything else, fully absorbed in his healings, but he looked around now to find his friends, the green woman, and three green children looking at him.

"Are there others who are injured?" he asked in a hoarse voice.

"No," Tere said. "The others were already dead. It's only these three and the children left."

One of the children sobbed at the statement and Tere winced as if realizing what he'd said in front of the child. His parents were probably lying dead in front of them.

The green woman dropped to her knees in the few inches of water she had been standing in. "Thank you, lord. Thank you for saving us and for the miracle of healing on Touri."

Urun stepped over and took her arm, helping her to her feet. "No. I am not a lord, but only a priest of Osulin." Shock painted her face, as it had the man earlier when he mentioned the goddess. "You know of her?"

"We do. The goddess and her mother are well known to the arba."

"What?" Marla said. "Arba? But the arba are extinct. There has been no record of them for several hundred years. The last was around the end of the Age of Magic."

The green woman cocked her head. "We do not leave the swamp. Perhaps we have been...overlooked."

Marla shook her head and muttered to herself. She seemed to be arguing both sides of a point. Urun turned his attention back to the woman.

"I am Urun Chinowa, priest of Osulin, as I've said."

"I am Misun," the woman said, "and this is my mate Rogen and my children Chuli and Nedu. Touri is the man you healed. Also here is Dob." She stepped closer to Urun and whispered, "His father lies there, dead." She pointed toward one of the corpses, shielding the child's view with her body.

"I'm so sorry we didn't arrive sooner," he said.

"Do not apologize for saving our lives. Had you not arrived when you did, we too would be face down in the water. Thank you."

Lily stepped up, and Misun bent her neck to look up at the tall archer. "Have you been attacked by those creatures before?"

"Our people have," Touri said, already standing though he'd been a hair's breadth from death only moments before. "But not us personally. Every one of our tribe that has encountered the monsters this closely is dead. The best we had hoped for was to delay them long enough for the children to escape. As Rogen said earlier, we have not been able to kill them. Yet you were able..."

"We have encountered ones similar to them before," Urun said. "Magic may injure them, but only life or light magic can kill them. Fortunately, we have such spells, one of which I use to coat our weapons with life magic. That's why we could kill them. How long have they been attacking you?"

"The first attacks were a few weeks ago," Misun said. "We had never seen them before that. The swamp has been... changing of late."

"That's why we're here," Urun said. "We're trying to find the source of the changes. Can you help us?"

Misun shared a look with her husband while worrying her lower lip with her teeth. "It is prohibited to associate with outsiders. Defiance may result in our expulsion from the tribe."

Urun didn't know what to say to that. Nor did any of his companions, it seemed. The silence stretched as he tried to think of what to do.

"Misun," Rogen said, "if they had not shown up, we would

be dead. What is expulsion compared to that? He is one of Osulin's own. When was the last time the goddess took a servant? I say we chance bringing them to the elders. If we are cast out, so be it. It may be, however, that these can help us. It is already clear they know more about how to fight the monsters than we."

"Yes. Perhaps you are correct." Misun turned to Urun. "We will take you to our village to see the wise ones. I hope we can help each other." She forced a smile, which Urun returned. He understood the risk she was taking. Being expelled from the only family one knew was a serious matter. Still, he was glad she had decided to bring them to the tribe. If anyone could tell them what had been happening in the swamp, it was the arba, a race also known as the forest people, staunch supporters of everything natural.

And, obviously, of the goddess Osulin.

❧ 15 ❧

The arba picked up their items just outside where the battle had occurred. There were several fish, some strange salamander-like creatures, and a fair amount of firewood. Urun thought it strange that they carried so much wood but then realized with most of the ground covered in water, wood dry enough to burn would be at a premium.

"Here," he said, helping to pick up some of the fuel. "Let me help you carry these."

The children looked confused, but Mlsun smiled at the priest. The expression didn't last long, though, as her eyes moved past Urun to where their dead lay.

"Do you...do you prepare your dead in some way?" he asked.

Marla answered before either of the arba could. "The arba were known to bury their dead."

"That is true, in general," Rogen said. "Our ancestors in the forest did so, but we cannot. Bury a body in the swamp and it is likely to pop up again in the future, perhaps where you least expect it. We burn our dead so that we may scatter the ashes on the soggy ground and allow the person to go back to the soil in that way."

"But we haven't the time or fuel enough to do so," Misun said. "With how many have fallen to the monsters lately, we must wait several days so that we can build pyres for more than one person. I am afraid we will have to leave them for the swamp and its creatures to take."

One of the children gasped. Urun recognized him as the one whose father had died.

"I am sorry, Dob."

Marla was inspecting the area, but Urun didn't know what she hoped to find. After a moment of contemplation, she spoke. "Wait. I think I can help with that. Let's bring them here." She pointed to a relatively dry spot on the raised section of the terrain.

The two arba threw quizzical glances toward her, but began to do as she said. Urun, Tere, and Lily helped, with Marla directing them where to put the bodies. She moved part of a downed tree next to a flat rock almost as long as a person, then motioned for the corpses to be lain across both, keeping them slightly off the ground.

Once the bodies were in place, Marla turned to the green people. "Do you have words to say or rituals to perform?"

Rogen pulled his eyes from the bodies. "We are simple people, and Osulin and Mellaine are not ones for flowery speeches. If we may say a few words?"

"Of course."

He cleared his throat, glanced to his wife and the children, and turned back to his former friends. "Osulin, goddess of nature, and Mellaine her mother, please accept these back into the cycle of life. Ever they strove to live according to their natural roles and we ask that, as they were created of the raw stuff of the land, they once again will walk Dizhelim to do further work in your service, even if as part of another type of living thing. We now consign their physical bodies to our home, the swamp and the land."

The children had bowed their heads, as did the adults. A soft sobbing came from Dob, his eyes glued to the form of his father. Urun and his friends bowed their heads in respect as well, but all looked up to Rogen when he finished speaking.

He seemed at a loss about what to do. "This is when we usually light the pyre."

Marla nodded and joined him near the corpses. "Step back now."

He did, rejoining his wife, their friend Touri, and the children.

Marla took a breath. She began a short incantation, thrust both hands out toward the bodies, and cast one of the fire spells Urun had seen her use before in combat. Jets of flame shot out from her fingers, licking the bodies. At first, the wet clothing steamed and smoked, but soon, the water evaporated and the cloth caught fire. The green and brown outfits seemed to be made of some natural fiber, most likely something from one of the plants in the swamp. It didn't burn like the clothing Urun was familiar with, almost as if it contained a high content of moisture in itself. Soon after, the bodies themselves began to melt and blacken. Spouts of flame appeared in some areas where body tissue burned more readily than others around it.

The air filled with the sweet, sickly smell of burned flesh. It soon mingled with another odor, one more reminiscent of meat charring over a cookfire. Marla continued to feed the flames with her magic. In a few minutes, the bodies were reduced to ash, the magical fire shortening the process considerably compared to a wood fire.

She finally ended the spell. A few small pieces smoldered,

but the work was essentially done. She dipped her head again, then turned toward the others.

All three of the adult arba were standing with their mouths open, blinking. Urun wondered why. Hadn't they seen her use magic during the battle?

The green people hit the ground with their knees. "Thank you," Misun said. "Thank you for using precious magic to aid in their spirits' passing. First we behold a priest of Osulin, and now a great mage the likes of which hasn't been seen in centuries. The wise ones must heed these signs."

Marla didn't seem to like being fawned over any more than Urun did. She helped the woman up, saying, "It's just a simple spell. Many at the Academy can cast it as well or better than me."

"The Academy?" Dob said. "You are a hero from the Hero Academy?"

"I am," Marla said. "Do you know of it?"

The young arba nodded, but seemed tongue tied.

Misun smiled at the boy. "He has for years told anyone who will listen that he will be the first of our people to go to the great Academy."

"Is this true?" Marla asked, crouching down in front of the young arba. He nodded vigorously. "Well, then, perhaps we can talk about this once the danger has passed and we have made the swamp safe again. I know the headmaster of the Academy at Sitor-Kanda. Personally. I might be able to bring you to talk to him. No promises, mind you, but if you can impress Master Qydus, maybe he will let you study there. We're always looking for brave and hard-working young people."

The boy seemed ready to explode, his eyes wide. His entire body vibrated, like he was preparing to jump as high as he could. "Thank you," he said, but couldn't seem to keep eye contact.

"You're welcome. First, though, we need to talk to your elders and see how we can help. These monsters must be stopped from hurting anyone else."

Misun tousled Dob's hair. "Yes, it is time for us to return to the village. Please, follow us."

❦ 16 ❦

It took the strange party several hours to make it to the arba village. Along the way, the adult arba unerringly led them through the easiest passage, finding narrow strips of relatively dry ground for them to travel upon. Urun had no doubt that without the green people to guide them, it would have taken twice as much time or more, even if they knew where the village was to begin with.

When they reached the outskirts of the village, structures began to appear. They were unlike any Urun had ever seen, a combination of erected buildings and living plants. He passed the first few without even realizing what they were, but once he figured it out, a glance cast back over his shoulder confirmed that the abnormal shapes were indeed homes.

The domiciles were low to the ground, though built on small stilts to keep their floors above the water level. Much wider than they were tall, it seemed that the owners wouldn't be able to stand up inside them, but it was an illusion. Because of the overall squat shapes, they didn't appear very tall until an arba male stepped out through the door opening and Urun could judge the relative size of the home.

Draped over the buildings were vines and even moss, a wetter equivalent to sod-roofed homes, Urun thought. The plants appeared to be living still and not only tight enough to keep the insides dry, but also able to absorb the moisture from rain.

Urun's inspection of the houses was interrupted as they came upon more and more of the green people. They didn't look shocked, exactly, but there was concern etched into some of their faces at the newcomers' arrival. Misun waved at them to allay their fears, but in the eyes of some, the concern deepened as they made a count of the arba entering the village. Urun understood. They had realized some of their number were missing.

The procession stopped in a wide, open area at the center of the village. A rack-like contraption dominated a large open space, ash sitting at its bottom. As with most of the other manufactured things in the village, it was raised above the ground, resting on stones as high as Urun's knees. It was likely that even the dry ground flooded occasionally in hard rains or as the swamp shifted. This was their answer to a fire pit.

An older arba woman exited a home nearby, and the three who had been leading the humans bowed their head to her in respect. The children, shedding nervous energy the entire trip, became still and bowed their heads to the woman as well.

"Leaf Talker Vora, Mother, we have brought news."

The green eyes of the woman—Urun wasn't sure if she was actually Misun's mother or if it was a title for her—swept over the humans. Her orbs were the pale color of moss that had dried in the sun, such as the clumps of beard moss Urun had seen often in his home within the Grundenwald Forest.

"You have brought more than news, it seems." Her mouth remained in a line, neither a frown nor a smile to indicate her mood. The tone could have been disapproving or merely an emotionless statement of fact.

"We have, Mother," Rogen said. "Forgive us for leading strangers to the village, but please hear our news first, before judging us too harshly."

"They're heroes," Dob said. "They saved us from the monsters."

Misun made a shushing noise, but too late.

The older woman's mouth twitched into a slight smile. "I will hear of these heroes. Come, the open air is no place for such tales." She turned and glided back to the home from which she had emerged. Misun whispered something to her children and motioned for another arba woman nearby to come to her. A few words and the other woman led the children off toward another home.

"Please," Misun said, motioning for the humans to follow after the elder woman.

Once inside—the space was larger than it looked from the outside—the humans and their arba guides took the seats provided. There were a number of short stools within, making Urun suspect they were not in a home, as he had first thought, but in some type of meeting room.

"Where are Bardun, Aleor, and Feras?" the older woman said.

"They are dead," Touri said, "as I would be had this man not healed me. The monsters, they caught us unawares. As we fought to allow the children to hide or flee, these came upon us and destroyed the beasts, but not before the others were fatally wounded. I was seriously injured, unto death, but this one,"—he pointed to Urun— "healed me of my injuries."

"Healed you? Of injuries that were serious enough to cause death?"

"Yes, Leaf Talker. He is a priest of Osulin."

Urun was watching the older woman's face; otherwise, he

wouldn't have noticed her eyes widen slightly. She controlled her emotions well, though, and brought her expression to neutral so quickly that the priest was sure no one else saw it.

"I see." She blinked. "Did you say...they destroyed the foul creatures?"

"I did."

This time, she was unable to control her shocked expression. "Our best warriors could not keep the beasts from getting back up after the most savage of blows. We have not been able to kill even one. How? How can you kill them?"

Urun looked to Marla and Tere. Both met his eyes but made no move to answer the question. Logical, considering the weight the arba put upon Osulin's name. "Life magic. Other magic can affect them, too, but only life or light magic can kill them."

"And you have such magic?"

"We do. Much of the magic Osulin grants me is of life. Marla has been trained at Sitor-Kanda and can use many types of magic, including life magic."

The elder arba considered Marla for a moment, then turned back to Touri. "The others, the ones who were killed, did you bring their bodies back so their spirits can be soothed with a sending?"

"No, Mother," Misun said. "We could not carry them so far. This one, Marla, used fire magic and reduced their bodies to ash so they could rejoin the cycle."

The leader of the arba closed her eyes for a moment, but whether it was in sorrow, respect, or something else, Urun couldn't tell. "You have our gratitude, strangers, both for rescuing these and for enabling our brothers to gain the rest they deserve. You are welcome here, priest of Osulin and wielders of magic. Perhaps it is Osulin's will that brings you here."

"About that," Urun said. "What you say is correct, in a

way, but probably not as you think. We weren't sent by Osulin so much as we came here looking for her. Our goddess is in trouble, and we are here to help."

"We seem to have goals that align," Vora said. "Perhaps we can aid each other. My people know the swamp, and you have the power to defeat the monsters that have recently plagued us. We can help you find what you seek, and in return, you can—"

A loud screech echoed in the room, seeming to pass without trouble through the walls from outside. Following immediately were shouts. Then screams.

Urun jumped to his feet, but his friends were faster than him. Tere was already halfway out the door, followed closely by Marla and Lily. The priest spared a moment to register the shocked look on the Leaf Talker's face and followed his friends outside.

What only a few minutes before was a peaceful picture of simple village life no longer resembled that. Figures were charging into the communal area, some loping like beasts and others slithering like slippery eels. Everywhere, green humanoid bodies strived to withstand the charge of creatures, but for the most part, to no avail.

Some of the attackers had the same forms the humans had met hours before, twisted animaru with elements of plants and trees embedded within them. The other assailants, though, were something Urun had never seen.

They looked like piles of rotting vegetation that had somehow been able to get up and move around. Bits of wood and leaves stuck out of their hides and Urun doubted there was anything but plant matter throughout their entire bodies. They leaned in one direction to begin moving and then toppled in the direction they had chosen. It was a sort of slithering, slipping, falling movement. If it weren't for the effect of the creatures colliding with the arba, Urun would have found their appearance laughable.

As it was, though, there was nothing funny about it. When one of the plant monsters came within reach of an arba, it lashed out with slimy appendages, like vines or tentacles, slamming into the victims so powerfully, it broke their bones. Snaps and cracks were the precursors to screams of agony.

In amongst the damage being done by the plants, the modified animaru did what they did best: tear and puncture with claws and teeth.

Tere and Lily were already firing arrows nonstop, taking out animaru left and right. The shafts didn't seem to do much damage to the plant creatures, possibly because they had no organs to target. For those, Marla was making her presence known.

The red-haired Academy graduate slashed out with her sword and dueling knife, cutting parts off the plant monsters. Occasionally, she threw magic at them, lances of light or fire that burned whole sections of the monsters away. There were several already dissolving into piles of loose vegetation.

Urun took Marla's lead and began throwing light lances at the plant creatures or at the animaru, if those were closest. The arba had mounted a defense, slashing at the attackers, warding off the monsters' attacks as best they could. Their efforts had little effect on the animaru, but they did better with the plant creatures.

Urun wiped sweat from his head. They'd been fighting for several minutes and probably two dozen attackers remained in front of the humans and arba. Suddenly, without a sound, all the creatures turned and fled, the animaru with their beast-like movements and the plant creatures in their own slippery gait. In moments, the only monsters left were the bodies of those that had been slain.

Urun wanted nothing more than to sit down or, even better, lie down and rest, but he knew he couldn't. There were injured arba he could help. He shuffled to the closest while getting Tere's attention. The archer nodded, already guessing what Urun wanted. He immediately moved among the injured, assessing the magnitude of injuries so that Urun could heal the most serious first.

Half an hour later, Urun wearily got to his feet, then stumbled. Four arba were dead, with more than a dozen injured in so short a time. He had healed them all, setting bones to regrow and closing up lacerations. It felt good to be able to help, but he couldn't help but to despair of those he couldn't help.

A hand squeezed his shoulder. "You can't save everyone, Urun."

The young priest wanted to argue, but he knew Tere was correct. He would know. He'd been a hero, saving people and —unfortunately—losing some long before Urun was born.

"I know, but that doesn't make it any easier on their families."

The arba leader stepped up to the humans and bowed. "You have saved more of my people. We owe you a great debt. I thank you. As we were discussing before the attack, my people can help you find what you are seeking. Anything we can do, we will do with our whole strength."

"Thank you," Urun said. "If you can help us find where the source of this corruption is centered, that will be appreciated."

"And if we can leave our horses here, that would be helpful, too," Marla said. She pointed toward where the mounts were tied to a building, arba children all around them.

The leader smiled. "Of course. The children want to spend more time looking at and petting the animals in any case. We have no such beasts, but some among us are familiar with them. We can provide them food and water as they wait for you. Out in the swamp is no place for them.

"It will be dark in another hour. It would be better if you waited until the morning light to begin searching. The dark monsters seem to be stronger at night, though even during the light, they have been invincible to us."

Urun was anxious to find the source of the problem, but he saw the sense in what the Leaf Talker said. With a sigh, he said, "Yes, it would probably be better."

"Very well. Please, join us for the evening meal, and then you can rest in two of the homes that are vacant."

The rest of the evening passed slowly, even dreamlike to Urun. Something ached inside of him, wanting him to go out immediately to find his goddess, but he sat through the meal and meeting their guide, nodding his head at what seemed to be the appropriate times and counting down when they could get to the search. He fell asleep early, confident that the village watchers would shout an alarm if they were attacked by more of the monsters. He wasn't sure when he would get a full night's sleep again.

The last rays of the setting sun filtered through the trees surrounding the small clearing where Aeden brought Khrazhti a small plate of the cooked fish Catriona and Greimich had prepared for their evening meal. He knew she didn't have to eat, but she had become accustomed to having a few bites when the humans ate. It helped others see her as more human, less the rampaging monster the other animaru were.

Of course, nothing convinced Dubhghall to provide her even the barest respect. He was, even now, scowling at the blue woman, his lip occasionally lifting to show a tooth or two.

Go ahead and try to intimidate her with hard looks, Aeden thought. *If you take one step more toward being rude, I'll drub you until your friends have to carry you the rest of the way.*

The touch of Khrazhti's hand on his brought his attention to his friend. "It is a little thing. Do not concern yourself over it. Posturing and glaring are second nature to animaru commanders and lords. It affects me not." She backed up her words by smiling at him.

How had he ever thought the expression unnatural on the animaru? She wore smiles comfortably and beautifully, as if she was born to do so. Aeden thought that might not be so far from the truth. After all, weren't all humans born to smile? It was only circumstances in life that squeezed the smiles out of people as they grew to adulthood. Some people, anyway.

"I don't like it," he told her. "It's disrespectful and I cannot abide disrespect toward my friends, especially those who are most deserving of respect."

She chuckled, another non-animaru thing. "If he begins to affect my mood and my thinking, I will take care of it." She cocked her head for a moment. "I will not kill him, however. That may cause problems. I will handle it as Marla Shrike did. Her display seemed very effective to me."

Aeden laughed. "Yes, I think it was."

The Trebhin spat in the dirt in front of him. "It's beginning to smell here. I'll eat where the air is fresher." He got up and headed toward the opposite end of their camp, muttering something about treating animals like humans.

Aeden tensed and began to stand up, but Khrazhti's hand on his arm pulled him back down.

"He has left. Leave him to his solitary meal. He will cause no more trouble tonight."

Greimich, sitting next to Aeden, shook his head. "Damn Trebhin."

"Come now, love," Catriona said. "Don't blame the whole clan, even if every one of them I have met are the same way. We need all the clans to come together as brothers and sisters. The simple truth is that *that* man would be an arse regardless of which clan he was in."

Greimich smirked and stared into his wife's eyes. "I do love you, Catriona Tannoch."

"Catriona *Ailgid* Tannoch, if you please, husband." She leaned over and kissed the tip of his nose.

"Aye, as you say."

Khrazhti watched the two. In fact, Aeden noticed her paying close attention to the interactions between all their fellow travelers. He wondered what went through her head at those times. She was obviously figuring out all the varied dealings between humans. How different were those from how the animaru dealt with each other?

"I do not understand this," Khrazhti said. "You speak of brothers and sisters, but you were not all born from the same mother. There are far too many for that."

"It's another use of the words," Aeden said. "For example, Greimich and I trained together, were partners during our training—"

"Braitharlan," Khrazhti said.

"Yes, exactly. He had his mother and father and I had mine, but we were brothers in that we became as family to each other. I would give my life for him and he for me. In that sense, we were brothers. So too with the rest of the clans. Originally, we came from the same parents thousands of years ago, so in a sense, we're all brothers and sisters."

"But you are cousins," she said. "How can it be that you are cousins—Marla Shrike explained the word to me—and still be brothers?"

Aeden's brow wrinkled. He knew what he wanted to say, but couldn't figure out how to make his point clear. "Uh, it's like with me and Fahtin. We are not related through blood family in any way, but I was adopted into her family and she is as much a sister to me as Marla, whom I didn't know existed until recently. So, there is blood family and there are brothers and sisters who are people you love and who are important to you. Important enough to sacrifice for."

Khrazhti rubbed her jaw for a moment. "I understand. You are my brother, and Fahtin and Marla are my sisters because I care for all of you and would put myself in danger to save you."

Aeden swallowed, a lump suddenly forming in his throat. "Yes. That's the non-blood family version. Then there is the blood-family type, which the rest of the clans are to us."

"This still seems strange to me," she said. "This blood family that you speak of."

"Maybe if you tell her the history of the clans, it would be clearer," Catriona said.

"Cat, you are too smart sometimes," Greimich said. "I think you're right. It would help." He turned toward Khrazhti. "Would you like to hear how the clans were formed? It could explain why we consider the others in the highlands as brothers and sisters, though to be accurate, that hasn't always been the attitude."

"Yes, please tell me."

"Good. I'll start off. If I forget anything, speak up, Aeden. I don't have to tell Cat. Her habit is to argue with everything I say and to correct me out of habit."

His wife mock glared at him but couldn't hold the expression. It broke to pieces, replaced by an impish grin. Greimich winked at her and began his tale.

"During the War of Magic, prisoners were taken by all sides when they were captured after a victory. Salaman troops would take Souveni prisoners or those from Gentason prisoners and the other nations would do the same with their enemies. Sometimes prisoners were mistreated and sometimes they were simply detained to be used for leverage in negotiations.

"It was one such group of prisoners that are important in this tale. They were of the Salaman army, from the northern part of Salamus. In that region, the people were not as dark-skinned as in the southern part of the empire, nor did they have the dark eyes of the southerners. Though their hair could be dark, many from the area were known to have red or lighter brown hair.

"As I said, the soldiers came from the north and were involved in a battle far from home, a conflict all the way across Dizhelim on the Souveni border. The battle went badly for the Salaman troops and the group was captured. They were moved to an area near the Grundenwald Forest, a place even wilder than it is today.

"Unsure of what would be their fate, some of the soldiers decided to attempt an escape rather than to be tortured or killed. They knew it would mean death to be caught, but they were an arrogant people, believing themselves superior to the Souveni. All they would have to do was to utilize their superior minds and abilities and they would be free.

"They planned the escape for more than a month, working out each detail. They had settled into a routine, going out to work each day building roads for the empire. It was hard work, but they were fed and were not treated too cruelly most of the time. Not yet. Some of the prisoners chose to stay in captivity, but the others went ahead with the plan.

"On one of their trips to the daily work site, they cooperated and overwhelmed the guards. Half of their captors with them that day were killed in the scuffle, and several of the others were injured.

"The plan progressed as they intended and those who chose to escape fled to the northeast, into the rugged highlands. The area was heavily wooded and covered with vegetation that resisted movement. Though cutting through the plants with the weapons they stole from the guards made a visible path their pursuers could follow, it was their only option for making their way toward the wilder terrain that was their goal.

"Fortunately, by the time the Souveni jailors organized

themselves and gave chase, the escaped prisoners found areas they could move through without cutting down plants and leaving an obvious trail. They disappeared from their former guards.

"But the Souveni were not going to give up their prisoners, their laborers, so easily. A captain of the Souveni army was sent to bring the escapees to heel, and he vowed to do so regardless of what measures it took. Along with him, he brought a thousand men, at a time when soldiers were sorely needed on the main battlefields of the war. Such was the importance of regaining the captives.

"The captain, whose name has been lost to history, scoured the highlands, gradually moving his way up through the pine, larch, and juniper interspersed with peat and brambles. But it seemed that the prisoners had disappeared.

"In fact, the escaped prisoners were desperately trying to stay one step ahead of the Souveni. Over long months of their flight, they became familiar with the land and the flora and fauna of the highlands. The area was rugged and essentially untouched by humans because of the harsh climate, lack of large areas to farm, and the danger from wild beasts. The former prisoners began to love the untamed terrain in all its beautiful danger.

"They quickly learned to make their way around the area, not forcing their way as the Souveni were doing, but by becoming part of the land. By the time the Souveni had cornered their prey, the former prisoners had learned enough to fight back effectively.

"Two of the escaped prisoners had been trackers for the army of Salamus, one of whom was accustomed to high elevations and rugged terrain, having spent several years as a scout in the mountains then known as the Wall of Salamus. Today, they're called the Shadowed Pinnacles.

"These two trained the others in surviving in the highlands, and thriving there. They made simple weapons and by the time the Souveni soldiers found them, they had prepared surprises.

"Across more than twenty miles of bleak, unforgiving terrain, the escaped prisoners whittled down the troops trying to recapture them. There were few wide-open spaces in that corner of the highlands, so the Souveni army could not take advantage of their numbers to simply charge the smaller group of men and women.

"Oh, maybe I forgot to mention it before, but there were women within the forces of the Salaman army that was captured. Some of them joined in the escape and so the group was mixed, male and female.

"The decisive battle was in an area with jagged red-rock pillars thrusting up from the ground. The escaped prisoners took a heavy toll on the Souveni there, and it is for this area —and the battle fought within it—that the highlands are named. Crionna Crodhearg Fiacla, old blood-red teeth, as said in what would be the language of the highlands. The shortened form, Cridheargla, was what it was commonly called, though, even to this day. Either that, or simply the highlands, for ones with no tongue for the language.

"In the end, the captain realized he could not win and turned what was left of his soldiers around to head back to the empire for reinforcements. Now the roles had been reversed. Every step of the way, the Souveni were harried. One or two at a time, the soldiers' numbers decreased.

"They never knew when attacks would come, so as they tried to carve their way through the forests and slog their way through the highland marshes, they got less and less sleep. And still the former prisoners attacked them in stealth, reducing their numbers.

"The captain and his last forty soldiers made it to within thirty miles of a major road that took a path close to what is today the North Road. They were goaded into a small box canyon by the escapees' attacks. When they ran up against the stone obstructions ahead and to their sides, the captain knew it was his end.

"The Souveni, leaner than they had been for lack of sufficient food, clothed in uniforms that were little more than rags, with weapons in disrepair because of the lack of sufficient tools, huddled in the wild terrain.

"There were only twenty-two of the escaped prisoners left, but they had become accustomed to the highlands. Their weapons, though simple, were well made and well maintained. Each of them carried a bow and weapons to cut or smash opponents up close.

"They chose to use the bows.

"From behind rocks and trees, the newly minted highlanders loosed their arrows at the Souveni. The soldiers dropped in groups until only the captain remained, standing in the center of the corpses of his troops, holding his sword up defiantly.

"The tracker who had become the defacto leader of the group came out of hiding and stepped into the clearing, several dozen feet from the Souveni captain.

"'You have been defeated,' he said. 'We will allow you, the last of your army, to return to your emperor. Tell him we have no quarrel with Souvenia. We are no longer the men and women we were. We only want to live, here in the highlands. If you or any of your fellow soldiers return, we will destroy you to a man. In the middle of a war, it would be a mistake to split your forces in such a way. We afford you this one chance. If we so much as see a Souveni uniform on our land, I will personally hunt you down and kill you in the most painful of ways, even should you be in the middle of your capital city. Believe that I can.'

"The captain had a choice between accepting his release or dying there and not reporting what had happened.

"'I am not the emperor. I can't promise he won't send troops.'

"'You had better be persuasive, then, unless you'd prefer to die now.'

"In the end, the captain agreed. The tracker threw a satchel—it was an official Souveni soldier's satchel that had been taken from one of the dead—with food and water in it. At a signal from the leader, the highlanders disappeared into the foliage, leaving the captain alone to make his way back to his commanders.

"The Souveni did not send more troops to the highlands. Not because they didn't believe they could root out the small band, but simply because the war was not going as smoothly as they liked and they needed every fighter for the main battle lines. The Prophet, Tsosin Ruus, had defected, weakening the power of the empire, and a handful of former prisoners were not seen as too great a threat.

"There were those who thought to simply burn the highlands, destroying it in a grand conflagration, but the emperor saw it as a waste, stating that he wasn't even sure if they could manage it with the wet climate in much of the area.

"So from the small group of escaped prisoners grew a new people. Their language, originally a dialect of Alaqotim, changed through the years, eventually transforming to a totally new tongue called Chorain. When the tracker-turned-leader had five sons, they eventually moved off to different areas of the highlands, taking numbers with them, and these became the clans we know today: Ailgid, Seachaid, Trebhin, Corcan, and Tannoch."

❧ 18 ❧

Khrazhti appreciated Aeden's friend Greimich sharing with her the story of their people. Each of the others sitting around the fire wore looks of pride and fierce determination at hearing their history, even Dubhghall sitting alone in the dark, clearly visible to her keen dark vision. These were a proud people who cared deeply about their past heroes.

"I thank you for sharing this story with me," she said to Greimich. "It is a good tale of honor and battle. A fitting way to start your family. I understand now why you would call your clans brothers and sisters."

"But what of you, Khrazhti?" Catriona asked. "Do you have no family where you are from? Any brothers or sisters?"

Aeden stiffened beside her, but Khrazhti herself took no offense. Catriona was ignorant of the animaru culture, as ignorant as Khrazhti was of human culture. More so, truly.

"All animaru but one were created at nearly the same time. We do not reproduce, nor have there been any added to their number but that one, three thousand years ago."

Catriona's mouth made a wide O. "What? How then have

the animaru not died out if they're not replaced when killed?" She thought for a moment, but then seemed to realize what she had said. "Ach, that's right. They don't die. Well, except for now with the life magic we discovered can kill them. But still, none added but one? Why was there one added if it never happened before or after?"

"One of the animaru lords...raped—is that the word you told me, Aeden?—a human visitor to Aruzhelim." Aeden nodded to the question, so she continued. "The human woman had a child, half animaru and half human. That child was me. I was the only animaru to be born. Three thousand years ago."

Catriona frowned. "But then, you have a father, though he is a rapist."

"I do not. I killed him a month ago."

A small gasp escaped Catriona's lips.

"Cat," Aeden said, "Suuksis was one of the god S'ru's top commanders. He had come here to try to bring Khrazhti back to S'ru's service or to kill her, then to do the work of destroying our world. If Khrazhti hadn't killed him, I would have."

"Perhaps we should talk about something else," Greimich interjected. "This subject will do nothing but bring my spirits down."

"Aye," Aeden said. "I think you have the right of it."

"Oh," Catriona said. "What about a story from your past, Khrazhti? Something not so depressing. I heard you were the high priestess of your god. That's quite an honor. How did you become elevated above all the others like that?"

Khrazhti was not sure that the subject of her former office was any less depressing than the circumstances of her birth. She was, after all, no longer in S'ru's service. Her god had been false, and to satisfy her honor she had left him, gone to the other side. The enemy's side. It was not pleasant to think upon.

"Uh," Aeden said, staring into Khrazhti's face. He obviously noticed her discomfort. "Maybe another subject. How about—"

She put her hand on his arm. "It is fine, Aeden. I have very few things in my entire existence that are not disheartening. Until I came to this world and joined my new friends. But all those stories you know. I will talk of attaining my position of high priestess, if you would like to know, Catriona."

The woman looked toward her husband, indecision on her face, but then turned back to Khrazhti and gave her a little nod.

"Very well. It was nearly two thousand years ago."

Another gasp from Catriona brought a small smile to Khrazhti's face. Sometimes she forgot how brief a time all her new friends lived.

"Yes, it is a long time. I am young as far as animaru go, but at times it seems that humans fit so much more into their shorter lives. Decades or centuries pass quickly but often with nothing notable happening. It is a matter of perspective, I believe.

"But as I said, it was two millennia ago when the tale begins. I was a commander of a force of animaru, a middle level commander at best and with a small contingent. Still, I faced prejudice, not only because of my impure makeup but because of my color."

"Your color?" Catriona said. "Your skin is a most beautiful shade, I think."

"Thank you, but we speak of animaru, not kind humans. If you have noticed, all animaru are dark. Some black, some grey, others brown, but all dark. When I was high priestess, S'ru's power infused me and my color was darker, but at the time of which I speak, my skin was as it is now, much too light for animaru to accept me readily.

"So, though I had proven myself through countless battles —for what else was there for us to do with our never-ending existence?—I was still treated as lesser. I was strict with my soldiers, demanding total obedience lest they face my wrath, because otherwise my orders would not be followed. In this, I developed a reputation for keeping a well-run army and for being victorious in battle, but I was looked down upon by the other commanders, especially my father.

"I had enjoyed S'ru's favor since the time he had found me and taken me from Suuksis, but I had not proved myself superior to all others. Not yet. And thus, he devised for me a test, one to demonstrate to him, to myself, and to all others, that I was as much animaru as all the rest.

"The high priest at the time was a powerful mage called Zhadril. My simple test was to travel to where his armies were camped and defeat him. I was not told if S'ru had warned Zhadril or not, but it mattered little. There was constant warfare among the different factions and lords. His scouts would notify him my army was approaching and we would do battle. It was a typical scenario.

"I knew Zhadril to be an arrogant leader, relying on his commanders and the large number of his troops. At this time he was encamped with twenty-six thousand in his army, most of what he could gather given a month's notice. I would not give him that month.

"My troops numbered almost nine thousand."

"Are you saying that you had nine thousand soldiers under your command?" Greimich asked.

"I did."

"And your enemy had twenty-six thousand?"

"Yes."

"There are not nine thousand total in all the highlands."

Khrazhti cocked her head at him. "Truly? When I was high priestess, I had over thirty thousand soldiers in my forces, nearly forty thousand at times."

Greimich shook his head. "I...oh, I'm sorry. Please continue. I never imagined those numbers against us."

Khrazhti nodded, wondering if he realized those numbers were small compared to how many animaru S'ru would bring over to Dizhelim to attack the humans' world.

"I mobilized my troops and began to march toward Zhadril's encampment. While we moved, however, I sent a few animaru ahead of us. Choosing three aliten—the winged, flying animaru you have seen—I had them each carry an important burden. One erfinchen and two urtumbra.

"Of the erfinchen, I do not believe you have knowledge. They are very rare and can be valuable in the correct circumstances. They can change their shape into essentially anything. Existing in Aruzhelim for thousands upon thousands of years at that point, my erfinchen could duplicate the form of any type of animaru and most of the higher-level commanders with such accuracy that they could pass for the original, at least in the short term. My erfinchen also had several lower forms they could hold to blend in with the normal troops.

"An urtumbrus is a type of animaru that is what amounts to a living shadow. They are not strong fighters and do not cast magic, but they can infiltrate places unseen and collect information that can be useful.

"The aliten dropped their passengers near the boundaries of Zhadril's forces and went to work. Because of the comfortable near-darkness of Aruzhelim, the urtumbra slipped into the camp easily. The erfinchen took the form of a pilae—an animaru type much like a ball of shadow—and infiltrated the camp that way. After choosing one of the seren on guard duty, the erfinchen took a form similar to it and strolled into the encampment.

"The spies spent a few days in camp, watching and listening as reports were received of my army moving toward them. More importantly, they heard the plans Zhadril's commanders developed.

"The erfinchen gave his information to an urtumbrus, and the shadows made their way back to where the aliten would pick them up to bring them back to me. The shapeshifter would stay to learn of any changes, coming back to me a week later.

"Meanwhile, I developed my own plan. I studied the terrain, even having aliten take me to the skies so I could scout out the land myself. Finally, we were ready for battle. But we wouldn't be attacking Zhadril's larger army where they were camped. I had a better plan than that.

"Three days out from Zhadril's camp, we halted and began preparations. I knew he was too experienced to come to the location we had chosen, so I decided to prod him.

"The aliten flew off again, this time with another erfinchen and the two urtumbra that had been to the camp before. With four spies within their camp, my plan began to take form.

"The shadows planted notes to be found by key members of the higher command staff. These appeared to be reports from aliten commanders and indicated troop movements that did not exist. I knew that there were few aliten with Zhadril's force—he was biased against the flying animaru for some reason—so the reports were not confirmed with further observation.

"The erfinchen that had been in the camp the entire time had observed one high level commander which he was familiar with and fine-tuned his knowledge of the commander's specific actions and manner of speaking. My erfinchen struck down the commander and took his place on the command council. He hid the commander's regenerating body in a place where the shadows could spirit it away so it was not located during its long recovery from the damage done to it.

"The other erfinchen did the same with another commander, one he had a thorough knowledge of from when the shapeshifter had worked with the officer in previous armies. With two on the council of ten upper commanders, it put my forces in a good position to manipulate strategy.

"More importantly, the commander who the second shapeshifter impersonated was in charge of the army's aliten.

"My spy told Zhadril in council that my troops were moving toward Desaru. It was the site of a great battle three hundred fourteen years before, one in which Zhadril defeated his foe, against conventional military wisdom. The high priest bragged afterward that, had he been on the opposite side of the conflict, he still would have destroyed his enemy.

"Zhadril smiled, making comments about how 'that light-skinned creature' was too stupid to devise her own strategy, but had to copy his own past battles. He gathered his troops and began the march to Desaru. It would take four days.

"Desaru was a rugged, twisted land, even more so than the other parts of Aruzhelim surrounding it. In the center, it rose several hundred feet and was clogged with jagged rocks, stunted and misshapen plants, and dotted with crevices and craters. There were not large areas for a mass advance, so much of the fighting needed to be in small groups. It was the kind of place where a smaller force could combat a larger force attacking them.

"In Zhadril's famous battle, the enemy general had the high ground. Zhadril's forces inched their way up the rise, taking heavy losses but inexorably moving upward. However, some of Zhadril's elite forces went wide of the obstacles and made their way up a steep section of terrain, unseen by the other forces' scouts. Their ascent was thought to have been impossible, but they had found a narrow, winding path to the top, much of it through cracks that hid them from view.

"The elites came upon the enemy and cut their way through to the main command post, where the highest-level officers determined the strategy for the battle. The enemy general was among them. Once they were brought to their lowest energy level, the battle was essentially over. Most of the elites' bodies joined those of the enemy officers to start the slow regeneration process so they could once again fight in several months' time.

"From behind, the remaining elites disrupted the forces on the battle lines while the bulk of Zhadril's army smashed into them from the front. He lost more than half his troops during the battle, but defeated the enemy, leaving torn and battered animaru bodies on the rocky ground.

"Of course, he thought he would do the same with my army, but this time he would prevent any from using the path they had found to the rise and he would be in the high position, proving what he had always claimed, that he could win from the opposite position on the field.

"And so, he marched his armies toward Desaru, already confident in his victory."

❧ 19 ☙

"On the way to the location, however, there was a canyon with sheer walls. They were not so high that they could not be scaled, especially for such as seren, with their sharp claws, but it obstructed the march, squeezing the troops through at only two dozen or so abreast. It was long enough that nearly the entire force could be within it at once.

"Zhadril, of course, trusted his aliten's reports that my forces were already arrayed at Desaru. It surprised him when my seren and kryzt attacked first the head of the army and then the tail, both sides of their mass. In the confines of the canyon, we tore into their ranks and defeated several thousand with lesser numbers. Only when their seren began to climb the walls to gain larger numbers on the battle lines did we leave.

"By the time my fast-moving forces fled, almost six thousand of Zhadril's forces had been damaged so severely it would be several months before they would be able to fight again. I had lost merely two hundred forty-seven.

"Incensed at the trickery, Zhadril pushed his forces hard

to get to the site of the *real* battle. On the way, small harrying forces attacked and then retreated, at times luring away groups of their fighters to be defeated before the commanders could call them back for fear of the army being strung out. They were beginning to suspect their intelligence was not completely accurate.

"My spy convinced them that their relatively few aliten had missed spotting the small forces, but suggested they continue with their plan. The other erfinchen lent support, easing the minds of the other commanders and of Zhadril. They continued, though the time was short for my spies.

"Zhadril's forces finally arrived at Desaru and mounted the heights. My own forces were a day away when they did so, lending credibility to the aliten commander's reports. Once in place on the rise, Zhadril smugly looked down as I, along with my troops, arrived. He called taunts down, challenging us to attack.

"We waited.

"In Aruzhelim, we have neither day nor night as you do here. It is always dim or dark, the weak light varying according to some cosmic movements no animaru ever deciphered. Because of this, attacks may be performed at any time with no advantage or disadvantage. After some time, my forces moved onto the softly sloping front of the rise, advancing in ranks.

"We do not use projectile weapons like humans do. Indeed, the only way enemies are attacked from afar is with magic, though it is rarely cast more than a few dozen feet. Our warfare is more...intimate. Claws and teeth, swords and the like for some of the higher-level animaru, that is our way. So, with my shouted command, my forces built up to a run, seren, kryzt, gulrae, and lesna at the front, with colechna, aliten, and the semhominus officers following.

"They clashed with the enemies and began to tear at each

other. After the initial assault, I moved forward, heading toward Zhadril, intent on battling him myself. All the while, he wore a smug expression.

"I looked past him, to the rim where he had, so many years before, sent his elites to attack his enemy from behind. He noticed my gaze and raised a hand, then pointed to the forces he had posted there to protect the rear.

"At that moment, I cast a bolt of power up high in front of me. Zhadril's eyes widened, but then, when he realized it would not hit him, merely shook his head at my poor aim.

"But I had not been aiming at him. The crackling bolt of power passed above the heads of his forces and fizzled harmlessly. It had been enough. A signal.

"My own elite forces, fully one thousand strong, poured out of crevices and cracks surrounding Zhadril's hastily constructed camp. My desid workers had dug tirelessly, widening places for my soldiers to hide. Then, they had waited patiently and silently as Zhadril's army had gathered nearby, focused on the sight of me and the rest of my army.

"My elites tore into his commanders, much like his own had done in his famous battle. The guards he had posted to prevent access from the narrow path were thrown off the sheer side of the rise. In very little time, we whittled down Zhadril's army so that we matched their numbers, and then further so we had greater numbers. Meanwhile, their inferior discipline prevented them from effectively resisting us without most of their higher-level officers.

"I cut my way through the lines and Zhadril's personal guards and soon faced my enemy. His satisfied expression had fled his face.

"He cast spell after spell at me, attempting to overwhelm me. I did not return magical attacks. Zhadril was renowned as a great mage, and though I believed I might equal him in power, I was not so proud that I needed to prove myself. Instead, I took a more cautious approach.

"I focused my magical energies on a shield and continued to let my swords cut a path toward him. His spells were reflected or absorbed by my shield, though it took much of my concentration and strength to keep it whole. Step by step, I moved closer as he stood in one place trying to break through with his magic to defeat me.

"Then I was in front of him. The shocked look on his face told me that he realized—too late—his position. He turned to run, but it was my turn to attack. I leapt at him and cut him down as he fled, my two swords severing parts of him as I carved my enemy. I ended the battle when I rammed both blades through his torso.

"His body dropped to the ground, where it would stay for as long as it took him to recuperate. I estimated it would take three months because of the damage I did to him. We might have fought again after that, but he had been defeated and would no longer have the acclaim he had. Even at that moment, most of the remaining troops raised their arms or other appendages in surrender. They would become my own troops, a common enough occurrence in battles.

"For defeating Zhadril, I gained S'ru's blessing and the appointment as his high priestess. As my god made the pronouncement, my skin color became darker and I felt his power infuse me even more strongly than ever before.

"After that, I gained more respect, but still perceived side-long looks at me or even comments between others when they thought I could not hear. By no means had all been turned to my side, but respect, though grudging, was mine in general."

"That is an impressive story," Catriona said. "You've commanded large armies. That will be helpful in our fight, I think."

A loud scoffing sound emanated from the darkened edges of the camp.

"You have a problem, Dubhghall?" Aeden asked. Khrazhti recognized the tone in his voice, one that entered only as his anger rose, a rare enough occasion she'd only seen twice in all the time she'd known him.

"You all believe the lies she tells," the man said. "A woman, commanding armies. Ridiculous. If you're all daft enough to take her at her word, you're all even stupider than I thought."

Aeden took a step toward the man, but Greimich grabbed his arm, shaking his head slightly. The others around the fire watched intently to see what would happen.

"You're the arse end of a leaper," Aeden said. "When we battled Khrazhti, she led all the animaru forces in Dizhelim, at least several thousand strong. The only reason it wasn't more was because at that time, there weren't any more in our world. She has more battle experience than every highlander combined."

"If you believe she's as old as she claims. Do you have proof, or are you blinded by her breasts?"

Aeden broke Greimich's grip to lunge toward Dubhghall, but Khrazhti caught the arm and spun him to her. "No, Aeden. He is unworthy of battling you. It is I he insults. It is perhaps time to address his disrespect?"

Aeden growled in his throat, but his head thrust into a savage nod.

"Thank you," she said, and turned to the Trebhin. He was tense, preparing for battle with Aeden. In his eyes, Khrazhti saw indecision, worry he may have said too much, pushed things too far. The humans' eyes conveyed so much emotion with their different colors and their pupils. She found them easier to read than animaru.

It was time to address the man's constant taunting, though, as she said to Aeden. Perhaps if she handled it correctly, she wouldn't cause the others to want to fight as well.

"Dubhghall," she said, being sure she pronounced his name correctly. It sounded awkward to her ears, but in the same way it sounded when the others said it. "You disrespect me. Is it because I am female, because I am animaru, or because you are intimidated by me?"

Instantly, his expression changed from indecision to anger. "You deserve no respect because you're an arrogant whore animaru bitch."

Khrazhti turned to Aeden, whose face was turning red. He shook with rage, his fist clenching and unclenching. He wanted to combat the man but held himself back because of his respect for her. The familiar feeling of warmth suffused her chest, the one that came when Aeden or her other friends showed her she was valued by them.

"That is bad?" she asked him. His eyes widened, then clenched down to narrow slits.

"Yes. Very bad. Like someone calling you the excretions of a forgren. Or worse."

"Ah," she said calmly. "That bad."

"Aye."

She turned back to Dubhghall. "Would you like to strike me?"

"What?"

"Would you like to attempt to strike me, since I am a... what was it, an *arrogant whore animaru bitch*? Is that not what men like you do with such as those?"

"Are you insane?" he spat. "Are you asking me to attack you?"

"Yes. Please." She put an exaggerated smile on her face she had seen when her friends meant it to be ironic. She had apparently gotten it correct.

"Aye," he said. "I'll drub you, teach you you're no better than the other whores *that one* keeps in his company."

Once again, Khrazhti looked to Aeden. "Did his words make an insult to you?"

"They did," he said through gritted teeth.

"Allow me, please, to answer his insults then, through combat."

"Khrazhti," Catriona said.

Khrazhti looked to the woman, Greimich's wife and...if she could be so forward, a friend of hers. "Yes?"

The woman raised her chin and looked directly into Khrazhti's eyes. "Don't kill him. We've enough messes to clean up."

"I will not kill him, but his insults will be rewarded accordingly."

"A bunch of women, all of you," Dubhghall said, as if it were another insult. "Will you talk all night? Where is this combat you've promised me?"

Khrazhti stepped away from the others, eyeing Aeden to make sure he stayed where he was. "You may attack me when you desire."

Dubhghall ran at her, fists raised.

🜺 20 🜺

The guide Leaf Talker Vora assigned to the group was named Saevel. She was about Urun's height, taller than most of the other arba, and was dressed in typical hunter garb with one exception. Her ensemble included a leather tunic with leather pants, with tall leather boots, all dyed green instead of the brown on most others. Her hair was an auburn color, long enough to reach the center of her back, and with her light green skin, the woman was striking. The young priest found himself staring into eyes that were midway between the color of her skin and the darker green of her clothing.

"Urun?" Tere's voice said.

He shook his head. "Ah, oh, right." He dropped the woman's hand—which, despite calluses on the pads of her palms and on her fingertips, were surprisingly soft—and cleared his throat. "Well met, Saevel. I'm Urun Chinowa—"

"The priest of Osulin," she said excitedly. "Yes, I know. I am so honored to meet the chosen of the goddess, and to guide you through the Mellafond." Her voice had a musical quality, almost magical.

He instantly felt a kinship with her, even more than the other arba. He thought it might be the natural magic the arba had been said to have. He watched her as she greeted the others, admiring the narrow lines of her face and chin and the long ear lobes poking out from where she swept her hair over one side.

Besides the leather clothing—which fit very well—she also had a hip quiver and several small pouches attached to a belt at her waist. She carried her bow casually, obviously comfortable with using the weapon. As she was introduced to Tere and Lily, he felt a pang of jealousy that they shared a love of archery with her. He wished he had that in common with the enchanting woman.

Where had that come from? She had just professed her respect for him as a priest of Osulin and he was thinking of arrows? He shook his head and looked away from her. Right into Marla's face.

The red-haired woman pursed her lips and nodded at him, a knowing look in her eyes. His face flushed and he searched the surroundings for something to take his mind off it all.

The introductions were concluded and the party prepared to head out. Urun went to Rainstorm and gave her half an apple as a treat, then handed the other half to one of the children so they could feed the horse.

"Stay here and be good," he told the beast. "We'll be back. Hopefully. Don't be a pest and don't bite the children." One large eye fixed on him and the horse snorted. Whether that meant agreement or not, Urun didn't know, but he'd accept that his equine friend would be on her best behavior.

They started off, Saevel in the front. Urun could only watch her swishing hips in her tight leather pants for so long before he moved toward his right and started up a conversation with Tere to distract him from his growing discomfort.

The guide knew the area well. When Misun had led them

from the site of their battle to the village, Urun had been impressed with the way she could find pieces of dry land for them to trod, but they had still spent nearly half the time sloshing through shallow water. With Saevel, they rarely got their feet wet.

She led them easily and casually toward what she said was the center of the Mellafond. What's more, she confirmed their suspicions by telling them that there were greater numbers of monsters in the middle. She had traveled farther inward than any other lately because of her abilities in stealth and combat, not to mention that she was the reigning champion in the annual races the arba held. When she told Urun about it, she winked one beautiful green eye at him.

"The plant creatures showed up first," she said. "That was a month or more back. Those, at least, we can kill, though they are hardy and rarely are found alone. For someone like me, out here without another to watch my back, the best course of action is to avoid them. Or failing that, to run until they give up the chase.

"The other things, those dark creatures that look like a cross between some kind of mythological monster and the plant creatures, showed up only in the last two weeks. They have killed many of us because we never knew how to defeat them. We didn't know they *could* be defeated. Not until you and your friends told us of the magic. Unfortunately, we no longer have much magic."

Marla shouldered her way in between Urun and Saevel. "I wanted to ask you about that. The arba were said to have strong nature magic. Of course, the last time anyone reported seeing one of your people, it was before the end of the War, so I suppose you could have lost it when the gods left and magic fled with them."

Saevel shook her head. "No, I don't think that's it. The history is unclear, and the Leaf Talker could tell you better than I can, but I think the arba died out when the magic left. We are only a shell of our ancestors, a mix of human and arba. I think our magic was diluted from the first."

"Hmm. That could be. Though humans can learn to use magic and some have an affinity for it, we are not magical by our nature. Not like the arba or astridae. It's still curious to me that no one has ever realized your people still exist."

The guide smiled, the expression causing her ears to shift and raise up. Urun thought maybe all ears did that when their owner smiled, but with the elongated lobes, it was more pronounced.

"The Mellafond has always been dangerous to those who do not live here. Few explore it. From ancient times, it has been a place the gods set apart as one that does not easily endure trespassers. There are other places in the world such as that, from what I understand. I myself have not been outside the swamp my entire life, but some few have chanced traveling and have told me of such places. One is called the Grundenwald, I believe?"

Marla gave Urun a smile and said, "Yes. Good point. Few explore the center of that forest. Urun used to live in the Grundenwald, as did Tere."

Saevel whirled toward Urun, eyes wide, and grabbed his arm. "Is it true? You lived in the forest of legend?"

"I did. It is where I first discovered Osulin's shrine and became her priest. Her presence is strong there, since it's one of the few untouched natural places in Dizhelim."

"Tell me about it," she demanded. "I want to hear everything. How does it look and feel? How does it smell? What kinds of creatures abide there?" She took a breath, then sighed. "I mean, if you would like to share. When we stop to rest. I should concentrate on finding our way." She dropped her hand from his arm and to Urun, it felt like the skin there went cold.

"I would love to tell you about it whenever I can. It's a wondrous place. Maybe when Osulin is safe and the Mellafond is back to normal, I can take you there."

The wide smile she gave him made his heart ache with the anticipation of the journey. "I will hold you to that, Urun Chinowa. Priests of Osulin do not idly make promises."

"We do not," he agreed at the same time he hoped they both survived their current mission.

Saevel stepped ahead and made a show of scanning the terrain ahead, though she occasionally cast a glance back at Urun and gave him a shy smile.

Marla elbowed him and gave him a sisterly smile. "I think she likes you."

"She is a follower of Osulin. She kind of has to like the goddess's only priest."

"Sure, sure. Keep telling yourself that, but not for too long, okay?" She winked at him.

He looked toward their green guide, imagining the wonder in those emerald eyes at seeing the majesty of his former home. He knew that wonder well, and suddenly, for the first time in his life, he wanted to share it with someone else instead of hoarding it all for himself.

But Osulin first. His goddess needed his help and it was his life's mission to provide it. Once he did, though, and she was safely out of whatever trouble she'd found, maybe he could get to know a bit more about the arba race, and one individual arba in particular.

They traveled until nearly sunset. Saevel knew of a good campsite, so they pushed on until they reached it. It looked surprisingly like the one the party had camped at before they met the arba, though Urun should have realized *all* dry sites to camp probably looked the same in the swamp. While the others were setting up camp, their guide stepped away for a time, promising to be back before dark. Urun raised his hand to suggest someone go with her, but she left so quickly, he was unable to say anything. At least he had imbued her weapons with light magic, as he had with his friends' weapons and those of the other arba before they left the village earlier in the day. The effects lasted several days, so she could defend herself if she couldn't avoid any of those animaru plant creatures.

By the time Saevel came back, the sun had gone down and twilight had fallen. She carried with her five large fish and a bundle of firewood. From what Urun had seen, the wood was probably worth quite a bit to the arba.

"I keep wood stashed nearby," she said, "and there is a pool not far where the fish grow fat with few predators. It's easy to shoot them with an arrow from the dry ground."

Tere set up the wood for a fire, nodding at Marla once he was done. He didn't even bother taking out his flint and steel, but allowed the Academy graduate to douse the wood with fire from a spell to begin the burning. Meanwhile, Urun and Lily prepared the fish for cooking. Saevel had even thought to bring spices in one of her belt pouches.

"You can eat fish without spices," she said, "but why would you?"

Urun laughed, glad that the guide had been so prepared.

"Won't the fire attract the monsters?" Lily asked.

Saevel shook her head. "No. We're not sure why, but it doesn't seem to catch their attention. The regular beasts of the swamp will stay away from the fire, but the plant creatures and dark creatures—animaru?—don't seem to care one way or another."

❧ 21 ❧

Urun stared out into the darkness, his vision obscured by the remnants of the fire, wondering where Osulin was and what she was enduring. Could gods die? She was half human, after all, though still immortal as far as he knew. She had already lived for thousands of years. Even if she couldn't die, he hated the thought of her having to endure pain or imprisonment.

The combination of the warmth of the fire and the temperate condition of the surrounding air caused his eyelids to become heavy, almost to the point where he had to chase where his thoughts were going. While he wrestled with fatigue, Tere and Lily were speaking to each other quietly, but loud enough for Urun to hear.

"I never heard of arba before today," Lily said. "I'm confused about what everyone keeps saying about them, that they use magic, that they *are* magic. What's the story with them?"

"They were thought to have died out around the end of the Age of Magic. It's thought that—"

"No. I heard that part of it earlier. I mean, what's their

story? Why haven't I ever heard of them? Where did they come from? Were they created by Surus along with the other races and they had their own place, like maybe one of the mysterious continents to the south?"

"They..." Tere turned his head toward Urun and caught him listening. "Urun, Lily wants to know about the origin of the arba. It's smack in the middle of your area of expertise. Do you want to tell her?"

Tere said it loudly enough that Marla and Saevel—softly chatting with each other—both turned their heads to look at the priest as well.

"Uh...I suppose I can tell it. Is this considered my turn in storytelling, because as I remember, I was the last one to tell a story for our mealtime tales, the evening before we left the Academy."

Tere chuckled. "Sure, you can count it as another turn. You have my permission to skip the next time you're up in the rotation."

"Oh, good. Story credit."

Saevel gave him a confused look, but he waved it away. He'd explain it to her later if she wanted.

"Fine. I'll tell you the short version. One that, by the way, is approved by Osulin herself, since she is in part of the story."

Urun moved closer to the fire, where Tere and Lily were already sitting. Marla and Saevel scooted closer to the trio, settling on a slightly raised lump of dirt.

"We all know the story of Trikus Phen, the great hero, and how Codaghan the God of War took offense to him showing mercy to an enemy and how he viciously beat the hero until the edge of death. Then how Mellaine, who had been watching the whole thing, rushed in as soon as Codaghan left, used her natural magic to bring the hero back, and healed him over a period of time. Then how the two fell in love and he decided to stay with her for the rest of his life. Of course, their child was Osulin, my goddess. You all know that part of it, right?"

The others all nodded, so he continued.

"Despite being brought back to health and living to a respectable age for a human who was not a mage, the hero was still mortal. So it was that he eventually weakened and died, simply because of old age. When he expired, Mellaine wept for one hundred days straight, and the world knew rains like they hadn't seen previously.

"Some of her tears leaked magic from the goddess, and as it mixed with the soil and the plant remnants on the forest floor near her home, the mixture came alive. The nature magic of the goddess and those natural ingredients spontaneously generated living tissue. But it was formless, simply like a soup of dirt, decaying plant matter, water, and magic.

"When Mellaine saw what had happened, she knew what she needed to do. She would not allow such new magical life to lay useless in the forest without a purpose or a will. So she took up handfuls of the composite and formed it into humanoid shapes.

"After she had created several dozen, she looked upon them standing before her. They were still not moving, nor could they think, but she delighted in them just the same. Her final step was to breathe air into their bodies, carrying with it more of Mellaine's magic. And so the people woke, able to think and move and feel like any of the other races.

"They recognized her instantly as their mother and their goddess and they dropped to their knees in thanks for the gift she had given them. She bade them to rise and charged them with defending and promoting nature, but especially with living in happiness and joy, something she felt she might not experience again for some time.

"And she called them arba. Green of skin, their very

essence was magical and they were able to cast spells, but not through study of books or through gifts from the gods. They tapped into nature itself, into the world's store of magic, and used it instinctively.

"They multiplied and spread out to different places in the world, but always where nature was strong. They were not meant for cities or large groups of people but felt more comfortable among the trees and wild places of Dizhelim. This was how they lived...until the natural world and magic itself was corrupted by the many activities of the War of Magic. But that's another tale."

"Wow," Lily said, glancing over at Saevel, whose eyes were shining in the firelight. "A race of people directly created by the sorrow of a goddess. They must have been very special to her."

"They were. She loved the arba above all others. Like Osulin, Mellaine rarely had priests, but when she did, they were always from the arba. Osulin told me one time that she and her mother did not have many priests because the arba were, in effect, an entire race of people who were priest-like, wholly dedicated to her. She said she missed them. I suppose it's possible that even she didn't know there were still arba here in the Mellafond."

"We're not really the arba they knew," Saevel said sadly. "Our people are not worthy of the goddess. We've lost our magic and are pale imitations of our ancestors."

Urun stared into Saevel's eyes. "I think not. When we rescue Osulin, we will ask her. You'll see then. My goddess doesn't cast off her chosen people because they've forgotten how to use magic. What matters to her is what is in their hearts, not what they can do."

Saevel's eyes glimmered, but she said no more. He knew Osulin's mind, and she would be ecstatic that there were still arba left alive, if in fact she didn't know already. He guessed she didn't or she would have made herself known to them. It was one more reason to rescue her. The happiness she would feel when finding out about Saevel's tribe would be immense.

The five conversed softly for a couple of hours after they ate and then set a watch—Urun first—while the others lay down to sleep. The swamp was peaceful and quiet but for the sound of insects, frogs, and a few screeches from night birds. The nature priest could see the allure of living there. Then he thought about the humidity, all the standing water, and the reek of putrid mud and thought maybe he wouldn't like for it to be his home.

He did miss his little house in the Grundenwald and wondered, not for the first time, if any animals had adopted it as their den or if the forest had reclaimed the space without him and his power there to prevent it. He sighed and bided his time, staring into the darkness, running his fingers over a chip in his staff's surface, and listening for any sign they might be attacked. When Marla got up just before he was to wake her, he greeted her quietly and settled into his own bed roll. He was soon asleep.

When Urun woke, Tere was sitting watch. Saevel was nowhere to be seen, though the nature priest swung his head around, scanning the area.

"She's scouting ahead," the archer said. "She'll be back before we're ready to leave."

Urun grunted and stuffed his bedroll into his pack.

After a light breakfast and Saevel's return, they headed out again. As before, the arba led them unerringly to paths where they could travel without stepping into the water.

The morning passed quickly. The lack of monsters and the ease of travel because of Saevel's guidance made Urun feel more comfortable with the swamp. He was still worried about his goddess, but they seemed to be making good progress toward finding her. For the first time since her message, things began to look up. They would find her, defeat the danger afflicting her, and then he could show Saevel the Grundenwald.

While he was thinking it, they passed through one of the few areas in which they had to walk through water and muck. The smile slid off his face when Lily, just ahead of him, disappeared into the water as if she had fallen into a deep hole.

A moment later, something stringy, slippery, and very strong grabbed his ankle and pulled him down as well.

❧ 22 ❧

Dubhghall Trebhin charged Khrazhti, hands clawed like he would tear her head off with his bare hands, a snarl twisting his face as if he were some kind of wild beast.

Aeden had to fight the urge to intercede. Khrazhti was fully capable of taking care of herself, but he felt as if Dubhghall had insulted him as much as Khrazhti. The Trebhin had not only cast aspersions on his friend, but he all but accused Aeden of being a dishonorable lech. Aeden thought he might do some head-tearing as well.

But he trusted Khrazhti, and she didn't want him to interfere. She was probably right, as hard as it was to watch without taking action.

He had known fighters like Dubhghall when he was in training with his clan. He appeared to be a brawler, relying on strength instead of technique and efficient movement. Aeden remembered one in particular, a bully he had taught a lesson in one of his trials.

The man swung his fist at Khrazhti and struck nothing but air. She easily evaded his blow, as well as the follow-up punch and the body slam he attempted. Her movements were graceful and lightning quick, but Aeden already knew that. He had sparred with her often enough. Being on the other side of her skills was not a pleasant experience for most people, though he enjoyed it because it pushed him to become a better fighter.

Dubhghall hissed as he tried to strike Khrazhti again. He was getting frustrated, which meant he was going to sacrifice his defense for a more concentrated offense. A classic error. As long as his opponent had a good defense themselves.

Which Khrazhti did.

Several more singular strikes evaded, and Dubhghall threw a flurry of blows at the blue woman. She dodged all but the last two, which she slapped aside with parries so fast, her arms blurred. If the man continued at this pace, he would be lying on the ground panting from his exertion without Khrazhti having to strike him at all.

Aeden's mouth turned up into an amused smile. Khrazhti had not once counterattacked. She was proving a point: the Trebhin could bluster all he wanted, but he couldn't even strike the animaru. He just wasn't skilled enough.

The thought seemed to occur to Dubhghall at the same time, because he drew his sword and stepped forward to attack Khrazhti with the weapon instead.

This time, it was Aeden who had to hold someone back. Of all people, it was Catriona who drew a long knife and attempted to attack the Trebhin.

"No, Cat," Aeden said. "Just watch. She's in no danger."

"How can you say that? The man bared steel on her."

"Do you remember how Marla taught him a lesson?"

"Aye, but—"

"Trust me," he said. "Between Khrazhti and Marla, Khrazhti is the better warrior. Watch and enjoy."

If anything, Aeden had become more relaxed. Combat

was where his friend was most comfortable. He doubted she would even draw her own weapons. Not for the likes of Dubhghall Trebhin.

The Trebhin's style was rudimentary. It was the first time Aeden had seen the man use a weapon and he was not impressed. As he'd expected, the brute relied too heavily on his strength and size. He was in for a rough education.

Khrazhti moved easily, her face emotionless and her body relaxed and supple. Wherever the man struck, she was simply not there. Her opponent began to breathe harder, hissing and spitting through clenched teeth, and then panting with an open mouth. Was she going to simply let him tire out?

"Will you strike me?" she said to him, the first taunt Aeden had ever heard her utter, if one didn't count the barbs she traded with her father. "I am waiting here patiently for you to strike me, yet you swing your weapon like you are chasing insects. You are not worthy of the honor of me striking you."

She turned her back on him and he screamed, charging at her with such rage, Aeden thought the man's head might explode.

She cut the timing very close. Dubhghall's sword whistled downward toward the back of Khrazhti's head and still she hadn't moved. Aeden tensed his whole body, clamping his fists so tightly to keep from interfering or screaming out that his knuckles popped. Was she going to let him sink his sword into her flesh to prove that he couldn't kill her? It would be painful for her and he didn't like the thought of that at all.

Then, at the last possible moment, Khrazhti twisted. It was a small movement, beautiful in its simplicity. A turn of the hips and shoulders, and the sword passed within a fraction of an inch of her head and torso.

As Dubhghall, off balance from committing so fully to the strike, stumbled, Khrazhti's arm flowed in a circle, matching the trajectory of the blade and catching it on the unsharpened back side. Her footwork was magnificent, worthy of an Aranir duelist or a professional dancer. In a movement Aeden would have to ask her to show him more slowly at a later time, she whirled, struck Dubhghall in the midsection with a knee, spun the man around to connect with an elbow to his jaw, then stopped his movement instantly by torquing her hips the opposite way.

Dubhghall's eyes went wide when he saw that he was bent backward over Khrazhti's knee, the blade of his own sword touching his neck. Aeden saw it in his eyes. The man understood that if she had stopped his movement a part of a second later, his throat would've been cut by his own blade.

The Trebhin wheezed from the strike to his abdomen and tried to take a breath, which pushed his throat against his blade and drew a thin line of blood as it split his skin. He still had a thin scab from when Marla had given him similar treatment a few days before.

Khrazhti stared into her opponent's eyes with her own softly glowing blue orbs, then showed him her teeth in a mix between a smile and a snarl.

"Do not test me again, little man. You will not survive it."

Just when Aeden thought the surprises were over, Khrazhti flung the sword from them, somehow generated the leverage to ram her knee upward into Dubhghall's back, and then performed a whirling movement that brought her other leg down in a circular motion to slam a kick into his chest, ramming his body to the ground. What was left of the air in his torso huffed out in a grunt.

Khrazhti rubbed her hands together as if cleaning them off, turned her back on the man, and resumed her place with her friends.

As Dubhghall groaned and tried to catch his breath, Catriona's laugh burst out over the campsite. She took

Khrazhti by the arm and hauled her back to their seats, whispering and gesturing to the blue woman.

Aeden spared a look at Dubhghall, then another at his sword, somehow stuck in a tree ten feet away, and shook his head. When would the Trebhin learn? He hoped soon. The next woman just might kill him.

❧ 23 ❧

The party of Croagh and the single animaru traveled quietly for the next several days. Or, at least, it seemed quiet and subdued without Dubhghall constantly trying to argue with everyone. Aeden would've been glad of it, were it not for his fear of the man trying to do something to get back at Khrazhti for losing face.

He probably had nothing to worry about. His friend had lived her whole life in Aruzhelim, where allies one minute might turn into enemies the next. If there was one person who, by their very upbringing, could withstand sudden attacks, it was Khrazhti.

On a deeper level, though, Aeden worried about the effects of what had happened on the negotiations with the rest of the Trebhin clan. Would they all have the same attitude as Dubhghall? He wondered what the other Trebhin in the party thought about the whole thing. He had, up to this point, kept a low profile.

Every warrior would be needed in the fight against the animaru. He didn't like to think that an entire clan would decline to be part of a united effort because of one man's misogynistic tendencies and his chance meeting with two women who trounced him in combat.

"Are you angry at my actions?" Khrazhti asked him.

"What? No, of course not. I am both pleased and impressed at how you handled the situation. You didn't harm him permanently but you decisively demonstrated that his actions were inappropriate. I want you to teach me how you twisted him around and put him into that position on your knee. It was fantastic."

She smiled. "I will show you when we have time without others watching. I do not believe in giving free things I have learned through hardship, except to my friends. Anything I know I will give freely to you, but not to bystanders."

"Thank you. I understand and appreciate it. I feel the same way. Maybe we will—"

Aeden spotted something on the road ahead. They were on the last few miles of the North Road before they would turn due north and enter the wild vegetation of the highlands. They hadn't seen many travelers, most likely because of the increased chance of anyone meeting animaru the farther east they went.

But the figure ahead was a mystery. Not simply because a man and a horse sitting on the side of the road was a curious sight, but because Aeden believed he recognized the man. And the horse.

"Dannel?" he called out and the man on the road snapped his head up.

When he caught sight of Aeden, a wide smile jumped to his mouth.

"Aeden Tannoch. Well met." He turned to Khrazhti. *"Haeusemica, iquidagise?"*

Khrazhti greeted the man in turn and Aeden hurried to reach him, clasping forearms with him.

"Dannel Powfrey. How is it that you turn up whenever I

travel on the North Road? Do you live nearby, perhaps, and lie in wait to find me?"

"I do not. It is ever my good fortune to find you during our travels."

"I have a quarrel with you," Aeden said. "I would speak of it."

"A quarrel, you say? Oh my. That sounds like hungry work. Perhaps we can make camp, share a meal? The day is drawing to a close and you will not lose more than an hour of travel time to do so."

Aeden looked to Greimich, who was as close to a leader as the group had. He was, after all, in charge of bringing the clan representatives to find Aeden and then bringing Aeden back to the clans. Aeden's friend nodded. The other highlanders looked ready to stop in any case. Dubhghall wisely remained silent.

"Splendid," Dannel said. "I happen to have meat and fish aplenty, along with some spices I have just obtained. Let me prepare the food and begin cooking, and you may scold me over my trespass."

Once the food was cooking and Dannel's horse, Blennus, was happily grazing nearby, the lanky man sat in front of Aeden with a chagrined look on his face. "Very well, tell me of this unknown quarrel."

Greimich, Cat, and Khrazhti sat nearby, but the other Croagh were separated in their own groups, like normal.

"I asked around at the Academy and none know you. If you indeed graduated, you have not done so recently, yet your years are not enough for it to be otherwise."

"Ah, that. I told you true, Aeden Tannoch. I graduated from the Academy, mastering the schools of history, language, and a few others. It was long before the time of those you might have asked, however. I am sorry to have caused you concern, but rest assured, what I have told you is true."

Aeden ran his fingers through his hair. "I don't know how that can be."

Dannel turned to Khrazhti and spoke to her in her own dialect of Alaqotim, doing it so quickly, Aeden only caught about half of it.

Khrazhti's mouth dropped open and she stared at the young man.

"Khrazhti?" Aeden said.

"I...I am sorry. He asked me of the Godan Chul, asked if I really knew what they were and what happened to them. Not the popular myth we heard from the man singing songs at the tavern. And he spoke of the Epradotirum."

She spoke in her own tongue to the man, as quickly as he had earlier.

"I asked him how he knew we met the Epra."

"I am sorry," Dannel said, in Ruthrin. "There are answers I prefer not to provide at this time. Suffice it to say, I am paying keen attention to you and your work, Aeden. You will have to trust me for now. Or not. It is your choice. But know that I will help where I can, if for no other reason than because I have not met one such as you for a long, long time. The age of heroes is long past, yet here you are, right in front of me."

"I'm not sure what that means, Dannel, if that's even your name."

"It is as good a name as any, I suppose." He readjusted the meat over the fire and sprinkled a few more spices on it. "But let us not get caught up in trivialities. Do you know the story of the princess mage?"

"The...the princess mage?" Aeden stammered.

"Yes, the princess mage. It's a very popular children's story, though I'm not sure if they tell such things in the Crid-heargla. It's not the most warlike of stories."

"I've never heard of it." Aeden looked to Greimich, who

shrugged. Catriona wore confusion on her face and Khrazhti stared blankly at the man in front of them.

"Wonderful. I do love to tell new tales. If you like, I could tell it to you."

"Tell us...a children's story?"

"Wonderful. Don't mind if I do. Thank you for asking. It's a very old story, and like all good children's stories, there is more to it than you realize at first hearing."

Dannel fussed over the dinner for a time, pronouncing it ready and serving it up on plates he pulled from his saddle-bags. Once he had taken a few bites of his own, he settled down to tell the tale.

Aeden absently shoved a piece of the spiced meat—venison, perhaps—into his mouth and couldn't help but close his eyes. It was the tastiest thing he had ever had the pleasure to eat. Even Khrazhti seemed to enjoy it, her large eyes narrowing in delight.

"There was once a princess mage," Dannel began. "Who lived in a grand castle with many servants, many rooms, and parents who could have been better.

"Her father, the king, was a weak and sickly man, so he could probably not be blamed for the situation. His wife had died years earlier and his new, younger wife was a power hungry, selfish woman, as second wives are wont to be in stories such as this.

"The princess, like all of her line, had a strong affinity for magic, and before the step-mother arrived, she had trained with the court mages to develop her power. Once her father's new wife joined the family, however, all lessons were stopped.

"The stepmother essentially ruled the kingdom. The only thing she dared not do was to harm the princess, because she knew the entire kingdom would rebel if she did. Instead, she hid the girl away, not allowing any but the servants who took care of her to see the girl. The stepmother was jealous of the princess's beauty, you see, among other things.

"Though deprived of lessons, the girl had time in abundance, and so with her time she studied in the castle library and she practiced her magic. In fact, she invented new spells and uses for magic, wondrous things that amazed all who saw or heard of them.

"Unfortunately, the stepmother had the princess explain them thoroughly and then the woman would take the ideas as her own and profit from the acclaim they granted her as a master mage.

"Though the princess was miserable, she did not try to escape so she did not cause problems for her father. Instead, she read and she experimented, and she befriended the servants, who delighted in the young girl and provided her with toys, clothing, and dolls created by their own hands.

"It was the dolls that ended up being the release the princess needed. Thirteen of them she had collected, and she played with them often. After a time, they became like a family to her, cherished children. She so wanted them to understand her affection, she worked on magic to make it so.

"First one of the dolls, then another, then another, she tested and devised and created magic to bring them to life. Finally, she was able to do so, transforming the first doll into a thinking, feeling person she could interact with.

"Soon, all thirteen of her dolls were moving about— though only when she was alone with them—and conversing with her. In fact, they varied in their personalities and their wisdom. She would listen to them, naming them her advisors and confidantes.

"It came to pass that her father began to decline, his age and illness getting the better of him. The princess knew that once the king passed, there would be nothing to stop her stepmother from killing her and crowning herself the ruler of the kingdom. Even worse, there was another evil growing in the world, one that could wipe out not only the kingdom of her father, but also the rest of the kingdoms. These things her advisors told her.

"The princess worked tirelessly to increase her magic, and especially to increase the magic of her dolls. Unfortunately, she had no talent for healing or she would have helped her father as well, but as her advisors told her, if she helped the kingdom, she would be helping her father, too.

"The time came when the dolls were powerful enough for the princess to stand up to her step-mother with their help. In a plan devised by her advisors, they took control from the stepmother and locked her away.

"Then the princess and her dolls turned their attention to the growing evil. For several years they battled it, utilizing both the magic that had been invested into the dolls as well as that inherent in the princess herself. Finally, they were victorious, vanquishing the evil forces.

"The kingdom recognized that the princess had saved not only their kingdom, but the world itself. She was hailed as their savior and queen and she was installed on the throne of her father. He lived for several more years, tenderly cared for by his daughter before, proud of his only child's achievements, he passed from his mortal life."

Dannel leaned back, a self-satisfied grin on his face, and took a bite of what was undoubtedly cold food.

"That was a nice story," Aeden said. "But why did you tell it? What does it have to do with what we're facing?"

Dannel didn't seem fazed by the question. "Do you know who Daana Vaskova is?"

"No."

"She was a prophetess, of sorts. She was the author of almost all the classic children's stories, and within those stories were hidden foretellings."

"Foretellings?" Catriona said. "The stories are prophecies?"

"Yes and no. They are a mixture of prophecy and entertaining stories."

Aeden was beginning to get impatient. "Dannel, just tell us what you want us to know. We've not time for games."

"Quite right," the Academy graduate said. "Do you know the main library at Sitor-Kanda?"

Aeden released a breath and closed his eyes for a moment. "Yes, I've been there."

"Good. When you get back, go to the third floor, to the history wing. On the fourth pillar from the end, there is a carving of a mythological beast, a manticore. Press its right eye and a compartment will open. Within you'll find a book."

"A book? In the library? How unexpected."

Dannel frowned at Aeden. "The book is unique, written by Daana's own hand. It is called Secret Meanings of Popular Children's Tales. Look up the story of the Princess Mage. It will be well worth your while."

"Third floor, history, fourth pillar, manticore's right eye. Got it."

"Excellent." Dannel walked to his horse and took the reins, his dishes cleaned by Greimich and Catriona while he told his tale and now in his saddle bags. "Don't forget. Search out the book as soon as you get back. You'll understand once you've read it."

"Are you leaving?" Aeden asked.

"I am afraid I must. Things to do, you know."

"Dannel, why can't you tell me what's in the book, what the story means?"

"I'm afraid I can't, Aeden. I would love to explain it to you, but I can't do that either. You'll just have to trust me."

"I've no real reason, but I find that I do," Aeden said.

"Thank you for your information. I hope to talk with you more about it the next time I see you."

"Will there be a next time?" the scholar said, winking. "I do hope so. I'm growing rather fond of you and your friends." He said a few words to Khrazhti in animaru Alaqotim, nodded toward the rest of the Croagh, and started to lead his horse back out onto the road. He stopped after several paces and looked Aeden in the eye. "Oh, and do keep in mind that Daana had a certain political leaning that may have affected some of her stories and commentary." Dannel started walking again and was soon out of sight.

"One day, I'll figure out who or what that man is," Aeden said. "I think I'm glad he's on our side."

❧ 24 ❧

Urun swung his arms—one still holding his staff—wildly as he took in a deep breath. The thing that grabbed his leg tugged at him, pulling him down into the water. Any attempt he made to resist was too weak to matter, especially considering there was nothing around for him to hold onto. His hands and arms slapped the water as first his feet, then his legs, then the rest of him was pulled downward.

In his panic, a spike of confusion shot through his thoughts. How could he be pulled under when the water had only been up to his calf? There was mud and muck beneath the surface of the liquid, but he had been standing on it. Now he was being pulled through it.

It was mere seconds until his head was at the level of the water, then under it. His scrabbling resulted in a handful of slimy mud and a staff so covered in mud that it felt like it was two feet thick, but didn't halt his downward progress in the least. The mud pressed against his body as he slithered through it. It seemed an embrace of sorts, but a cold and slimy one. The thought of dying through suffocation in the muck made his pulse race. Not the thing he needed when his air was limited. He gave in to the panic, though. What was an extra few seconds of life?

With a wet, slurping sound, he felt air on his body, then on his face. He didn't have time to try to take a breath before his feet slammed into what felt like stone under a thin layer of mud. The bones in his legs jammed into his hips painfully as he collapsed on impact, not ready for the sudden landing.

Then he did gasp, pulling in air, though with some water and mud as well. He coughed, spitting out the foul pollutants. He tore at the muck covering his eyes, clearing it enough so he could see. At least, he tried to see. Everything was black, but he thought he saw gradations, some darker black spots amongst the greys.

Sounds like barking nearby drew his attention and the priest put his hands out toward the sound, hoping whatever it was would run into his hands before it got to the rest of him. He remained perfectly still, suppressing the urge to continue coughing so as not to give his position away.

The sound came again, from the same place. It sounded less like barking now than something else. Coughing, maybe?

Indecision warred within him. Should he take the risk? He decided he would.

"Hello?" he called.

The coughing came again, but followed by words. "Urun?"

"Yes, it's me. Saevel?"

"Yes. Where are you? I can't see."

Before he could answer, a slurp and then the slap of a hard impact burst through the relative silence. It seemed to be to his right, while Saevel's voice had been to his left. Instead of coughing, a pain-filled grunt came.

"Who's there?" he asked.

"Ugh. It's Marla. I turned my ankle when I landed. Are we all here?"

"No, it's just me and Saevel."

Two more slurps announced someone else coming through the mud, along with the duller thuds of two people landing.

"Tere, Lily?" Urun said, wondering why it took Lily so long to arrive, since she was taken down before him.

"I'm here," Tere said. "Has anything come out at you from the tunnel yet?"

"Tunnel? What tunnel?" Urun realized as he said it that Tere could see where they were. With only a shred of light, barely enough to see beyond pitch black, they were all blind but the archer.

"The one we're in. Oh, you can't see, can you? Hold on, I'll get my flint and steel."

"Don't bother," Marla said. "Everyone, shield your eyes." She waited a few seconds, then a small ball of pale light appeared at about shoulder height. It was tiny, maybe as big as a candle flame, but it seemed like a sun in the darkness.

As Tere said, they were in a cavern seven or eight feet high and a bit wider. It stretched off in two directions as far as they could see, but considering that their sight was based on the tiny flame, that meant less than ten feet.

Once his eyes adjusted, Urun could see his friends, all of them dark shapes like some type of slime monsters. They had an eerie resemblance to the plant creatures they had fought not so long before. He noticed Marla was holding up her light with one hand but holding herself upright, braced against the wall with the other. She stood on one leg, the other pulled up so it wouldn't bear any weight.

"Let me take care of that ankle," he said, kneeling down on the mud-slick floor. He was already covered in the stuff, so he thought nothing of putting his knee in it. He ran his hand over her leg. "It's broken. You must have landed awkwardly on it. Anyone else injured?"

No one was, though Lily was sprawled on the floor, swaying gently like she was dazed. He set to casting healing magic to fix Marla's ankle, planning on checking on the archer after that. In a few minutes, she tested her weight on the foot and sighed. "Thank you, Urun. It would have been difficult to do anything with that injury."

"You're welcome."

Lily had perked up. Tere traded looks with Urun. "She was without air for a little while and it made her groggy."

A simple delving and a healing spell had her as good as new, though still as filthy as the rest of them.

Urun stared at the ceiling of the tunnel for a moment, then raised his staff up—luckily, he had kept hold of it—and poked at the mud there. The wood sank a couple of inches into the goo, but then met resistance. It didn't really feel like stone, but it also didn't allow his weapon to move any farther. "Hmm."

"How could that happen?" Saevel asked. "We were standing on the mud and it was holding our weight until the vines grabbed us." She snapped her head up, eyes scanning the tunnel, and especially the ceiling. "Where are the vines?"

Lily scooped some of the muck off her face and threw it at the tunnel wall. "Is that what those things were? Vines? I thought maybe they were tentacles on some monster."

"They could be a little of both," Tere said. "The important thing is that they brought us here. But why? Are we to be food for something or is something or someone helping us?"

His questions were sobering. Considering, however, that Urun thought he was dying a few minutes before, he would take sober.

Wet, slapping sounds echoed from farther down the tunnel. "Maybe we should try to find a way out," Urun said, "or we may get an answer from a source we'd rather not get it from."

"Urun," Marla shouted. "Hurry, bring your staff here."

He did as she asked, stepping closer and lowering his weapon so the tip was near Marla. She said a few words and another ball of light flared to life on the wood.

"You take the lead," she said. "I'll guard from the rear."

The slapping sounds grew louder and seemed to grow in number as well. Just as Urun turned to lead the others down the tunnel away from the noise, a figure came into Marla's light.

It was shaped vaguely like a man, and it was about the same height, though it was wider all the way through. Instead of flaring at the shoulders and tapering at the waist like a human, it was the same thickness all the way through until its body split into two wide legs at the bottom. Instead of two arms, it had many waving, flexible appendages Urun could only think of as tentacles, though without suction cups like he'd seen on sea creatures.

The thing's head wasn't defined well, making the monster look like a giant pile of seaweed and kelp that had somehow come to life, but denser. It was a grey-green color and even from two dozen feet away, Urun smelled its wet, putrid scent.

"Go!" Marla yelled as she launched several of her little fire pellets that normally caused so much damage. They sank into the creature with a squelching sound and the flames went out with a hiss.

As he turned and ran as fast as he could down the tunnel, Urun heard the red-haired Academy graduate say, "Okay, fire won't work. How about air?"

Urun didn't see or hear any more because he was too busy running while trying to watch for any obstacles his light might reveal at the last moment. Lily's heavy breaths panted right behind him, and he hoped that the others were right on her heels.

Saevel surged forward, almost brushing Urun's left shoulder. She ran even with him, seeming more comfortable in the position than he did. He heard her breathing occasionally, but not nearly as hard and loud as his own gasping. Priests were not meant for strenuous physical activity, he thought.

"This way," Saevel said, darting toward a branch on her side of the tunnel, and pulling on his robe to guide him along with her.

The walls of the tunnel fell away, disappearing from the small globe of light. Urun raised his staff as well as he could while running, but they ran in an endless sea of black, nothing visible in the entire field of the illumination.

"Stop," Marla said from close by.

Urun did so, happy for the chance to rest. He wheezed his breaths in and out and supported himself on his staff. He had become more fit since traveling with Tere and Aeden and the others, but he was no hero. His legs throbbed to remind him of that fact, and the pounding pulse in his head confirmed it.

Everyone was there, all within the small ball of light attached to Urun's staff.

"I think I lost them back there," Marla said. "They don't run very fast, thankfully."

"What...what were they?" Urun panted. "Saevel?"

The arba was right next to him and when she spoke, it startled him. He'd been looking at Marla. "I don't know. I've never seen anything like those creatures before."

"But you live in the swamp."

"True, but still, I've never seen them. Maybe they have always been here, beneath us, or maybe they have only recently come to be. I don't know."

"These tunnels aren't new," Tere said. "If these monsters are new, they took the caverns from something else."

"They seem to have the hang of pulling things through the mud," Lily said. "My bet is that they've been here for a while, but there's nothing saying that they weren't affected by the corruption. They could have been passive and solitary but now they're...not."

"Good point," Tere said.

"That's all great," Marla said, "but it doesn't help. We need to get out of here. Unless the corruption we're seeking is in these tunnels, we need to get back to the surface. Saevel, do you know where we are in relation to where we were going? I'm all turned around."

The arba closed her eyes for a moment, then turned to her right. "We need to head that way. Toward the tunnel we were in before."

"The tunnel where those monsters are still looking for us," Urun clarified.

"Yes."

"Great."

✸ 25 ✸

"Okay," Marla said, "I think that should do it."

The Academy graduate had cast her spell to create little balls of light several times over. In addition to the one she had been carrying—which she dropped to the ground so she had both hands free—she had made more of the little light sources and stuck them to each of her companions.

Urun appreciated the ingenuity. Marla had attached them to the tops of each of their heads. He could, even now, feel his hair adhering to something, though the spheres had no weight. It was strange, but not so irritating that it would distract him. The sphere lit a circle around him, with a radius of four or five feet, but it didn't glare in his eyes or affect his vision adversely. Now he could see without having to use his staff as a light source.

The globe on Marla's head was crooked, since she had to cast it without seeing where she was placing it, but she seemed content as she picked up from the floor the light she had created earlier.

"Now if we could only go through the tunnels without catching the attention of those evil monsters," Tere said.

"Actually," Urun said, "I don't think they're evil. Or corrupted. I think they are simply what they are. Dangerous, yes, but still only creatures living in the way they know how."

"What do you mean?" Saevel asked.

"I don't sense any wrongness to them. I don't doubt they'd kill us, maybe even eat us in some way, but they're not part of what's corrupting the swamp. They...belong here."

Saevel twisted her face in confusion and disbelief. "How can you say that? They're monsters and they pulled us under into their tunnels to kill us."

"Like I said, I think they would kill us if given a chance, but not out of some twisted, evil intent brought on by some sort of corruption. It's just their nature. Some creatures are more passive and some are more aggressive. Though it's strange that you've never heard of them attacking before, I don't think they are wrong to be here. They belong."

"Well, maybe we should ask them for tea or sit down to eat lunch with them," Tere said.

"I..." Urun started.

"No, no," the archer said. "I'm sorry, Urun. I understand. We'll fight them, kill them if we can, if they attack again, but they're neither the root cause nor the symptom of the Mellafond's corruption. Best for all of us if we can somehow slip by them."

Marla snorted at that. "You keep wishing. Maybe a magic rainbow with candy raining down will suck us up and bring us to our world above ground. While you do that, don't mind me if I try my best to kill them before they kill us."

Tere laughed, but didn't respond. Urun wasn't sure how serious Marla had been, but Tere was a great judge of character, so if he thought the intent was humorous, Urun would accept that he knew what he was doing.

"Okay, so we should get going," Marla continued. "The lights will last for almost half an hour, and I would be very happy if we can get out to daylight before then. Tere, do you want to go first?"

"Yeah. Lily and I can scout ahead a little bit, though it probably doesn't make a difference with all of us wearing lights on our heads."

Urun raised his finger to tell them he didn't think the creatures saw things the way the humans did, with light and images, but decided they didn't need to discuss it. Instead, he picked up his staff and followed the archers, Saevel at his side and Marla taking up the rear.

They sloshed through the mud-covered floor for a while, Tere asking the arba to let him know if they should take one of the side tunnels to get closer to where she sensed the corruption.

Just when Urun started to relax, daring to believe that they might actually find their way out without meeting more of the creatures, squelching sounds traveled down the tunnel.

They were in a long stretch of the cavern without any side openings. Tere scanned their faces, eyebrows slightly raised to invite suggestions.

"There's nothing for it," Marla said. "Keep on ahead."

They got to an intersection as the sloshing grew louder. Down a branch of tunnel to the left, Urun saw a flicker of movement in Lily's circle of light. On the other side, other sounds emanated from a tunnel on the right side, though nothing was in view. The sounds—reminiscent of palms slapping the water in a pond—sped up.

"Shit!" Tere said, unlimbering his bow.

"Straight ahead," Marla shouted. "We can't stop to fight or we'll be surrounded. Just hope there aren't any monsters ahead of us."

Tere grumbled as he nocked an arrow, but did as Marla

suggested. He broke into a fast jog, scanning ahead and to his sides. Lily had her bow out with an arrow on her string as well, but hadn't drawn it back.

Urun and Saevel passed the two side tunnels. The priest looked around cautiously, hoping he didn't see any movement. The stirrings he had seen to the left resolved themselves into two of the tentacled seaweed monsters, but though the sounds from the right side grew louder all the time, there was nothing visible yet.

A stirring in the tunnel formed into an almost visible object as it passed by Urun's head with a whoosh. The weapon—seemingly made of air—slammed into one of the plant beasts and cut deeply into its shoulder. It howled in a voice that sounded much too high-pitched for the size of the monster.

"Go," Marla shouted and began casting another spell.

She didn't have to tell Urun twice. He charged down the tunnel with Saevel at his side. He wondered if he should do something to help, but decided that running as fast as he could without getting in someone else's way was the best contribution he could make.

Until he slammed into Lily's muscular back and bounced off like he had hit a tree. Goddess, the woman was built like a boulder.

Saevel, apparently more agile than the nature priest, avoided a collision and slowed to a stop safely.

"Trouble," Tere said, releasing an arrow that embedded itself in something with a wet squish. "More up front."

Lily pulled one of her red-fletched arrows from her quiver, nocked, drew back, paused, and released in the blink of an eye. In midair, the head of the projectile burst into flame as the alchemical mixture Marla had created for the archer activated. The arrow sank into one of the creatures' heads with a *fwump* sound and immediately extinguished.

Lily spat a string of curses that raised Tere's eyebrow and made Urun's ears go warm. Apparently her fire-tipped arrows had no greater effect on the monsters than Marla's fire spells.

Urun thought at first to cast his shield spell, but then frowned at the decision. He was always shielding himself, not taking part in the combat, not helping his friends except healing them afterward. The priest needed to aid them in a way that mattered, a way that would damage their enemies.

He cast his Life Spike spell and a triangular shape appeared in front of him, zipping toward one of the monsters blocking their way. It picked up speed as it flew, generating a whooshing sound as it sped toward the creature. It slammed into the thing's chest. The moist thump didn't sound right to Urun. He was hoping for more of a cutting sound, a swishing or a zipping.

The target stumbled back half a step, but that was all. It regained its lost distance and pushed inexorably forward toward the humans.

Urun thought of curses of his own, though kept them silent. The spell was devastating to animaru, if only one at a time, but it hardly affected the swampy shape in front of him. It made sense. Life magic was a particular weakness of the monsters from Aruzhelim, but the current enemies were actually creatures of life magic. Urun was just happy it hadn't healed the creatures.

Thinking furiously, he cast a shield around himself. He had no other spells that could be used offensively on such adversaries.

A barely discernible shape cut the air between Urun and Tere, heading straight for the lead monster. It struck and parted the creature's head down the middle, causing it to stumble and flail its arm appendages wildly. At least that spell was effective.

"Try to go around them," Marla yelled. "There are more behind than ahead."

Tere and Lily slung their bows over their chests and drew their long knives. The older archer nodded toward the younger and they set to work cutting into the creatures in front of the party, chunks of wet vegetation flying with each swing.

Saevel stepped up behind Tere, just to the side, and used her short sword to cut at any of the creatures that tried to flank the archer.

Urun swung about with his staff, battering at the monsters with the hardened wood. It didn't seem to do any damage, but he was at least able to knock one of them around and keep it off balance. When his opponent finally got an opportunity to strike back, its thick, swampy arm bounced off Urun's shield, pushing him backward a little, but not nearly as much as would have been the case without the protection.

Marla was suddenly there behind Urun, carving pieces off several of the monsters with her sword and dueling dagger. She sheathed the shorter blade and threw her hand out. Wind sprang up from her outstretched palm and forced four of the monsters back from her.

"We need to push through the ones in front," she said. "There are more coming from behind."

Tere growled, but doubled his efforts, as did Lily and Saevel. Urun forced his staff to fly faster as well, but it seemed they were lost. Two of the swamp creatures crowded Urun, battering his shield, and he could already feel it failing. The monsters were strong and heavy—heavy as piles of dead, wet vegetation—and he wouldn't last much longer.

Marla took a glancing strike from one of the enemies, spinning her to the side, but she turned the movement into the casting motions for another spell and the wind picked up again, a howling gale that originated with her and flew off toward the monsters in front of Tere and Lily.

One of them was thrown a dozen feet back, while two others didn't leave the ground but were pushed out of the way.

"Go," Marla commanded through gritted teeth, spinning to slash at more of the creatures.

Tere and Lily didn't say a word, nor did they look to Urun or Saevel, simply leaned forward and sprinted through the gap Marla had made. Saevel followed on their heels, apparently having decided already that Marla was one to be listened to.

Urun glanced at Marla, concerned about his friend, but she growled for him to go, though he didn't know if she could even see him.

He took off running after the others.

It was a strange sight, the bobbing globes of light affixed to his friends' heads, speeding through the dark caverns. Urun saw flashes ahead of walls, obstructions like small stalagmites, and even openings that resolved into other tunnels as he passed, but it seemed they had gotten around the tunnel's monsters. For the moment.

A soft slapping behind him made him feel like something was literally breathing down his neck, but he turned enough to see the bulb of illumination attached to Marla's head. The other one she had apparently left behind. He detected a flash further behind her as figures passed in front of the light, making it flicker.

They ran for what seemed hours, but which must only have been minutes, if for no other reason than that Urun wouldn't have been able to run at such a pace for long. Tere finally slowed the group at a fork in the tunnels.

Both branches were larger than what they had been traveling through, widening out to nearly twenty feet wide and more than ten high.

"Which way?" the archer asked. His head moved back and forth as he scanned the tunnel behind them.

"Saevel?" Marla said.

The arba looked intently at the left tunnel, then the right. "They both seem—"

The familiar sloshing that signified the monsters' appearance sounded from the left tunnel, followed shortly by the return of the sound from behind the party.

"The right one it is," Tere said, and took off running down that corridor.

Twice more they got to intersections at the same time more of the swamp creatures arrived, so they took the other fork in the tunnel. First they ran down the right tunnel, and for the second, they had to dodge the monsters in the right-hand tunnel and go left.

Urun had lost count long before, but there had to be several dozen of the things chasing after them, many more than they could defeat because of the creatures' resistance to most damage the party could inflict. The only thing keeping them alive was that they kept running and—even if just by a hair—they took empty tunnels before their pursuers could get around to their front so the humans and arba would be surrounded.

Even if they figured out how to kill the creatures, Urun pondered what he had sensed when he had first seen them. They weren't evil; they were simply acting according to their nature. Did hunting cats all deserve to be destroyed because they attacked other animals and sometimes humans to eat and survive? Part of him was glad they couldn't kill the strange creatures. But he didn't want them to kill him and his friends, either.

But how long could they continue to have good luck?

"There," Tere yelled back over his shoulder.

Urun's vision was swimming, his head pounding from the exertion of running for so long. He swung his head to where Tere was and noticed light on the other side of the archer.

Daylight.

Somehow, Urun pushed himself a little bit harder, speeding up slightly. Tere and Lily had already thrown themselves into pulling mud and plant matter away from the hole where the sunlight came through. They were trying to widen it, though they constantly slipped atop of a pile of muddy debris.

The footsteps of the monsters could barely be heard behind them. Despite their fatigue, the party had put some distance between them and the denizens of the tunnels. If they got out, there was no way the swamp creatures could catch them in the open air. If the things would even follow them to the surface.

It was a race then. Still. They had to get through the obstruction and flee to above ground.

Urun stuck his staff in a thick pile of mud and threw himself at the wall of the stuff, digging at it with his hands. It seemed that for every handful he scooped away and threw behind him, twice as much oozed down from the top, covering any progress he made. If the muttered curses from Tere were any indication, the archer was having the same problem.

Trying a new method, Urun pulled his staff from its resting place with a slurping sound and jabbed it at the wall. When he thrust it hard enough, it left a hole when he pulled it back out, allowing a little more light through. Saevel saw what he was doing and joined him, her shoulders touching his because of the close proximity. He punched holes in the mud and she scooped the slop out before the holes could close up.

In a very short time, the main opening grew, letting even more sunlight through.

The creatures had not given up on their prey, though, and the sounds of their heavy plant feet slapping the muddy water only increased. Urun glanced over his shoulder—almost slamming his staff into Saevel's hand from the distraction—and saw Marla standing there alone, weapons out and waiting for the monsters to come near enough to attack.

But they didn't.

The creatures moved in a wide arc around the humans and then stopped, waiting less than a dozen feet away.

But what were they waiting for?

"The sunlight," Marla said. "I think they are afraid of the sunlight."

Tere grunted and joined Saevel in clearing the holes Urun was making with his staff. The technique worked too well for it to be just the wood. It must have been the life magic infused in the staff from using it as a focal point for his magic. Soon, all three of the other humans were clearing out large areas of the mud where Urun's staff seemed to weaken it. Marla continued her standoff with the swamp monsters waiting so close to her.

Finally, enough of the mud was cleared away that Lily slogged up the slight incline and pushed her way through the opening to step out into the daylight. Tere and Saevel followed.

"Marla," Urun said. "Come on."

"Go ahead. I'm right behind you."

The priest did as she suggested, using his staff to keep his balance as he slipped and slid while trying to make it outside. He finally squeezed through an opening not quite as large as his body. For a wonder, he had stepped out on dry ground. Marla's footsteps slapped the mud behind him.

The air was suddenly clean and sweet. Though the entire

swamp smelled of wet and rot, compared to the tunnels, it seemed like air at the top of a mountain, with a breeze blowing by. He sucked in a breath and closed his eyes.

"Move, Urun," Marla said, and the priest realized he had stopped in the opening, blocking the woman's path.

"Oh, sorry."

Marla lunged past him and joined the others a few feet away. Through the mud opening—already starting to melt closed—Urun saw the monsters lined up, keeping outside the circle of sunlight pouring in. There had to be close to fifty of them. He shivered when he thought of what would have happened if they hadn't found the way out.

"Well," Tere said. "That's something I wouldn't want to repeat."

They all looked a mess. Mud, bits of rotting vegetation, and other muck covered them from head to toe. What Urun wouldn't have given for a bath. He cocked his head. Actually...

The nature priest scanned the area, looking for the closest body of water deep enough to actually wash off in, and froze.

On two sides of the humans, dark shapes turned to consider them. Not as many as the number of swamp creatures they had been running from, but he saw more than twelve, along with movement among the twisted trees around them. They seemed to be radiating out from one particular dark creature, this one looking more like a regular animaru than the half plant, half animaru monsters the others were.

Without anything more than a gesture from the one, the creatures charged the tired humans.

❧ 26 ❧

eden peered from the foliage of a tall hill out over the sea of dark bodies, shaking his head. There had to be more than a thousand of the creatures in front of him. If he were to guess, he'd put the number at close to three thousand. He'd seen large groups of the animaru before, but at the time they were swarming him, trying their best to kill him, so he hadn't been afforded the opportunity to consider them the way he was doing now.

Aeden, Khrazhti, and the group of Croagh had seen evidence of a large host moving through an area south of the North Road. Before leaving the road themselves to go north, the humans decided to see what had made such a wide swath of trampled vegetation.

The young warrior had expected another human army like the one he had seen while trying to find Izhrod Benzal, but it ended up being the animaru force he was looking at now.

He nodded to Greimich, and the humans and Khrazhti descended the hill. A few minutes later, they were far enough away from the dark beasts that Aeden felt comfortable speaking.

"They were lined up, as if in ranks. They're more orga-nized than they were before."

Khrazhti nodded, but Aeden noticed her teeth were gritted.

"What's wrong?" he asked.

"When I directly oversaw them, my troops had good discipline. Some of my officers, though, were more lax. The troops you saw knew better than to resort to their baser instincts and battle haphazardly, yet they did so when they knew I could not see them. It angers me."

"Sorry, I didn't mean it like that. It's just that they actually look like an army down there, rather than a large mob. That's not a good thing."

"Of course it is not. Discipline and organization are key to an effective campaign. There are few animaru commanders who demand discipline. I wonder if Zhadril, Agthiros, or Sastiroz is now responsible for the troops in this world."

Aeden tried to assimilate the information. He sometimes forgot that though it seemed like the dark creatures simply gave in to their lust and attacked without thought, they were actually armies. It made everything that much scarier.

"I thought they were just groups and they did whatever they wanted," Greimich said. "How are the animaru organized?"

It was a good question, one Aeden would have asked. He leaned in to hear the answer.

"As with any army," Khrazhti said, "the attitude and effec-tiveness are dependent upon the one in command. There is no one animaru army, though S'ru will force those in this world to be one of purpose.

"In Aruzhelim, there are animaru lords, most of whom are commanders of military forces. You must understand that we cannot be destroyed—or at least, we could not before Aeden discovered that life magic can accomplish this. S'ru has always had the power, but no other. Because of this, animaru live forever. All except I have been in existence for more than eleven thousand years.

"In those vast amounts of time, there is little to do besides trying to gain favor from S'ru and gain power over others. This requires not only political maneuvering but also warfare.

"Aside from the more important animaru—the lords, priests, and commanders—there are only layers of followers. These range from the erfinchen, which are high-level animaru that are not lords, down to the forgren and biuri. All of the animaru who are not in a command position are free to become part of any force they choose. There are cases in which some may owe service to one lord or another, but aside from that, they can belong to any army that will accept them.

"Most stay with the same commander, but some do change, trying to gain a more favorable situation by joining another host. They do as they are told, and thus they have a group to call their own so that some of the more bestial animaru will not find them and feast on them. They cannot be destroyed, but being eaten is painful and unpleasant, even if the attacker derives no sustenance from the eating.

"As for the commanders, and especially the lords, they spend their time vying for positions of power and influence, attacking others and defending in turns. Each lord has its own army and at any given time, the majority of these forces are at conflict with others.

"We are a warlike race, and almost all interactions are military in nature. Only now that S'ru wants all the animaru to work together to destroy all life and light on Dizhelim are they cooperating.

"I had my own forces, and I controlled them as should be done with an army, with discipline and efficiency. Other lords and commanders do not, and it was always these whom I had the easiest time defeating. Without proper discipline, a war machine does not function as efficiently as it could. Thus does it trouble me as well that it appears one of the organized commanders is in charge of these we saw."

"I had no idea," Greimich said.

"How many animaru are there?" Catriona asked.

"Between three hundred fifty-one thousand and three hundred fifty-two thousand," Khrazhti said, "though my figures may be off because I am not sure what has happened recently. I do not know how many are in this world at the current time. At least three thousand, for there are more than that in the host we just witnessed.

The humans silently considered what Khrazhti had said. Aeden looked at each and saw varying degrees of concern. Dubhghall was pale and his mouth twisted like he might be getting sick. He said the first words Aeden had heard him utter that didn't deserve a fist in the mouth.

"I thought the few hundred we had heard of were a formidable force, but we are Croagh and no band of monsters could overpower us, even if they're difficult to kill. But this... how can we fight against so many, and with their ability to think and use battle tactics?"

"Only by uniting," Aeden said. "You can see now how important it is for the clans to band together. All our petty differences and squabbles are nothing compared to this threat. Our enemies are not human, not even alive, and they will suffer neither on this world if they have their way.

"Their goal is to destroy all life on Dizhelim. It's not mere talk, Dubhghall. You can see they are deadly serious. The numbers we just saw are a tiny fraction of their total strength. If every human in the world—no, every living, thinking being of any species or race—comes together, we *may* be able to fight off their whole force. Then again, we may not. They have magic, and they have the advantage of being indestructible to most opponents."

"Then what?" the Trebhin said. "We should give in, let them kill us?"

"Of course not," Catriona said. "Don't be stupid."

Dubhghall glared at her, but then turned his attention back to Aeden. He wanted affirmation that there was hope. Aeden understood.

"The best course lies in not only gathering our forces together, but also working to prevent any more of the monsters from coming to our world. With the numbers they have in this world right now, we could defeat them if we cooperate. In the meantime, we need to find those making the portals from their world and put an end to them. We need to do both."

Dubhghall nodded, seeming at least partially mollified.

"For now, though," Greimich said, "we need to get to the other clans and bring them together. If we insist on trying to handle this as individual clans, there will be no Croagh left. It's up to us to make sure that doesn't happen. Aeden and I have lost our clan, Cat almost so, but the rest of you have the opportunity to prevent the same from happening to your own clans."

"What're we waiting for, then?" Tamhas Seachaid said. "Let's get out of here and back into the highlands where we belong."

That was the first thing Aeden could recall being said by anyone in the group that everyone seemed to agree on, judging by the firm nods and resolute looks on the others' faces. It was something. It was a start.

❦ 27 ❦

Urun threw up his shield in preparation for the strange animaru charging him. He took a moment to really study one of them. It looked like one of the seren, but with some modifications. Mixed in with the coarse hair some of the normal creatures had, there seemed to be plant material, even small vines and leaves that looked to be growing. It was as if someone had literally, physically, mixed the essence of the swamp with the animaru. They moved just as fast as normal, but also seemed somehow more at home in the water, almost like they gained strength from it.

The life magic the priest had cast upon his friends' weapons was still evident. It would be hours until it wore off and needed to be reapplied. Urun hoped they would be finished with their foes before then.

Arrows flew between the enemies, enough to be coming from three times the number of archers actually shooting. Tere and Lily, of course, were responsible for most of them, but Saevel made a good accounting of herself as well.

Marla fired the fiery bullets she preferred and this time,

they did significant damage. Maybe not quite as much as they would with the normal animaru, but much more than the effect they had on the swamp creatures in the tunnels.

Before the lead monsters reached him, Urun cast his Life Spike spell and skewered two of the charging enemies. The projectile made of pure life magic punched through one, then the other, and both dropped and slid to a stop where they would never get up again.

Two of the dark creatures caught arrows in their eye or head and disappeared completely. It was what Khrazhti had called the twinkling. Urun wondered if they would arrive at their transference points in Aruzhelim and be able to rise again, or if there would only be the corpses that appeared. He hoped it was the latter.

Apparently the animaru had passed on information about Urun and his shield because none of them bothered to attack him. Instead, they veered toward the others, leaping toward the humans with their claws out and their mouths open with teeth bared.

He took the opportunity to more closely inspect their leader. It looked like one of the semhominus animaru, the humanoid ones that led the animaru forces. This one didn't have weapons, which was strange, but it obviously knew how to wield magic. As Urun watched, it finished a spell that caused a dark blob to shoot toward him, seeming to solidify in midair.

When the projectile hit Urun's shield, the entire world turned upside down. Urun slid to a stop and realized it hadn't been the world at all, but he that had turned upside down. In fact, he had been thrown head over heels from the force of the attack. His shield had disintegrated, absorbing the vast energy of the attack.

He shook his head to try to stop the ringing in his ears. If he had faced an attack like that before Osulin had granted him increased power, it would have torn through his shield and killed him.

As Urun got to his feet, he noticed something he had missed before. Some of the animaru seemed to be resistant to the life-magic attacks. Not to the extent they were immune to the life-imbued weapons, but the attacks were less effective than they normally were.

The archers were having to "kill" the animaru more than once after they took an arrow in a critical spot but got up again to shamble—albeit at a slower pace—toward the humans. Even Marla's spells weren't damaging them as much as he'd seen in previous battles. The two he had killed with his life spike stayed dead—thank the goddess—but the priest didn't like what he was seeing.

It had to be whatever caused the monsters to grow plant parts. The source of corruption, whatever it was, must be giving them an extra resistance to magic of all kinds, even life magic. That was definitely not good news. Already, more than three dozen of the creatures swarmed them. This strange new resistance could be the thing that tipped the balance in their fight.

Tere's curses told Urun the archer had figured it out, too. Or, at least, he had realized shots that should have killed the monsters didn't do so, even if he hadn't puzzled out the reason.

What could the priest do? He could keep casting offensive life magic and hope they'd get through an apparently endless supply of the monsters, or he could try something else.

He went through the short list of spells he could cast. It had never bothered him that he had fewer than ten of them, but that was before he had been called on repeatedly to enter combat and do more than sit behind his shield while his friends fought.

Life Spike worked well enough, but it wasn't nearly as fast as Tere and Lily's arrows. Life Blast worked if there were several animaru in close proximity, but it was meant to force them back, not to severely damage or kill them. His healing spells were not offensive. The rest of his spells were either defensive in nature or they did one specific thing that would help if they were fighting one very powerful enemy, but not when they were being swarmed.

It would be nice if he had something other than Life Blast that could reliably damage more than one enemy, but he might as well wish Osulin herself was standing at his side, feeding him power he could throw about without having to learn how to utilize it.

The creatures circled his friends and Urun threw up another shield. He had to think of a way to help. He was so weary of not being able to do anything significant in their fights.

Marla had both blades out, slashing about her, doing some damage but not as much as she should have. Tere and Lily had their long knives out, carving through the animaru surrounding them but taking wounds, too. As Urun watched, Tere was knocked back by an animaru colliding with him and he stumbled, allowing another animaru to catch him with a glancing slice of its claws. The archer gritted his teeth as a bloody spot spread from his shoulder to the chest of his tunic, but then he regained his control and dodged the other creatures while tearing out the throat of the one that clawed him. He turned and used the momentum to slash out with his knives, nearly taking the head of the one that ran into him.

Saevel was momentarily lost within a group of dark bodies. Urun gasped, thinking she might have gone down, but the arba slashed madly with her sword and was able to edge closer to the two archers so they could cooperate and protect each other.

For the time being, the attackers were ignoring Urun, though the animaru mage continued to eye him. The priest wasn't sure why it was not attacking him. Maybe it was casting a complex spell that took some time. Its face was twisted in rage or hate or some other strong emotion. It was hard to tell with the beasts.

That gave Urun an idea. The half plant, half animaru creatures seemed to take their commands from the mage. If that was the case, taking out the magic user would seriously affect the efficiency of the monsters.

He began to cast Life Spike again, his most powerful offensive life magic spell.

The mage's eyes snapped to Urun and motioned with its clawed hands. The nature priest's spike of glowing light magic shot from him, heading toward the animaru mage. At the last moment, it struck something and was deflected slightly. Enough to keep it from hitting the intended target.

The monster had a shield that could block—or at least deflect—life missiles. Wonderful.

Marla grunted and Urun looked to her in time to see the end of a vicious slash of an animaru's claws that raked across the red-haired woman's back. She twisted, cutting into the attacker, but the damage was already done. When she turned again to face the larger group of animaru, Urun could see the deep cut through a tear in her armor.

They wouldn't last long like this, not with the resistance to damage the animaru were showing. Something else needed to be done.

Something by one who wasn't mired in combat with enemies four ranks deep.

Someone like Urun.

The problem was, he had no idea what he could do to help.

❧ 28 ❧

Urun's friends were desperately trying to fight off the dozens of creatures assaulting them. So far, they hadn't succumbed, but it would happen eventually.

Think, Urun, he thought with the force of a physical scourge. *Your friends rely on you.* Osulin *relies on you.*

The animaru mage seemed to be occupied with striking out at Marla, all but ignoring Urun. Its shield was still in place, Urun sensed, so attacking it as he had done before wouldn't do any good. He had to think of something else.

He started sweating, trying by sheer force of will to wrangle his thoughts in new ways. The priest was tired of failing, tired of not being able to take a significant part in the battles his friends always seemed to fight for him. They needed him, and he had no idea how to help.

"Aauuuggghhh!" he screamed in frustration. Why didn't he have more spells? Why hadn't he ever learned to fight better? Why?

The young man sighed, shoulders slumping in defeat. He looked forlornly at the animaru mage. It didn't have as many bits of plants attached to it as the lesser animaru did, but its color was off. Slightly more green than the dark grey most of the monsters were. It was being affected by some kind of plant magic, at least in part.

Urun's eyes widened as a thought blossomed in his mind. He purposely narrowed his eyes again and stared hard at the mage, willing information to come to him.

There! He had gotten so used to seeing nothing magical in the creatures, he had gotten in the habit of not looking. Not *really* looking, that is. Sure, he saw them, but he didn't search for life or nature magic in them as he did when he looked at most things. Now that he focused on the monster, softening his eyes a bit to look for nature emanations, he noticed something that shocked him.

The mage had a bit of nature magic within it.

Not sure how that could be, Urun swept his eyes over the other animaru. They, too, had the faint emanations of life magic, nature magic. It should have been obvious with the vines and tubers erupting from their skin, but it hadn't been. Not until he thought his way through it.

Observing the mage, though, made him realize that the lesser animaru were under complete control of the magic—and their animaru leader, too, of course. The mage seemed to be battling with the magic, using its own to try to wrest control. The battle happened subconsciously, Urun thought, something inside the mage's mind that recognized something was wrong without registering it consciously.

Maybe the nature priest could bring it to the creature's waking mind.

At first, he thought he'd taunt the animaru with the knowledge of what was really happening, but the nature priest was not good with speaking Alaqotim, let alone the animaru dialect. No, he'd have to do it in another way. If he could put enough doubt in the mage's mind, maybe...

Urun shook his head. No time to overanalyze. Instead, he focused his mind and tried to commune with the monster.

Normally, he wouldn't have had a chance. The animaru was unalive, and nature magic was anathema to it. With the effects of the corrupted nature magic, though, maybe—just maybe—he could do something. He concentrated, willing his thoughts into the mage's awareness.

Though the mage stopped the casting he had been working on and looked toward Urun, the priest didn't feel like he had established a connection.

He tried harder.

Their thought patterns were too different, the animaru's too alien, for there to be a real understanding. It began casting again, turning back toward Marla, who was sorely pressed already by the lesser animaru surrounding her.

Urun grumbled to himself. How he wished Khrazhti was here to speak to the thing. He realized that Tere would be able to communicate with it and he searched out the archer. He found the white-eyed hero twenty feet away, in the midst of so many animaru, Urun had hardly been able to see him. If it weren't for Lily's red hair—and her height—Urun wouldn't have known where to look. Both of the archers were in a life and death struggle of their own. The priest would never be able to explain everything to Tere and then have the other man talk to the mage before they were all overwhelmed.

Another thought entered the priest's mind, something Saevel had spoken about earlier. She said the arba, her ancestors, could commune with nature. Speak with nature. If a whole race of people could do so, shouldn't he be able to use his affinity granted by the goddess herself? Then it came to him. He knew what he needed to do.

"Urun," Marla called to him. "A little help. Maybe some healing?"

It stabbed him with regret, but he ignored the Academy

graduate. There was no time. If what he was thinking worked, it would do more good than healing individuals.

The priest closed his eyes and focused on his own magic, on the gift of the natural world that flowed through his body. In so doing, he tweaked the magic slightly, causing it to make him glow. He recognized the feeling from when Osulin had granted him more power. He had literally glowed that night. Now he forced himself to do so again.

Urun lifted his hand in front of his face. He was lambent. Catching the mage's attention by waving his arms and yelling at it, he succeeded in making the animaru see the glow. It cocked its head in confusion, but this was only half of Urun's plan.

This is the hard part, Urun thought as he turned his attention fully to the mage. With a flexing of his will, he latched onto the mage's substance, specifically on the nature magic—corrupted though it was—battling to take over the entire body of the creature.

It was easier than he thought it would be. Perhaps because the magic was already dedicated to taking the mage over in full. Urun didn't know, but the result was that he made a connection with the nature magic, and it started glowing as well.

The animaru mage noticed its own claw as it continued to gesture in its spellcasting. Its already too-large eyes widened even more. It stopped the movements and looked its own body over. Then it looked at Urun as if comparing the two.

The monster's mouth twisted into a grimace and it bared its gritted teeth.

"Yes," Urun said aloud. "Yes, you understand. We're the same, you and I. We both have nature magic. Yours is your weakness, trying to take over. Will you let it?"

There was no way the thing understood his words, but it seemed to grasp the meaning anyway. Its claws balled into fists and all its muscles tightened, tension rippling through its form.

"Fight it," Urun said. "Fight the corrupted nature magic. Don't let it take you."

The priest didn't really care one way or another if the animaru was its normal dark self or if it succumbed to the corrupted magic and became a plant creature. What he hoped for, what he was counting on, was that the two halves of the monster would fight it out, giving his friends precious time to kill the thing. If they did so, maybe the plant animaru would scatter without a leader. It was the best he could come up with.

The result was better than Urun ever could have hoped.

As the mage's magic fought with the corrupted magic, Urun observed carefully. More, he paid attention to the feeling of the magic—of both types—to understand them better. He stared at the conflicted creature, knowing that he should probably have been helping his friends, but still analyzing without acting. The priest had a feeling that it was important to understand what was happening.

The animaru mage grew more and more agitated. It almost seemed as if something physical was inhabiting him and fighting with the rest of him. It was *exactly* that, Urun realized with a start. The corruption was not only magical, but there were plant fibers within the mage, and they were trying to take over its body as the magical corruption laid siege to its mind and its abilities.

Suddenly, the creature threw its head back and roared to the sky. It was a howl of pain and an act of defiance.

Because the corruption was winning. It was visible at the edge of the priest's vision. The sickly green glowing power slowly but surely consumed the grey animaru magic that, until that moment, he had never been able to see. How was he seeing it now?

More seconds passed. The animaru mage jerked and writhed in its effort, then it did something unexpected. With another shout, this one sounding more like a spell incantation, a flare of dark magic exploded outward, taking back the area in its body the corruption had just taken, and then some. The spell quickly diminished the green magic in Urun's sight, shrinking it to a quarter of the size it had been.

With a victorious shout, the animaru mage straightened and turned its eyes toward the humans. It looked less conflicted than earlier, its large, pupilless eyes clearer than before, more akin to the monsters' eyes he had seen when battling animaru over the last few months. The mage spat out words in its own language. They sounded like commands.

The plant animaru all stopped for a brief moment and Urun thought they might fall into some kind of organized offense against him and his friends. One of the only reasons the humans were still standing was that most animaru didn't do well with cooperating, instead attacking individually in whatever way they felt best.

He needn't have worried.

As one, all the animaru tilted their heads and looked at the mage. Then, they all rushed to attack their supposed leader.

Within a minute, the plant animaru had nearly torn the mage apart.

"Hurry," Marla said. "While they're distracted. Kill them."

And they did.

In the time it took for the creatures to rip the mage to shreds, the concerted attacks from the humans had reduced the number of enemies to just a bare handful. By the time they shifted their focus to their enemies—Marla especially—Tere, Lily, Saevel, Marla, and even Urun rained destruction upon them in the form of arrows and spells.

The last of the creatures fell and Urun slumped. He felt

like he'd carried his horse for fifty miles. While running. The others must be more fatigued than he was. After all, they did most of the work.

"What did you do?" Marla asked, sinking to the ground where she was. It didn't seem to bother her that the dirt-colored animaru blood was everywhere. "To the mage, I mean."

Urun knew she was talking to him, though she was looking at the ground. "I pointed out to it that the corruption of the swamp was taking over its body and its magic, and that though corrupted, it was a type of life magic. It didn't like the idea. I suggested it fight the power, and it took my advice."

"Clever thinking, Urun," Tere said. "Good job. That move likely saved all our lives. Very fine job."

Urun's face went hot, especially when he noticed Saevel looking at him like he was some kind of hero. He thought of it and, yes, maybe he had done well. Perhaps there was not only offense and defense in combat, but different things in between.

He took a breath of the fetid air and closed his eyes. Maybe he could take a nap. He was so tired. But then, something occurred to him. Somewhere deep in his senses, something stirred. It was not unlike what he had felt within the animaru mage. It was...

"I can sense it," he said. "I can feel the corruption now. I know where it's coming from. I can lead us to the source."

❧ 29 ❧

A eden's eyes skimmed over what had been the largest
of the Ailgid clan villages. The hard-packed dirt
road they traveled passed right through it, making it
easy for the infrequent traders to bring their wagons through
the forested and hilly highlands.

The community had been slightly north and to the east of
where Aeden was born. He'd seen Ailgids before, but mostly
because some were captured in the constant battles between
the two clans.

Never again, though.

Though he'd been raised to spare no love for the
bordering Croagh clan, Aeden swallowed to force a lump
down and out of his throat. The village looked so much like
his had, down to the burned-out husks of buildings that could
have fit right into his own village.

His entire life, before he was cast out of his clan, was
spent hating the people of the other clans, and most especially their closest neighbors the Ailgid. When it came down
to it, though, they seemed to share more things than not. The

young Croagh mourned the thought that it took him being cast out and the shared slaughter by animaru to realize it.

"Oh Cat," he said. "I'm so sorry. It looks just like my village, when I found it after the animaru attack."

The woman's eyes glistened, but no tears fell. Her chin, raised defiantly, quivered the slightest bit, but she gave no other signs of the impact of her loss. "Thank you, Aeden. I saw your village, too, after you had cleaned it up a bit. Our clans are essentially gone, living only in the history books now."

"Not gone, Cat," her husband said. "As long as there exist one or two, the clans still live. We need only to survive the end of the world and we can rebuild them. Stronger. With more wisdom learned from hard lessons." He squeezed her hand and she closed her eyes for a moment.

She nodded. Anything more, Aeden thought, might break her composure. Hells, it almost broke his to witness it.

The other Croagh were not unaffected. They had apparently not come the same way when they had left the highlands to find Aeden, so it was their first time witnessing the destruction wrought by the dark monsters. Or at least the first time seeing the annihilation of an entire community. Some of the other clans had been attacked, but it had not been wholesale slaughter like with Tannoch and Ailgid.

The other clan members bowed their heads as they passed through, uncharacteristically quiet. Even Dubhghall didn't utter a word.

In a daze, Aeden stepped on something and almost tripped. When he stopped and looked back, he found a doll. It wore a simple highland dress and had red yarn for hair, its eyes bits of green stone that had been sewn to the cloth face above its tiny wooden dot of a nose and a yarn mouth.

It made Aeden think of Marla. She had escaped death, but

the child to whom the doll belonged had not. He thought to ask Cat if she knew if the girl had lived, but didn't want confirmation that she did not. His understanding was that, like his own village, this one had been wiped clean of all life.

He clenched his fists, gritted his teeth, and continued north. The sooner they left the graveyard of a village, the better. One thought burned in his mind: he would make the monsters pay for what they did.

A soft touch on his shoulder nearly made him strike out. He looked down and found the blue fingers on him and he relaxed. Putting his hand on top of Khrazhti's, he let out a breath and with it, some of his anger. Some.

How must she feel? Her people had done this deed. Most likely, it had been on her orders. Aeden didn't blame her, though. She had been deceived into thinking that the people on Dizhelim, like the animaru, couldn't be killed. She had been led to believe they would simply be brought low, and that they would recuperate over time. When she found out humans died forever when killed, she had switched sides.

He tried to smile at her, but his heart was still too raw. He left his hand on hers for a few seconds, then removed it. She took her own back soon after. The gesture was appreciated, and he'd tell her so later.

For now, he wanted to get lost in taking each footstep, moving slowly closer to other living Croagh.

Through the Ailgid territory, Cat and Greimich took the lead, guiding the party on smaller roads and hunting paths, some of which were nothing more than animal trails made through the underbrush.

As they traveled, Aeden's mind churned, thinking of his clan and what he had seen of the Ailgid clan. They didn't pass through any other villages, but he didn't know if there weren't any along the route or if Cat purposely avoided them. They had apparently all been wiped out, one of the sad results of being one of the more southern clan areas. He understood that situation well.

Along the way, the young Tannoch noticed interactions between the other Croagh and Khrazhti had changed. Before, they had been aloof—other than Cat and Greimich—but now he caught looks from the others. Some of them—such as the brother and sister from the Seachaid clan—looked at her worriedly, while others' faces twisted in a way that made Aeden think of a person being affronted by a foul odor.

There was even the infrequent glare of hatred.

Of course, the latter was usually on the face of the Trebhin. Surprisingly, though, he saw a hint of it on the other Trebhin, Naomhan, as well.

Aeden had just about had enough of it, and prepared himself to have a discussion about it with Dubhghall when the party reached the edge of Trebhin territory. The man strode up to the front and took over the guide position from Cat and Greimich. He wouldn't have time to glare at Khrazhti while picking out their path, so Aeden let it be.

"You have to understand," Greimich told him later as they dropped back to the rear of the group so no one else could hear. "Especially after seeing Cat's village, everyone's emotions are raw."

"Aye, I can see that. Mine are, too."

"But Aeden, they see the devastation, think of what they've seen with their own eyes, and it all points to one thing: the animaru. Khrazhti is animaru. Of course they're going to have hard feelings."

"I can understand that, too. It's true that every animaru I've met except her is a right bastard and deserves to be destroyed, but she's not that way. She is the most honorable person I've ever met. She has sacrificed everything to help the enemies of her people. And for that, she gets mean looks and challenges?"

Greimich put his hand on Aeden's shoulder. "I know. It bothers me, too, but people don't feel with their minds. The emotions are too high to think clearly for some of them. Give them some time."

"I'll give them time, but not too much. If this is the kind of reception she'll get with the clans, then there will be a problem. I'm telling you now, Greimich, if I must choose between the clans and Khrazhti, I'm afraid that the clans will be on their own. If they can't get past their stupid bigotry—for other clan members as well as other races—maybe they don't deserve to exist."

Cat caught the last part of what Aeden said and her eyes went wide. Aeden calmly looked into her eyes. After a moment, she nodded, though she did it with sad eyes.

The clans were arranged in the highlands like nations would be in other parts of Dizhelim. The Tannoch land was on the southwest portion of the highlands, bordering the North Road and closest to the Grundenwald, though sepa rated from it by more than fifty miles of hilly terrain and grasslands. North of the Tannochs was the Corcan clan, their territory stretching up to the Lisinis Ocean. They were some-times called the people of the lakes because their section of the highlands held hundreds of small lakes.

On the eastern edge of the Corcan clan's lands were both the Seachaid and Trebhin clans, the Seachaid on the north extending to both the Lisinis Ocean and the Netali Ocean. Below the Trebhin were the Ailgid in the southeastern part of the highlands, closest to Kruzekstan, though separated by wild territory at the edge of the highlands.

The Croagh passed through Trebhin territory without incident. They saw neither animaru nor evidence of their attacks. According to Dubhghall, animaru had found a few small villages, but they were groups consisting of only hand-fuls of the monsters and once they destroyed what they found, they disappeared back to wherever it was they came from.

Again, Aeden was struck by the similarity between the villages in his clan territory and the Trebhin. He didn't know why he thought they'd be so much different, but he did. Apparently, his prejudice also ran deep. Not as deep as the others, thankfully, but still more pervasive than he liked to admit.

The small emissary group wended its way through the people of the Trebhin clan. They were met with curiosity, which Aeden expected, but also something else. Many of the people did a double-take when they saw Khrazhti pass by, but others were not so passive. Sneers, glares, and expressions of outright hatred were not uncommon.

Khrazhti had foregone using her hood and cloak despite the weather getting cooler, and though most of the people they passed probably didn't know who or what she was, they equated her with something not human. The things that had attacked the clans were not human; therefore, other not-humans would be enemies.

Aeden didn't like the reception.

He growled in his throat, his fingers itching to wrap around his blades. Before the animaru, if he had seen any of these people, he would have attacked immediately because they were from another clan. Now, aggression against anyone in the clans would ruin what he was trying to accomplish here. But he'd had enough. No one was going to treat his friend like this.

The young Tannoch managed to hold himself back from direct confrontation, but he had no problem glaring back at the rudest of the onlookers. None of them were able to hold his steely gaze.

Except one.

A Trebhin man, maybe a handful of years older than Aeden, met him glare for glare. The large man reminded Aeden of Donagh, which instantly doubled his hatred. Donagh had been a bully and a hateful person. Until Aeden beat him so severely in his trial of combat that the boy took weeks to recuperate.

"What're you looking at, boy?" the Trebhin said.

Aeden smiled at him, showing all his teeth but without any real mirth or feeling. Though it looked predatory, Aeden was slightly amused. What the man said reminded him of his confrontation with Marla when he first met her. She had called him boy, too.

"I'll wipe that silly look off your face," the big man bellowed.

Aeden merely continued looking at the other man, though his senses had gone on alert and his body prepared for combat. As soon as this man attacked him, Aeden would unleash his anger in the form of an offensive that might have deadly effect. It depended on whether the Trebhin came at him with a weapon or empty-handed. At this point, the Tannoch didn't really care which.

Surprisingly, Dubhghall stepped between them, shaking his head at his fellow clan member.

"You'll not be wanting to try this one, Tasgall. Take my word for it."

Tasgall looked shocked to hear the words from his clans-man. He swung his gaze to Khrazhti, who was calmly watching the drama progress.

"Nor that one. Let it go."

If the man was confused before, he was befuddled now. After noting that everyone was watching him, he nodded quickly and turned his back to walk away. He paused, turned around, and spat at the ground between himself and Aeden, then resumed his exit.

Aeden met eyes with Dubhghall. The other man shrugged. "No use in injuring Tasgall. He's good enough in a fight. We'll need every man we've got."

This time, it was Aeden nodding to Dubhghall.

❧ 30 ❧

Urun couldn't believe he hadn't been able to distinguish the source of the corruption earlier. It seemed so clear now, like a bright blue flag against the backdrop of dense trees. It was true still that the Mellafond didn't consider the power to be corruption, but simply another type of nature, but Urun knew that was incorrect. He saw it now, in all its devastating and deadly glory.

"It's this way," he told the others, starting off in the direction he indicated.

"Hold up there," Tere said. "We should try to recuperate a bit before going off to battle again. We barely survived the last one."

The priest felt his face go hot. Of course. The others still had injuries from battling the plant animaru and the mage. Just because he had been out of the battle and protected by a shield didn't mean the others were in fighting shape.

"Sorry. I got a little carried away. Here, let me help." He went to each of them and healed their injuries. They all had some, even Tere. When he was done, they were whole again, though not quite ready to move on.

After she was healed, Marla went into her pack to pull out a snack to eat. As she did, she mumbled something and pulled out the message tablet.

"There's a message here from Evon," she said. "They are headed for Shinyan, as they planned. They're still in the Great Enclave, about to go into Arania. They wanted to see how the rest of us are doing. Give me a few minutes so I can answer them. I'll tell them we're hip-deep in hostile monsters and that we'll give them a full account when we have a chance to do so. I'll also tell them not to worry...too much."

Tere laughed. "I'm sure that will keep them from worrying."

"I'll make it sound better than I just explained it. Don't worry."

Marla pulled the stylus from the side of the tablet and scratched out her reply. Urun hoped the others would stay safe. He wondered if Aeden would answer with his own tablet.

"Urun," Marla said, after she put the tablet back into her pack. "Can you tell how far away the center of corruption is, or just the direction?"

"I think I know how far. It's not more than a few miles from us."

The red-haired Academy graduate nodded. She got a pensive look on her face and her mouth twisted slightly. Urun thought she was probably arguing with herself.

Finally, she spoke. "We might as well go on now. If we stopped to make camp this close, we'd probably be attacked by something else tonight anyway. Better to try to end this. Quickly. I don't want to be facing whatever it is when it's dark."

The others seemed to agree, though Tere still looked unhappy about it.

With that settled, Urun stepped up to the front of the

group, where he was joined by Saevel and Tere; her because she could help pick out their path, and the archer because he spotted hazards faster than even Saevel could.

As they threaded their way between cypress and tupelo trees, passing by growths of duckweed covering the surface of some of the deeper pools, Saevel looked toward him often, once even opening her mouth to speak but not saying anything.

"Did you want to ask me something?" Urun asked.

The arba looked toward the ground, for all the world looking like a child asking permission to go on an extended trip. "Did you really connect with the swamp, so much so that you can tell the difference between her magic and that of the corruption?"

"I did. When I was analyzing the animaru mage, it sort of came to me. It's as if I learned the Mellafond, way down deep in its core. I think I could recognize a small part of swamp life if someone showed it to me a thousand miles from here. After that, it was easy to distinguish the corruption, even though it's still strangely nature based. I'm not sure what that means in general, but for our specific situation, it means I can take us right to the origin of the corruption."

"It's like the legends of my people," she said. "They were said to have been part of the place, just another aspect of the nature of their home. In this case, the Mellafond. It must be magnificent."

Urun loosened his tunic around his neck. "Um, yeah. It does seem to be pretty helpful." His head snapped up, and the conversation was forgotten completely. "We're here." He pointed past a dense group of trees. "Just through there."

Saevel and Tere flanked Urun as they inched their way through the trees and underbrush. They barely made any sound, the archer and the arba being accustomed to moving about in vegetation and Urun having his special affinity toward nature, even if it was partially corrupted.

They got to the edge of a clearing and Urun stopped. Tere, a quizzical look on his face, halted alongside him, but Saevel kept picking her way as if she was still traveling through the low-lying bushes between the trees.

"Saevel," he whispered. "Stop. What are you doing?"

The arba turned, then saw everyone else had halted. She retraced her strange, crooked path back to him.

"I'm continuing on until we find something," she whispered back. "Why did you stop?"

"I didn't want to enter the clearing until we've looked around first," he said, quirking an eyebrow at her. Why didn't she understand that simple idea? She was a hunter and a guide, after all.

"Wait," Tere said. "Clearing? What clearing?"

Urun glared at the other man. They were choosing *now* to play practical jokes on him? Had some spell affected them, making them stupid? "The clearing two feet in front of where we're standing."

Tere and Saevel shared a look.

"Urun, there's no clearing in front of us," Tere said. "Only trees and vegetation, just like what we've been walking through. The ground is fairly dry here, the plants are thick, and our visibility is limited to what we can see between the trees."

"Does everyone see the same thing?" the priest asked, watching Lily and Marla as well as the two right next to him.

They all did.

"Huh," he said. "I guess that explains how it's stayed hidden. There's a clearing in front of us, at least two hundred feet long and about the same in its width. There are grasses, a few bushes, and one strange tree in the middle. And a large clump of vegetation that looks kind of like a huge ball of seaweed. It's mostly dry ground around it."

Tere held up his hand. "Even in my magical sight, I see only forest. Maybe something is affecting you, Urun."

Urun closed his eyes. Even without seeing, he could feel that the space before him was relatively empty. He thought for a moment.

"Where is the closest tree to where I'm standing?" he asked. Tere and Saevel both pointed directly in front of him and a bit to the right.

Urun scanned the clearing for signs of enemies and, when he saw none, stepped up to where the two had pointed. "Here?" They nodded. "Watch carefully." He hoped this worked. He swung his arm out through where they had told him the tree was. "Did you see anything strange?"

"It's like you did one of those sleight of hand tricks," Lily said. "It almost looked like your arm passed right through the tree."

Urun sighed. He took a half step to where the tree was supposed to be. "Now?"

"You..." Saevel said. "How are you standing inside the...oh!"

The arba swayed like she had been struck, then blinked rapidly, closed her eyes as if she had a migraine headache, and finally opened them again. Her mouth formed into an O.

"Where did the trees go?"

"Everything just disappeared," Marla said. "All but the clearing. Is this what you were talking about, Urun?"

"Yes. It must be an illusion to keep people from finding the corruption's center. I can still sense it. It's coming from that strange tree in the middle of the grass."

All eyes turned to the shape. It was huge, more than three feet in diameter, but only twenty feet or so tall. While it had a fair amount of foliage near the top, the two main branches coming out from the sides, eight feet off the ground, were too symmetrical. The split in the trunk, too, seemed mysterious. It was almost like...

"Those are legs and arms," Saevel said, just as the two huge side branches started swinging toward the group.

They scattered, Tere and Marla diving to the ground and rolling, Saevel and Lily jumping out of the way off to the side, and Urun backpedaling so fast he ended up tripping over an exposed root and falling flat on his back in the midst of damp grass. One of the massive arm branches made a whomping sound in the air as it passed over him.

"That's it," he yelled. "That thing is the source of the corruption. We have to destroy it."

He needn't have spoken. His friends were already in combat mode. The archers had launched several arrows and Marla was letting loose a fire missile spell. As always, Urun was the last to enter the fray. Once his shield sprang up around him, he cast a life spike at the center of the tree monster's trunk.

It glanced off harmlessly. Either its bark was that strong or it simply had an immunity to life magic.

Off to Urun's left, Lily rapidly launched her special fire arrows Marla had made for her. Each left her bow and, within a dozen feet, burst into flames as they raced toward the creature. When they struck, it was with a sound that was a combination of the shaft whistling through the air and the huff of fire thunking into the thing's bark. At the same time, the sounds of Tere whipping arrows from his quiver and the slap of the bowstrings on the archers' arms added to the cacophony. Saevel, too, launched arrows at a respectable interval, though she was no match for the others' speed.

The sharpened missiles had no effect on the monster. Even Lily's fire arrows didn't explode like they should have.

The woody creature continued to swing its branch arms and shuffle its stubby trunk feet toward Marla.

It was no wonder the thing had focused on Marla. She continued to shoot those fire pellets she seemed to prefer. While they didn't seem to be doing much harm to the tree monster, bits of fire pelting its bark time and time again had to be annoying.

Urun racked his mind, trying to think of what he could do to help. He'd already tried Life Spike, one of his most powerful spells, to no avail. Maybe he could use the strategy that worked with the animaru mage. Narrowing his eyes, he concentrated on the monster, trying to find a weakness to exploit, a way to battle the corruption.

His eyes widened when he realized it was made up entirely of that corruption.

One of the tree's massive branch arms came down where Marla had been a fraction of a second before. She had dived and rolled, drawing her weapons more out of habit than anything else, Urun thought. He read the frustration on her face. Nothing she did seemed to harm the creature.

Motion from the edge of the clearing caught Urun's attention. He let out a groan when he saw what was coming.

More than a dozen of the plant animaru were shambling toward the arba and the two archers. Reinforcements had arrived, but not for the humans. More help for the bad guys.

❧ 31 ❧

Aeden's group finally made it to the Seachaid clan territory, the farthest north of any of the clans. They had camped on the edge of Trebhin land the night before. As they were setting up camp, Aeden glanced at the message tablet Marla had given him and found messages from Evon and from her. It seemed that the group with Jia was traveling toward Shinyan—though they planned on stopping to visit the Gypta caravan—and Urun's group had faced some danger from strange creatures, but were safe at the moment. He wrote on his own tablet that they were in the Cridheargla, but not quite to their final destination yet, the place where the bulk of the remaining clans were gathered. It was good to hear that everyone was doing well, though he worried about what Urun and his companions were facing.

The Seachaid domain consisted of quite a large amount of land bordering the oceans. It was also secluded more than any of the other clans, at least as far as non-Croagh invaders were concerned. Few animaru had made their way to the territory. Yet.

The Seachaid were a slighter people than Aeden's own

clan, and even the others, in fact. They still had substantial figures, but they were not nearly the bear-like warriors the other clans boasted. When Aeden was with his clan, others used to joke about the Seachaid, saying they all had the form of women. Minus the breasts.

The bigger Croagh seemed to underestimate the Seachaid because of this, but Aeden knew better. It was true that size and mass could give one an advantage in battle, but that was not the end of the argument. A skilled warrior could generate power through speed and technique. Lighter, lither fighters could continue to battle long after larger warriors tired out from hauling their significant weight around.

A case in point was Khrazhti herself. She was taller than Aeden, but her slighter figure weighed less than his. He'd been on the other side of combat with her—both in practice and in truth—and she could hit harder than most others he'd ever fought.

The point was, he didn't look down on the Seachaid for their slenderer builds. As far as he was concerned, any Croagh was dangerous, and he would not disparage allies because they didn't look exactly like him.

The main village of the clan was packed with people from several clans. Makeshift camps—all separated by empty buffer zones—were spread around the village, and the roads were kept clear. They were hardly better than small dirt paths anyway. The Croagh didn't put a lot of thought or value on such things as paved roads.

One of the clan warriors led the group to the center of the village, to a building that could only have been the elders' lodge. All the important business of the village would be carried out there. The building, similar to the one that had been in Aeden's own village, was round with a domed roof made of thatch. There were other types of roofs on the buildings in the community, but community buildings such as the elders' lodge were historically thatch roofed. No one knew why, only that it was the way they'd always done it.

Greimich stopped at the door to the building and motioned that Aeden could go in first. Aeden supposed it was fitting. After all, the party of the different clan representatives had gone all the way to Sitor-Kanda to fetch him. He entered the elders' lodge and the others followed him, Khrazhti first on his heels.

Four men sat around a fire in the large room, each dressed in typical highland attire, but slightly different than one another. They stood—one of them doing so quickly as if he thought they were being attacked—and considered the newcomers. The first man, to Aeden's right, was the oldest of the group. He was of a height with Aeden, though his stance was slightly stooped, his grey-covered hair dipping in what might be construed as a respectful greeting. Aeden dipped his own head in acknowledgement.

The man smiled at Catriona and she returned the gesture.

"This is Touhas Ailgid, elder of the Ailgid clan," Greimich said. "The clan has not yet made formal one of the few remaining warriors as chieftain?" He said it like a question, and Touhas nodded. They hadn't decided even though it had been at least a month and a half since Greimich had been in their midst. "This is Aeden Tannoch, son of Sartan, the one for whom you sent me and the clan representatives to fetch."

Was that irritation in Greimich's voice? Aeden hadn't detected that before. Was there something his friend wasn't telling him, or was he simply tired and letting the irritation of being sent as a messenger getting to him?

"Next is Padraig Seachaid, clan chief of the Seachaid clan, whose hospitality we are enjoying." This man was a couple of inches taller than Aeden's five feet and ten inches, but he wasn't as broad in the shoulders or muscled around his limbs. Precisely what the Tannoch expected in a Seachaid. His dark brown hair, with a few grey streaks within, was tied back into a tail, keeping his blue eyes unobstructed.

Aeden nodded to the clan chief, who lifted his chin and looked down his nose at the younger man.

"Seoras Corcan, clan chief, is here," Greimich said, gesturing to a man that could have worn Aeden's clothes, their body shapes were so similar. With his blue eyes and red hair, he even looked to be a Tannoch, except for his clothes consisting of more furs than Aeden's more southern tribe typically wore.

The man broke the somber mood of the gathering by smiling a wide smile at Aeden. It stretched his skin and made a wicked scar across his throat shine in the firelight. Gods, that scar looked like he'd had his head half cut from his body. Aeden's eyes widened slightly, but he returned the smile.

"Well met, son of Sartan," he said, his voice firm with an air of command. "I knew your father and have wept to have heard of his passing."

"Thank you, Clan Chief. I appreciate that."

An exhalation of breath, almost a scoff, came from the last of the four men. No one needed to tell Aeden which clan he was from, and not only because it was the only one left to whom he had not been introduced.

"This is Daibhidh Trebhin, clan chief of the Trebhin clan," Greimich said, a bit of tension in his voice. Aeden hoped the others didn't pick up on it, but knowing his bratharlain as he did, he heard it loud and clear.

The chief was a massive warrior. He was nearly half a foot taller than Aeden and wider besides. Though muscular, he wasn't as toned as Aeden and Seoras were. The young Tannoch had no doubt the man outweighed him by a hundred pounds. A huge double-bladed axe leaned against the chair he had been sitting in.

Of course he used an axe. Why wouldn't he?

Daibhidh's shaggy auburn hair swayed as he looked Aeden up and down with his light hazel eyes. Then, so suddenly it almost made Aeden jump, the man threw back his head and bellowed a laugh.

Aeden didn't know how to respond to that. Was he laughing at Aeden, something he should challenge the man for, or was there truly something funny?

"Don't mind Daibhidh," Seoras said. "He often finds humor in nothing at all. Mayhap he is half mad from the state of the world and the clans."

The bigger man glared at the other clan chief, but kept laughing for a few more seconds. When his laughter stopped, his face grew emotionless and he waved toward the visitors. "Enough of the introductions. Begone, women. The men have things to discuss."

Catriona's lips tightened into a straight line as she met her husband's eyes. He shrugged and nodded, then the woman exited the building.

Khrazhti stayed where she was.

"Did you not hear me?" Daibhidh said to her. "Out with you. None with teats are to remain when men's business needs to be done."

Khrazhti stared at the man for a moment, then turned her attention to Aeden. In her own language, she asked, "The man speaks strangely. Is this oaf telling me to leave? What is the reason?"

Aeden smiled and answered her in the animaru Alaqotim. "He says that the women should leave so the men can talk."

She scoffed and continued to glare at the clan chief.

"Khrazhti will stay," Aeden said to the clan chiefs. "She has information that is invaluable to our efforts. She is also more experienced in warfare than everyone else here put together."

That caused a flurry of comments from all four men, each trying to explain how that was not possible.

"She is three thousand years old and was the commander for all the animaru in Dizhelim. If you insist on being ignorant and not listening to her, I'm afraid I have come for no reason at all."

"Now, on that we agree," Daibhidh said. "It's a fool's folly to bring you here, the disgraced pup of a substandard clan chief."

The next thing Aeden knew, strong blue arms were around his chest, pulling him back. His sword was halfway out of his scabbard and he was already visualizing the pieces he would be cutting off the Trebhin. Greimich's arms joined Khrazhti's a few seconds later.

"Maybe we should meet after we've had a chance to rest," Greimich said.

They didn't wait for the clan leaders to answer. Instead, Khrazhti and Greimich pulled Aeden out through the doorway and into the open air. Until the door closed to cut off his view, his eyes continued drilling into the man who had insulted his father.

Aeden stood several feet away from the opening of the elders' lodge, forcing his breathing under control. Cat stood in front of him, eyes large with her hand on her sword hilt.

"*Percipius pental tuu caenare. Andorin recoat du acci rudis flagranti. Gealich claidhimh d'araesh slaoch!* What is it with the Trebhin?" he asked no one in particular. "Are they all ruddy assholes or is it simply my bad fortune to meet each and every one who is?"

❧ 32 ❧

Greimich opened his mouth to answer, but his eyes darted over Aeden's shoulder and he closed his mouth, dipping his head to whoever he had seen there. Aeden didn't want to turn around. If it was Daibhidh, he might just lose control of his temper. Again. The man had insulted his father, the single greatest man Aeden had ever known and the epitome of a fine clan chief.

When Khrazhti's eyes went to the one behind him and she dipped her head as well, Aeden relaxed. He took another breath and turned to greet the mystery person.

"I am sorry for that," Seoras Corcan said. "Some of the Trebhin...take a bit of getting used to. We have all learned that in the last several weeks. Things were easier when we killed them on sight."

A weak chuckle escaped Aeden's lips, but died quickly.

"Walk with me?" the Corcan clan chief asked.

"Aye. The air is foul around here."

Seoras stepped off toward his left, threading through some of the buildings where people were busy working at various crafts.

"I'll have you know," the clan chief said, "I very nearly challenged Daibhidh myself for his words. I don't know how the contest would turn out—he's younger and stronger than me—but I don't like insults being hurled about a man I respect more than many in my own clan, let alone others."

"It's much appreciated." The older man's words did take some of the sting from the Trebhin pig's insult. "Did you know my father well?"

"Not so well as I'd have liked to, I'll tell you. The first time we met, it was in combat. A skirmish on the borders of our clans. No, not a skirmish, I think, not with as many warriors as were fighting, but still a chance meeting. We were both hunting. To this day, I can't recall if we met in our territory or in Tannoch land. The borders are not so well defined.

"I had thirty-six warriors with me and your father had twenty-nine with him. Large for hunting parties, but winter was coming and highland bison had been spotted in great numbers, so we wanted to be prepared. Besides, when near the border of another clan, it's wise to bring extra swords.

"The battle didn't last long. The death toll was not high, but neither were there warriors captured. That was a strange thing in itself. Even stranger was two clan chiefs meeting in combat.

"After casualties were dispensed on both sides, I caught sight of your father. I didn't know who he was, but the skill with which he fought mesmerized me. I thought to test myself against him. If I killed the enemy champion, the spirit of his men would falter and we would win the day.

"We fought for several minutes, an eternity in battle, as you well know. I used every technique I knew and still barely kept myself from being cut into pieces. I even used the Raibrech, which he countered with his own magic. I realized I could not win, but continued on, hoping to have a turn of luck.

"I didn't receive it.

"Your father expertly maneuvered me and then, in a burst of speed I still half unbelieve, slashed with his sword, scoring my neck." The clan chief lifted his chin so Aeden could get a good look at the scar etched across his throat.

"It was the most precise, controlled strike I have ever seen. He cut to the perfect depth, slicing through the skin but not cutting the air pipe or any of the major blood vessels beneath. He could have killed me, more easily than I am comfortable with remembering. In fact, I thought he *had* killed me.

"I dropped to my knees, not even able to counterattack because he had danced back out of my range.

"I will remember that day for as long as I am able to draw breath. I put my hand on my neck and saw that it was bloody, yet I could breathe. I'd seen enough cut throats and knew then it wasn't a fatal blow. My eyes found your father's as he did two things.

"First, he threw me a scarf off his own neck. Second, he whistled and, to my shock, his warriors disengaged, backstepping so quickly that my own warriors, who had seen my defeat, didn't have the time to press the attack.

"'We've hunting to do, Corcan,' he said to me. 'Go about your business and we'll go about ours. Maybe we'll meet again.'

"I gestured to my men to stand down, and we watched as your clan helped the wounded and headed back south. My own wound was dressed to stop the bleeding. I lived, which is obvious, but only by the grace of the clan chief of the Tannoch clan.

"I met your father a few more times after that, in negotiations over borderlands. After the third time, I asked him why he had spared me that day. He said he had heard what kind of man the Corcan clan chief was and it would be a shame to waste his wisdom and allow some hot-headed fool to take his place.

"I thought about that statement for years and came to realize that he had been wrong. I had not been wise. Yet. Meeting your father was the start of my wisdom. We are from different clans, but the news of your father's demise saddened me more than the death of my own father. I wish I could have known him better, Aeden Tannoch, but maybe I can learn more of him through you."

Aeden swallowed, his breathing growing difficult. He had missed so many years with his father because of his expulsion. What kind of man was Sartan Tannoch that even enemy clans mourned his loss? He thought, not for the first time, that he had been too wrapped up in his own training to realize exactly what a unique man his father was.

"I thank you," Aeden said. "To hear words of respect, especially from another clan, lightens my heart. Only recently have I realized how wise he was. I miss him."

The clan chief put his hand on Aeden's shoulder. "As do I. I would like to tell you, young Aeden, that I see your father in you. You are the Tannoch clan chief now, and would be if your clan was still whole. You are a warrior"—he gestured toward Aeden's wrists and the tattoos there—"and the firstborn son of the previous chief. Do not let the others look down on you. We are all on equal footing."

Aeden reeled back as if struck. Seoras had put it so bluntly, while Aeden had been carefully dancing around the subject in his own mind. The older man was correct, he supposed. He *was* the Tannoch clan chief, even if only over a scant few clan members.

The two men, with Greimich, Cat, and Khrazhti just behind, continued on one of the small paths. They passed by one of the younger men wearing Corcan clan colors trying to light a fire with wet, green wood. Aeden hadn't been paying much attention, but they seemed to have wandered into the area where the Corcan clan was making camp.

The young man muttered frustrated curses at the wood, but kept trying to strike flint to steel to start the blaze.

Apparently without thought, Seoras made familiar motions with his hands and pronounced three words of power and made gestures that were familiar, though they seemed backward to Aeden.

"*Crosen, sitingham, batorum.*"

Flame shot up from the wood like it was being generated from the fuel itself. When it stopped, a few of the branches had caught, starting the fire in the pile the young man had made.

"Thank you, clan chief," he said.

"Drier wood, Staefan. You'll never start a fire with that wood only using flint and steel."

"Yes, clan chief. It was the only wood available. The Seachaid are controlling the wood allowed outsiders."

"I see. I will try to do something about that."

They had only taken a few more steps when Aeden had to ask.

"Seoras, what was that spell you used?"

The older man's eyebrows climbed his forehead. "It's the third in the Raibrech. You don't recognize it?"

"The motions were slightly different than what my clan uses and the words, they were in Alaqotim."

"I don't know of Alaqotim, but they are the words of power for the spell. But yes, they might be different than what you're used to. Does that surprise you?"

"Aye. I've come to learn that the words used in the Tannoch Raibrech are actually in another language. It's called Dantogyptain, the same language the Song of Prophecy is written in."

"Is this true?" the clan chief asked. "I have never heard

that. Of course, the clans have never cooperated like they do currently, so there was never an opportunity to compare the different clan magic systems. I had assumed they were all the same, or very close."

"As did I. These differences between the clans, and the similarities, it gives me an idea. Thank you. That use of clan magic may help me to be more effective against the animaru."

The Corcan shook his head. "Too bad it won't help you against hard-headed clan chiefs."

Aeden rubbed his chin. "It just might at that."

❧ 33 ❧

Urun stared as his friends fought a desperate battle against the plant creatures. Marla fought the tree alone while the other three fired off arrows at the plant animaru monsters and the other swamp things that were rushing them. Soon, there wouldn't be room left to use their bows and they would have to fight in close quarters.

All the while, Urun stood in his shield, apparently forgotten.

No, that wasn't entirely true. A few of the attackers noticed the priest and lumbered toward him, but without the urgency with which their fellows charged the others. Even coming to kill him, the monsters didn't see him as a high priority.

Lily launched fire arrow after fire arrow. By far, they had the most effect of all the missile attacks against the creatures. Tere's and Saevel's projectiles didn't even seem to slow the enemies down.

"No more fire," Lily shouted as her last arrow struck the face of a swamp creature and the fire went out with a hiss. "Only regular arrows left, and not many of them."

Tere shrugged his shoulders as Urun had seen him do before to gauge the weight of his quiver. "I have a dozen. It doesn't matter. They'll be here before I can use them."

Saevel, her face scrunched up in concentration, didn't join the conversation. She threw her bow down, drew her sword, and rushed a group of three of the plain animaru. The monsters lurched toward her, swinging their slime-covered claws to disembowel her.

The arba slipped skillfully in between the dark creatures' attacks and cut into them. One of them made a sound that wasn't quite a scream, but the others were eerily silent.

Urun shivered. It was bad enough fighting animaru that growled and screeched, but this? It was...unnatural. He mentally kicked himself. Of course it was. That was the whole problem.

Tere and Lily followed the arba's lead a few seconds later, tossing their bows to the side and drawing their long knives. In moments, Urun couldn't see much besides dark green plant matter and even darker animaru flesh with vegetation adhering to it, with just the barest flashes of the lighter colored humans.

Marla cursed and rolled across Urun's field of vision. She came to her feet smoothly, throwing her hands out to shoot fiery missiles at the tree monster, but they did little damage other than to score its bark with burn spots. It was too damp to catch fire.

Still, Urun was frozen, watching his friends as he so often did. Doing nothing. Battles with normal animaru, so many they couldn't be counted, flashed through his mind. He had always taken a support role, sitting behind his shield while trying to help heal his friends while they put their lives on the line.

His failure in Praesturi pelted him. Because of his inaction, his friends were put in prison. He was with them, of course, but it was his fault for not reacting when Tere debated resisting the men who captured them. After that, he was unresponsive, no help to them at all during their imprisonment.

He'd needed their help just to eat. Without them, he would have died of starvation or thirst. And yet, he only sat there, staring into the dark.

The priest didn't deserve his friends. They were always looking out for him, protecting him, and what did he give in return? He healed them when they needed it, but other than that, he served no real purpose.

Urun shook his head, dispelling the thoughts and images. Two of the plant animaru, and one creature that looked like a large animal had eaten foliage and then vomited it into a moving pile, slammed against his shield.

He was daydreaming while his friends fought for their lives.

Enough of his cowardice and his worthlessness. They were here because of him. He would join the battle and help with more than simple healing.

But what?

"Saevel!" Lily shouted and Urun's eyes snapped toward where the archers and the arba were fighting. They had cleared a little space around them, arranged in a triangle formation, trying to fight off the monsters.

The reason for the scream, however, was evident. The creatures had grouped around Saevel and were charging with no thought to the consequences for them.

Tere and Lily tried to provide the arba support, but they were maneuvered away from her by the others surrounding them. Saevel slashed and spun, cutting into several of the attackers, but then she stumbled, only slightly, on the body of one of the animaru under her feet. Her sword dipped and Urun could predict what would happen next.

He wanted to close his eyes, but couldn't.

One of the swamp creatures swung a vine that looked more like a tentacle at her feet. She dodged, but then two of the plant animaru slashed at her with their claws from opposite sides. There was no way she could avoid or block them.

Sharp claws tore into her body and, worse, into her throat, tearing the skin in jagged rents. Her head flopped backward in a way it shouldn't have been able to.

Urun screamed, and as he did, involuntarily cast his Life Blast spell. The yellow-white light of life magic shot out from him, more violently than it ever had. The power seemed to go *through* his shield, which he hadn't expected. It was so much power, it scared even the priest himself.

His fear was nothing compared to the effects of the spell.

All the plant animaru around him disintegrated into lumps of pulpy green and grey mush, up to and including the ones in combat with Tere and Lily. The swamp creatures were thrown back, though it was difficult to tell if they had been harmed by the magic. The two archers swayed, as if assaulted by a strong wind, but seemed unharmed by the spell.

Urun slumped, and not only from the exertion of having so much magic flow through him. Saevel! The arba lay where she had fallen, blood pooled around her, somehow unaffected by the magic he had unleashed. He supposed it was logical. It was life magic, after all, and she was...

A sob escaped the young priest's lips and a few tears—not nearly enough to signify the heartache he felt—made tracks down his cheeks.

He gritted his teeth and straightened. There would be time for mourning Saevel later. Hopefully. For now, though, he and his friends were still in danger. Fewer monsters attacked, but there were still plenty to end their human existence. Especially the tree creature fighting Marla. It had been too far away to feel the effects of his spell. Urun wasn't sure it would have affected the monster anyway.

Tere and Lily danced between the remaining attackers, slashing and stabbing with their long knives. It was still possible they would be overwhelmed, but they appeared to have things under control for the moment.

Marla, on the other hand, was having problems. The tree had her on the run. It was pummeling the ground around her with its branches, which seemed to be able to stretch or change shape at will. The Academy graduate couldn't even get out of range to take a breath. The monster was relentless.

Urun made his decision. If he were more of a hero, if he had attacked the creatures and helped his friends instead of hiding in his shield, Saevel—oh, precious nature-loving Saevel —would still be alive. He'd had enough. No longer would he stand idly by while his friends bled.

He dropped his shield.

There were no monsters around him any longer. The swamp creature that had been pounding on his shield had been picked up and thrown a dozen feet away by his spell. It had pulled itself to its feet and staggered toward Tere and Lily. He used his relative isolation to move closer to the tree monster, though not too close to its swinging branches.

Marla dodged the woody attacks, successfully so far, but every time a branch missed her and hit the ground, it struck so hard the soil shook. It would only take one hit like that to kill Aeden's sister.

Urun focused on the tree, much as he did with the animaru mage. The sensation was similar, though a thousand times stronger. Whereas the animaru's two parts—its animaru nature and the corruption—warred with each other for ultimate control over the creature, the tree had no such battle raging within.

What Urun found was that the monster looming in front

of him was entirely the corrupted nature magic he had learned to identify with the animaru mage. There was no way the priest could use the same technique he used before, manipulating two warring halves into fighting each other. He'd have to find another way.

The tree stopped abruptly, then swung its trunk around as if searching for something. The part that had been facing Marla, recognizable from an old burn scar on the trunk at about human eye level, swung around to point toward Urun. Was that some kind of face or eye?

During that brief pause, Urun felt in his bones that he had been recognized, accounted for, and weighed. That wasn't good.

The tree charged the priest, ignoring Marla completely.

Damn, damn, damn, he thought. His analysis of the monster had somehow called its attention to him. He wondered if his shield would even work against something so powerful. One of those branches could probably smash right through. Well, he had wanted to distract it, give Marla a chance to attack. He'd accomplished that.

His first thought was to turn and run, but the thing moved much too fast. He'd never survive to find shelter. Instead, he narrowed his eyes and drilled into it with his mind, trying to find any information that might be helpful. If he could glean the slightest clue or gain the tiniest advantage, it might help his friends. Even if he was crushed by a branch before they could take advantage of it.

And so, he stood tall, facing down the monster streaking toward him, burrowing into its essence with his mind, trying to find a way to keep them all from dying.

Marla, a hero through and through as far as Urun was concerned, leaped through the air, both her blades in the midst of powerful downward strikes. She intercepted the tree with perfect timing, slashing down with a flash of magical energy. She had charged her blades with some kind of spell.

The strikes were more effective than anything she had done before. First her dagger, then her sword, slashed into the same spot on one of the branches. The appendage was too thick to cut all the way through, but she made it halfway.

The tree screamed, though Urun couldn't tell if he heard it only in his mind, or if it was actual sound. Its damaged branch swung back around to attack Marla, but she had landed and immediately rolled away from the monster.

"Whatever you're doing," she panted, "continue to do it. I used that spell earlier and it didn't have nearly the effect. You're weakening it."

Urun wasn't sure if she was correct, but it wasn't the time to argue. He redoubled his mental attack, diving deep into the corrupted nature magic of the creature, and tried to wrest it from the thing's control. It was nature magic, after all—though tainted—so maybe he could do something after all.

The priest and the Academy graduate continued to taunt the monster, causing it to turn toward Urun when he pressed it mentally and magically and then back to Marla as she danced in, struck at it, and moved back away. She cast a few spells from a distance, too, including her fire missile spell, and though it had more of an effect than before, it still couldn't take the creature down.

Marla used another spell Urun had not seen before, something that imbued her blades with flame. The magic finally cut through the branch she had been working on. With only one appendage, the monster's attacks slowed enough that Marla landed several more blows.

Then, the red-haired warrior stumbled as she tried to get some distance after a strike. The monster's remaining branch shot out like a striking snake and slammed into her. It threw her twenty feet, and though she landed in a roll to minimize the damage from falling, she had obviously been injured. Surprisingly, she had kept hold of her weapons.

The tree rushed to her to finish the job. Marla tried to move away, but her body didn't seem to want to perform as she directed it.

She wasn't going to make it. If the tree reached her, she would be killed.

"No!" Urun screamed. He barely noticed Tere and Lily still fighting for their lives on the other side of him. Marla was his biggest concern at the moment. He had to do something or another of his friends would die.

All because of him.

He had continued to wrestle with the tree monster during Marla's fight, and had come to realize its magic was not so different from his own. If he looked at his enemy's power as simply a polluted form of the power he possessed, he could almost...

A thought came from nowhere, something Saevel had said. Her people, the full-blooded arba, had been able to extract power from nature itself. They had used it for many purposes. Including combat, when necessary.

The priest closed his eyes and concentrated on what he was feeling with his mind, what he sensed from the monster and his surroundings. There was something he could grasp in the creature's magic, something he should be able to grab hold of. If he only had the power to do it.

It occurred to him that the difference between the arba's power and that which he wielded was that he got his directly from Osulin herself. But what if he could harness the power of nature magic without going through that conduit? Would that be blasphemy? Would it even be possible?

Marla's life might hinge on the answers.

With a deep breath, he decided to find out. He spread his

mind out to the surrounding swamp, so full of life, natural and corrupted.

Then he pulled.

Bits of energy flowed from everything around him and made itself available for his use. It all happened in the fraction of a second, before the tree monster could reach Marla. Urun continued to pull on the energy, the nature magic, and it began to fill him with power. If he wasn't glowing, it would surprise him. He felt like the sun.

When he held as much as he thought he was able to, the priest utilized some of it to latch onto the core of corrupted power in the tree's center. He snatched it with his mental fist and squeezed it, exerting his control.

The tree stopped all physical motion, and Urun felt the battle shift to a mental and magical combat.

He had caused the monster to pause for a moment, but Marla wasn't safe yet. Neither were the rest of them.

❧ 34 ❧

Aeden asked Seoras to lead him back to the elder's lodge.

"I have an idea that may solve our problems," he said.

"It must be a grand idea if you think it will smooth over the difficulties of the last hour," the clan chief said. "Would you care to share it with me?"

The young Tannoch almost told the Corcan, but decided that all the involved parties should hear it at the same time. Not because he didn't trust Seoras—the man definitely seemed to have honor—but because if he waited, no one could legitimately claim that the clan chief knew about what Aeden planned to do and was complicit in it.

"I think it would be better to have everyone hear it at the same time. I'm sorry, Seoras."

The man's skin crinkled around his eyes as he smiled. "No need for apologies. I understand. It will be much more dramatic if no one else knows what you're about. Besides, we wouldn't want anyone to think I am coordinating with you if this is something that will upset the other leaders."

Aeden blinked at the man. Was he really that transparent that the clan chief could guess what he was doing so quickly?

Seoras tapped his index finger to his temple. "These grey hairs aren't just a sign that I've lived a longer time than you, Aeden. I've learned a thing or two in my time as clan chief. I trust you. You have the demeanor of your father and the mind, too, I think. Let's go and try out your idea."

"Thank you, Seoras. I appreciate your help."

"Bah. I literally owe your father my life. It's my pleasure to transfer that debt from him to you. I think you can do what I cannot. Shall we find out?"

"Yes. Let's."

On the way back to where they had left the other leaders, Khrazhti questioned what had made Aeden change his mind about going back to those unreasonable men. They spoke in Alaqotim, so there was little chance anyone overhearing would understand them.

"It's an idea I have," he told her. "I can explain it all thoroughly later. I think you'll like it, though."

Her face took on a satisfied look. "I am sure I will."

The small group arrived at the elders' lodge. Aeden took a breath and calmed himself. He needed to remain focused for this, and to keep a rein on his emotions. The Trebhin clan chief would try to bait him again, but Aeden couldn't let him draw his attention away from what he had to say.

"Are you ready for this?" he asked to those with him. They all nodded.

"For what?" Greimich asked.

"I'm about to pick a fight."

His friend's mouth split wide into a grin Aeden hadn't seen since they were boys planning mischief.

"Let's go," Greimich said.

Aeden pushed open the doors and strode into the room he had vacated not long before. As he did, he swung his head to take an inventory of the men present. As he had hoped, none of the leaders had left yet. That would make the entire thing easier.

"What are you—" the Trebhin clan chief said.

"Come outside, into the center of the village," Aeden said in as commanding a voice as he could manage. "You all will participate in a solemn ceremony with me and by tradition, others in the clans are to be given an opportunity to witness it."

With that, he turned on his heels and glided outside, chin high as if he were the king of the world.

Seoras, who had entered right behind Aeden, turned and followed the younger man back outside. Greimich, Cat, and Khrazhti did the same.

Once outside, Aeden stood tall a few dozen feet from the door to the building, waiting.

First, Touhas Ailgid stepped out into the sunlight, blinking to let his eyes get accustomed to the light. After a few minutes, the Seachaid clan chief Padraig joined them.

Aeden waited, and the others waited with them. If Daibhidh didn't come out, Aeden would have to shout at him from without, trying to either taunt him or shame him into exiting the building, possibly escalating the situation. It was a tense few minutes.

Finally, the Trebhin clan chief walked through the doorway, disgust on his face. "Boy, you—"

Again Aeden cut him off. "In front of these witnesses, I invoke the *Mionn Bhais*, the Death Oath."

The Trebhin's mouth snapped shut and everyone around the leaders went quiet, even the children playing nearby.

Then Daibhidh Trebhin started to laugh.

Aeden stood before him, straight and tall. Waiting.

He continued waiting until the clan chief was able to control himself and speak. Still, the man wasn't able to complete what he said without a few laughs sneaking through his words.

"That's it? That is your plan. You would try to invoke something out of legend? Something that has never once in all the history of the clans been used?"

"It is one of our strongest traditions," Aeden said, unaffected by how humorous the clan chief found his idea.

The Trebhin looked around at the others present, his face showing disbelief as he shook his head. "You really are stretching yourself thin in trying to save face, boy. The biggest reason no one has ever invoked the *Mionn Bhais* is that the magic to perform it is lost."

"Is it?" Aeden asked.

Then he began to move. At first, his motions looked to be another of the exercises, the fighting forms each warrior practiced to train their bodies to move in the ways of combat. As he progressed through the actions, though, his body started to glow, then to flash, and finally to shine so brightly that onlookers were putting their hands up in front of their faces to shield them.

Aeden continued the forms until his feet came together and his hands clapped in front of his chest with a motion of finality, the light around him exploding out to bathe all those around him.

"So do I invoke the *Mionn Bhais* and so are we, the leaders of the five clans, charged with deciding on our duty. Thus is the Death Oath now in effect. You have one hour to respond, and may your honor and your life be forfeit should you fail in the requirements of this ritual."

The young Tannoch took a breath and slumped slightly—hopefully not noticeably—more tired than he could have imagined from such a simple form. He looked around and saw, as he expected, shocked looks on each face. Wide eyes, open mouths, and hands rubbing temples were common among both the leaders and the common clan people within the area. Of course, most of the common clan members were from the Seachaid clan, but there were others, from the other clans, mixed in as well.

As soon as each person regained his or her composure, they ran off, most likely to tell everyone they knew that an ancient ritual no one had ever seen had been enacted.

"How?" Padraig Seachaid asked softly.

"I used to enjoy researching old clan scrolls when I was younger. Many partial references, along with a few things I read after my time with the clan, came together and I discovered how to invoke the ritual. Recent information about how the Raibrech of the different clans vary"—he nodded toward Seoras—"allowed me to complete the picture."

"What did you just do?" Khrazhti asked him in Ruthrin.

"It is the *Mionn Bhais*," Greimich said. "The Death Oath. He has put the other clan leaders on notice that he is demanding all clans be made one, with him as the clan high chief. They can respond in one of two ways. They can either submit to him, retaining a station as under chief, or they may choose to refuse."

"And if one refuses?" Khrazhti asked.

"Then they must enter combat with Aeden," Cat said. "To the death."

"Though a combatant may also submit during the fight, if he can do so quickly enough to prevent being killed," Greimich added.

Khrazhti gave Aeden the biggest smile he had ever seen on her. In her own language, she told him, "You are correct. I like your idea."

Immediately, Seoras Corcan dropped to a knee. "I submit to Aeden Tannoch as the high chieftain."

The Ailgid elder slowly eased himself into a kneeling position also and repeated, "I submit to Aeden Tannoch as the high chieftain." As he did, he looked toward Cat and smiled. Aeden thought he could pick out relief on the man's face. The move would solve his problems in trying to choose a new chief with so few clan members left.

The Seachaid chief and the Trebhin chief shared looks, but neither spoke for a moment.

"One hour," Aeden said.

The Seachaid chief swallowed. The Trebhin's eyes drilled into Aeden's. He didn't seem to find the situation funny anymore.

"I'll not let a green boy try to steal my clan," Daibhidh Trebhin said. "I choose combat."

❦ 35 ❦

Urun Chinowa and the monster in the shape of a tree battled for their lives. Anyone looking on wouldn't know it, though. They both stood stock still, the human barely breathing and the tree with barely a ripple of its leaves.

It was the most strenuous thing Urun had ever done.

Physically, he appeared placid. In his mind, he was tossed about on a sea, clinging to a small piece of driftwood he had found and adopted as his only salvation. It seemed that his body was moving, even causing him to be dizzy.

The power drowning him was thick like molasses but thin enough to force its way into his ears, nose, and eyes. Except that in his mind, he had none of these things.

He could see the tree, two dozen feet in front of him, but more, he saw the lines of energy that made up the thing. It glowed brightly like it was, in fact, made of the glowing traces of light. They pulsed, similar to the blood vessels in his own body, carrying magical power to every part of the root, trunk, and foliage.

Every tiny fraction of it assailed Urun, trying to break the hold the man had dared to apply to the monster.

Urun mentally dodged lines of power whipping out toward him, retained his hold on the creature despite its thrashing to try to break free. With all that, though, they were at a stalemate, neither able to prevail over the other.

Marla, hardly able to stand, limped over to the motionless creature and began hacking at it with her sword and dagger. The priest wasn't sure it would do any damage, but if it distracted his opponent, he was all for it.

So tired. He was so, so tired.

The tree twitched. At least, its magical self did. Urun didn't think it actually moved physically, but he was almost too fatigued even to focus his eyes.

If he didn't figure out what to do to tip the strange magical battle to his favor, he was going to fail. He would become too tired to maintain his focus, and then the monster would have them.

Closing his eyes to conserve every last bit of energy he had and to keep himself from distraction, he delved into his enemy, inspecting the lines of power for any kind of weakness.

He found nothing.

The priest wanted to cry, to give up, to just die. That would be fine for him, but if he faltered, his friends would die, too. Like Saevel. Could he muster the strength to tell those left to flee? He didn't think so. Even if he did, they'd never leave him. They would never allow him to sacrifice himself so they could escape.

Very well. It had to be another way, then.

The thought of Saevel came to his tired mind again. Her greenish tint, the way her slightly darker emerald lips formed when she smiled. She had been so excited to meet a priest of Osulin and to hear about the Academy. She had felt honored to be able to guide the hero Erent Caahs and the Malatirsay —the actual Malatirsay!—into the swamp.

Then she had been killed. Senselessly. Needlessly.

The thought threatened to overwhelm him, but Urun could not afford to let it. If he did, more of his friends would die, including one half of what was needed to stop the animaru for good.

Saevel. Oh Saevel. With her connection to nature, and her reverence for it...

Connection!

Hadn't Urun just tapped into nature's magic itself? Hadn't he used it to force the tree to become immobile? He was utilizing its power at that very moment, leaning on it to battle the monster. Why not go further? Nature was infinite. It could spare a bit more of its precious vitality for him.

He had already tapped the energy without going through Osulin once. Even if it was inappropriate, what could happen if he took a little more? Ultimately, it was for her benefit.

Still watching the tree creature through his mind's eye, he shifted a piece of his focus to the surroundings. The water was teeming with life, as was the soil. The plants themselves were alive, though not sentient in a conventional way.

Urun touched them, like a handshake or a caress. They responded as to a brother, though some areas with more corruption reacted as if he were an undesirable sibling. He began to understand them more fully, to recognize their power, their magic.

Tears came to Urun's eyes. Or had they already been there but were now flowing more freely? His perception of all around him took his breath away. It was so beautiful. Even parts that contained corruption were beautiful in their own way.

Slowly, he begged energy from the life entities around him, pleaded for them to share their essence with him.

They agreed.

Power flowed into Osulin's priest like buckets of cold water dumped over his head on a hot day. Shocking. Refreshing. It washed away his fatigue, replacing it with confidence and power.

Urun turned his newfound energy on the tree creature. Their stalemate was over. He pushed and pulled and wrapped the monster up in power of his own making.

But it was not enough. He had to do more than simply hold his enemy motionless. He had to do away with the corruption of which the creature was the source.

In viewing the tree creature, he had developed an understanding of the way the energy flowed throughout its body. He used that now. Not to harm or to negate, but to nurture. Attacking the monster directly would not work. It was too powerful, too much a force of nature in itself and too tied into the entire swamp. If he battled it directly, even if he won, it would cause unknowable damage to many others.

Instead, he simply accelerated its natural processes. The flow of energy, even the amount, he changed. He increased the speed, added more power, and prayed to his goddess that he could accomplish what he was planning.

Energy swelled. Urun pulled more and more from the surroundings and channeled it into the monster. Its aura flickered, became muddied, and swirled. The turbulence indicated it was getting frantic, knowing somehow that what was happening was not good, but not able to do anything about it. As the power built, Urun's entire body grew hot.

He didn't know it, but both he and the tree were glowing brightly to anyone looking on. All he felt was the heat, and soon a panic of his own that he might not be able to control what he was doing after all, that he might burst into flames or melt because of it. Still, he continued. What else could he do? His friends' lives—at the very least—were at stake.

His brain seemed hot enough to melt his skull, and sharp pains radiated through his chest and lanced to a spot just below his navel.

Still he continued.

The tree began to vibrate violently. Urun snapped his eyes open and looked at it, seeing for the first time its luminescence with his real eyes. Its bark rippled and the crevices in it deepened. The branches thinned, taking on a gnarled appearance like old roots. Leaves fell off in clumps, crumbling before they touched the ground.

Then something inside Urun broke.

There was really no other way to describe it. The sensation was what he imagined he would feel if he had swallowed a head-sized chunk of metal, and then someone used the most powerful lodestone in the world to rip it out of his body, right up through his chest and neck and out of his skull.

The next thing the priest knew, he had the sensation of falling, right after everything went black.

❧ 36 ❧

Urun opened his eyes to a green glow somewhere in front of him and off to his right. It was where the tree had been standing, just before the priest blacked out and fell. How long had he been lying there?

Marla was standing—barely—near the glow, hands on her knees and her two blades on the ground in front of her. Ah, so he hadn't been on the ground long. Maybe only a few seconds.

"What happened?" he asked.

"I was going to ask you the same thing," she said. "What did you do? Nothing I was doing had any effect."

"I, uh," he said, but then remembered Tere and Lily. He turned his head quickly to find them and the entire world spun. "Oh."

"Easy," Marla said. "If you feel anything like I do, it would be best not to move too quickly."

"Yeah. I think you're right." When he was able to focus again, he finally found the archers. They were standing side-by-side. There were no monsters around them.

"What—?" he started to ask again.

"Don't know," Tere said. "They disappeared when you killed the tree." He kicked at a body at his feet. "Well, the swamp creatures disappeared into piles of plants. The animaru reverted to their normal form and dropped where they stood."

"I'll ask you again, Urun," Marla said. "What did you do?"

There was an edge to her voice that triggered Urun's self-preservation instincts. He hadn't heard her voice like that since the first time she had met Aeden and did her level best to beat him into the ground. He looked carefully at her. She was exhausted, injured, and probably in pain. It wasn't personal, he knew. Hoped, anyway.

"I..." He realized that he didn't actually know. "I gathered some energy from the surroundings, the plants and other types of life. Then I...I think I actually took some of the monster's energy, siphoned it off. I used it not only to make it weaker, but to make me more powerful. The way it processed its power became clear to me and I tinkered with it."

"You tinkered with it," Marla said. A statement and not a question.

"Yeah. I think. I tried to use my new knowledge against it somehow. Speeding up its use of the magic it had. Making it head toward..."

"You aged it," Tere said. "I didn't see much, but it looked to me like it burned through its magic and its lifespan and became more feeble. I've seen very old people in the magical matrix, and their magical signature is different than younger people. They have some aspect that makes me think of decay and drying, even if the person is still healthy and hale. It looked like the tree got that."

"Yes," Urun said. "That's it. Now that you mention it, I think something inside of me realized that bringing it toward the end of its natural life could weaken it."

Marla stared at the priest, wide-eyed. "You aged a creature

that was essentially immortal to the extent that it ceased to exist. Can you do that with other creatures?"

The spike of panic in Urun's middle caused him to take a sharp breath in. "I don't know. Goddess, I hope not."

"Why the hells not?" she asked. "Imagine what you could do to the powerful animaru against us with a power like that."

"It's unnatural!" he shouted. "I'd be no better than the creature made of corruption we just destroyed. I'm a *nature* priest, for Osulin's sake. I can't go around wielding unnatural energies. What have I done?"

"Tere," Lily said, but the other archer ignored her. Instead, he met Urun's eyes with his own milky white orbs. It was more than a little uncomfortable.

"Urun, calm down. I caught small glimpses of what you did. You harnessed the monster's own power, used it against the thing, but you didn't wield anything unnatural. From what I saw, you actually used nature to circumvent its corruption. In essence, you used the pure power of nature to overwhelm and influence the unnatural."

"Marla," Lily said.

"Oh," Urun said with a sigh. "That makes me feel a bit better. I'll need to think about it, pray, ask..."

"Urun," Lily said, this time more insistently.

"Lily, what is it?" Tere asked.

All eyes went to the beautiful archer. She pointed toward a green object half the size of Urun's fist on the ground where the tree creature had been. It resembled a rough, uncut gemstone, something like green-tinted quartz, uneven but still beautiful in its form. That was the source of the glow Urun had seen earlier, but he'd been so caught up in explaining what he did, he hadn't really taken a good look at it.

"When you did whatever you did," she said, "the tree

seemed to crush in on itself and dissolve. The glow that had surrounded it condensed into that."

Urun realized she wasn't pointing at the jewel, though, but past it. On the other side of the gemstone, the massive growth of vines and other vegetation he had seen earlier was melting. Disintegrating as if it was made of ice and sitting in the middle of a desert.

No one spoke. They all watched as parts of the plant matter sloughed off and puddled at the ground, some flowing into the surrounding water. Marla huffed, picked up her weapons, and straightened with a groan.

But there was no monster there to attack them. As the verdant covering fell off, more quickly with each second, grey stone appeared. After half a minute, it was clear that it wasn't a natural rock formation, but something built with the material. Worked stone.

"A well," Marla said.

Within a few minutes there stood an ancient stone well surrounded by a small wall. A fist-sized alcove was carved into the wall and on either side of it were identical carved symbols.

"Is that..." Urun asked. He inspected the swirls and flowing lines. It was a beautiful script, he had to admit.

"Yep," Marla answered. "It's Cogiscro, just like with the well underneath Ebenrau. "This time, it says *Iracundamel*."

"What does it mean?" Lily asked.

"Mellaine's Wrath," Tere answered. "Or something like that."

"That's about as close as I can figure, too," Marla said.

"Mellaine's Wrath?" Urun said. He swung his head around, searching the area. "That reminds me. Where is Osulin? She's who we came here for."

"The gem, Urun." Marla pointed at the green, glowing gemstone in front of them. "Put it in the little indentation in the wall."

Urun started. It did look like the niche in the well's wall was the same size as the gem, even the same uneven shape. But why was Marla telling *him* to put it there?

"You saved us," she said. "You beat the guardian. You do the honors."

He nodded, then stooped to pick up the glowing gem. He could almost see through it, but could only distinguish cloudy shadows through it. It radiated magic, but not the corrupted type the tree used. He felt an affinity for its power, some kind of recognition. When he touched it, it felt like a warm embrace.

The nature priest stepped up to the well and fitted the stone into the indentation in the well's wall. At the last instant, it seemed that the jewel jumped out of his hand and traveled the rest of the way to seat itself firmly in the wall.

A blinding flash shot out from deep in the well, forcing the others to put their hands up to shield their eyes. To Urun, though, it didn't seem too bright. He watched it with wonder, sensing the energy explode outward. It coalesced twenty feet above the well, swirled in the air, then expanded until it seemed to cover the world.

In a moment, it had all disappeared. In its place was what felt like a new world, one in which nature and its magic seemed to have increased. A new world, and another small stone with the Cogiscro symbol on it.

"Oh!" Marla said.

"Gods!" cried Tere.

Urun had no words. It felt to him like witnessing the birth of a world.

"Did you feel that shift?" Marla asked. "Something in the world's magic just changed significantly. Like it did with the other well."

Urun opened his mouth to answer as he knelt to pick up the Cogiscro stone, but what he saw in the corner of his vision threw everything else out of his head.

A slender shape with long green hair appeared two feet off the ground, bound in gossamer rope. Once fully solid, she fell.

🦋 37 🦋

Urun sprinted faster than he ever remembered moving. Even the others seemed surprised by his actions. He made it to his destination with not a second to spare, catching his goddess before she could strike the ground.

He grunted with the sudden weight, and his knees bent and he almost fell himself, but refused to do so because it would mean dropping Osulin.

When he regained his balance, he carefully set her on the ground, then watched as the strands securing her arms and legs melted away. Her eyes fluttered open and found his own.

"Urun, my beloved priest," she said. "You came to me."

"I did, my lady. As will I always."

"I knew you would. Somehow. Just as I knew you would find a way to defeat that which held me captive."

The others stood, watching silently as Urun and his goddess conversed. They looked more reserved, more out of their depth than the priest had ever seen. It took a moment for it to sink in: he was accustomed to speaking with his goddess. They had probably never seen a deity before.

"My friends," Urun said, a bit too loudly. "These are my friends, without whom I never would have found my way here, let alone survived."

Osulin turned her gaze on the others as if she had not noticed them before. "Yes. I am aware of your friends, one of whom is a famous hero of yesteryear and another who is half of the one foretold. I have witnessed some of your deeds and you, also, have my appreciation for aiding me."

"It is an honor to serve," Tere said, his voice more respectful than Urun had ever heard.

"My lady," Urun said. "What happened? How is it that you were captured, and what does it all mean? It felt like a massive amount of magic was just released."

The goddesses stood regally before them, her expression conflicted. Her priest recognized that she was considering what she could tell them.

"I am a creature of the magic of nature. While my mother is the true matron of that power, I am merely subject to it. True, I may control it, act as its mistress, but it does not originate with me. Call nature magic my subservient younger sister." She smiled at the statement.

"What you witnessed was a vast concentration of the magical essence of nature, of my mother, Mellaine. Iracundamel, the words etched into the wall there, means 'Mellaine's Wrath,' referring to the creation of the Mellafond centuries ago.

"I do not know how or why the power coalesced into this...well, but it did so. Further, it in some way developed a kind of intelligence and life of its own. Such things are not too rare when dealing with magic. This new intelligence apparently decided it needed a guardian."

"The tree monster," Urun said.

"Yes. I do not know how long this creature and the well existed. It was hidden even from me, hidden by its own nature magic. Something must have happened recently, for I had never seen this type of corruption before. I sensed it and came to investigate.

"Know this, my priest and his friends: magic has been... unstable of late. You know well of the difficulties I have had with my own powers, being assaulted by other forces I will not discuss at this time. That weakness, I believe, compounded with the corruption here and trapped me. It took all my remaining power to send a message to you, in hopes that you—and your friends—would come to my aid.

"I am still uncertain exactly what happened, but when you destroyed the guardian of this place, the magic was released. The corruption, it seems, died with the tree entity, but the pure nature magic that had been hidden in the well expanded to the entire world. This it was that revived me and loosed my bonds."

"So," Marla said, "does that mean the magic had to be recaptured?"

Osulin laughed, a soft tinkling sound reminiscent of the burble of a gentle stream mixed with birdsong. "No, Malatir-say. This is conjecture, but I believe the magic had been captured by the well, making it unavailable for use. For how many years or millennia, I do not know, but now that it is free, it is as it used to be, before the War of Magic. It is now available for use by those in tune with it. Can you not feel it?"

Urun closed his eyes and connected more fully with the world around him. He did feel it. It was different than before, like there was more power at his fingertips. Like right after Osulin had given him more of her power so recently. He gasped, realizing something.

Osulin's lips curved into a smile. "Ah, yes. You feel it, Urun, do you not? But I have a question for you. How was it that you did what you did? How did you defeat the guardian when my own power could not?" She still wore her smile, making Urun think it was a trick question.

"I don't know, my goddess. As I explained to Marla a few minutes ago, I was able to tap the energies of things around me, even of the tree creature itself. I used it against the monster."

"Its own energy?" she asked. "Its own magic? You used these things, aside from the gifts I have given you?"

The priest felt his face go hot. "I...I did, my lady."

"And how did you do so?"

"I don't know. It merely occurred to me. I thought of what Saevel..." He stopped mid-sentence, his eyes going liquid and his throat closing up. He took a breath, with difficulty, and shuddered. It took two more deep breaths to finish his sentence. By the time he did, tears were streaming down his face. "Saevel told me how the arba of old could use nature's magic without a conduit, such as you or your mother. Not like priests, but like mages who had a great affinity for nature."

"I see," she said. "I was aware of the descendants of the arba who populate the swamp, but had not approached them. But why is it you are so heart-stricken?"

Urun couldn't say it. His eyes were blurry and he looked at the ground, not able to meet his goddess's eyes. Instead of telling her, he simply pointed to the green-tinted corpse laying a few feet away, its neck torn out and blood soaking her clothing.

For the first time he had ever seen, his goddess looked shocked, her eyes widening. Not so much as a human would, but definitely more than he thought a goddess would.

"Oh. A casualty of your battle with the monsters of corruption?" Her eyes showed sympathy, which wrenched his heart even further.

He nodded.

"The arba were truly a wondrous race," she said. "They were the favored of my mother and, of course, myself. They did indeed utilize nature magic, so great was their connection with the natural world. No full-blooded arba exist today, only those of diluted blood, none of which wield the power of their ancestors."

A sob escaped Urun's lips, making him feel even more ashamed of his emotions.

"However," the goddess continued, "arba are connected to the nature of the world, and especially of the place where they have set their roots. There is power in these things. Maybe power enough."

The young priest didn't know what his goddess was talking about, but he remained silent, fighting with his grief. For a few minutes, he had been too preoccupied to think about Saevel's demise, but now it crashed down on him like a tidal wave.

A glow pulled Urun's head up. Osulin was throwing off enough light to illuminate the entire swamp at night. Even in the daylight, it was so bright it almost hurt his eyes.

What was she doing?

Magic flowed through Osulin, swirling and exiting her fingers. Urun locked his eyes on the glowing eddies of magical energy intently, committed to not missing a thing.

She pointed to Saevel's corpse.

The world could have ended during the few minutes Osulin directed her magic at the arba's body. Urun never would have noticed. There was only Osulin, her power, and Saevel.

After what seemed like a thousand years, the magic abruptly cut off. Osulin sighed and her shoulders dipped the slightest amount. Urun couldn't imagine the amount of power she had just expended.

"Ungh," a voice said. Urun's eyes snapped to where Saevel lay.

She turned her head and blinked at him.

"Urun?"

He couldn't help himself. He dove at the ground and pulled her into an awkward hug. She grunted again.

"Sorry," he said. "Sorry. I just...you were...it's good to see you."

She smiled as she relaxed into his embrace. "It's good to see you, too."

38

Osulin observed the interaction between her priest and the arba. She didn't respond in any way. Urun had been afraid she would scold him for acting un-priestlike.

"As for the conversation of a few moments ago," she said, "I do not think you understand what you have done."

"Done?" he asked, climbing to his feet and holding out a hand to Saevel to help her up.

"Yes. You drew power from nature itself, from the life surrounding you. I did not channel magic to you, nor could I, other than that which had already been granted you.

"The relationship of a deity to her priest is a powerful one. You represent me with other mortals and I grant you abilities that are drawn directly from me. When possible, and merited, I increase the power you may wield, as I did the last time we met. That power is a constant, something that I need not think about to allow your access. You can use it freely.

"Then there are times when you need additional resources, new spells or increased power because of some specific situation. In these cases, you pray for my additional help and, again if merited, I may grant you increased abilities. That is assuming I can afford to let you take more power. In these last few months, that has been difficult.

"But you, my priest, bypassed that conduit and instead took power directly from nature, as the most powerful of arba of old did. That should not have been possible."

Urun dropped to his knees in front of the goddess. "I'm sorry, my lady. I hardly knew what I was doing. My friends were dying." He looked at Saevel. "One had already done so. If we had fallen, it may have crippled our fight against the animaru as well, and I would not have been able to aid you. Marla is too important to the world. I..."

"Peace, Urun Chinowa," Osulin said, a wry smile returning to her lips. "I am merely explaining what occurred. I cast no accusations, nor do I scold. Allow me to continue."

"Of course. I'm sorry."

"Stand, my priest. There is no need for you to be on your knees."

Urun stood, waiting for what his goddess would say next.

"As I said, you did what has not been done in thousands of years, something that had never been done by any non arba priest of myself or my mother. Only have I seen it with the pure blooded arba. I know you, Urun, and you have no arba blood in your veins. I am unsure how you managed it, but it is good. It is very good."

"It is?" he asked.

"Yes. In this time of corruption and attack on all life, every power and ability we can bring to bear will help our cause. You are not only my priest, but are now the champion of nature. She has chosen you, it seems, to carry not only my blessing, but hers as well.

"I am regaining my power, but do not know what lies ahead. Practice with your new abilities, commune with the natural world, and learn to be more than you are. I know you are conflicted, that you feel unworthy of certain tasks in certain company. Do not feel this way. Learn and grow. Even the smallest seed or living creature in nature has a purpose, and not all of them were meant to battle dragons. Find your own path. Perhaps rely on those who can help." The goddess gazed at Saevel and Urun's heart jumped.

"I will," he said. "Thank you. But I'm still confused about what happened and what is happening."

"As am I. I intend to find answers to my questions, and when I do so, I will share what information I may with you. Nothing should have been able to bind me so, but it did. The wonder of the flood of nature magic is something I have never experienced as long as I have existed. It bodes well for the world, I think, but may also provide a warning. There are many powers in the world, magical and not. What of the others? Are they contained as well? If so, what happens if the animaru or someone else is able to utilize the captured power?"

"Pardon, your highness," Marla said, "but are you saying that instead of releasing power into the world like Urun just did, someone might be able to take the power in themselves, becoming powerful enough to do things like trap a goddess?"

Osulin's laugh was as light and magical as ever, and it made Urun's body vibrate in the most pleasurable way possible. "You needn't call me 'highness,' Malatirsay. 'My lady' will do. To answer your question, however, I do not know for sure. Until I can learn more, it is merely conjecture. Be wary, however. There are movements and magical currents in the world I have not felt in millennia, and some I have never experienced."

"We will," Marla said. "Thank you."

"Thank *you*, Malatirsay, and you, hero Erent Caahs, as well as your protégé. To my priest, I have already expressed my thanks, and I hope the small service I rendered to the descendent of my mother's favored people is an indication of my appreciation as well. One more thing can I do before I must go."

Osulin waved her hand, almost casually, and a glow sprang up around all five of the figures before her. It energized Urun, erased his fatigue and the aches he hadn't realized he had been feeling. A cut on Lily's face disappeared and the blood that had been dripping from it flaked off, showing perfect, unblemished skin. From the sighs coming from Tere and Marla, their injuries were being healed, too.

"Now, I must depart," Osulin said. "Express my appreciation to your other comrades, for they have aided me and mine more than once in recent times. Return to them with my blessings. As to your people, brave arba, give them my special thanks for their devotion. When the world is less troubled, I will visit and thank them in person."

She turned to Urun. "Do not ever underestimate your abilities or your courage, my priest. It is true that nature is nurturing, but at times it is also aggressive, even violent. I would prefer that you heal, but perhaps I should have given you the tools to protect more effectively. Meditate upon what you have learned, and you will realize new ways to use your powers. I regret it is all I can do for now."

"Thank you," Urun said. "I will. As ever, my life is dedicated to your service."

"I know it is, and it is because of this that I feel better about the future of the world. Farewell for now, my beloved priest, and his brave companions."

A bright light flared around Osulin, this time bright enough for Urun to have to shut his eyes. When the light was gone, so was the goddess.

"Well," Tere said. "That was something I had never experienced before." He rotated one shoulder and Urun noticed a slash in the armor there. The archer smiled. "I guess our job here is done. Are you ready to head back to the village to fetch our horses? I think there are some folks back at the Academy that would like to hear about what just happened. And I'm sure they'll be interested in that stone."

EPILOGUE

L ucio Sanctus eyed the three men before him. As the Patr Pruma of the Church of Vanda, he had been involved in many meetings with his high Itera, the three most influential and powerful of his underlings. He'd been in his position for over twenty years, the youngest to ever attain to the top position in the Church. He wasn't so young anymore.

He had dealt with problems before. But nothing like this.

"There are strange things happening," Raimund Bainer said. The man seemed obsessed with stroking his mustaches. Three strokes, then he would twist the ends to points, only to brush them again backwards to undo what he had just done. "Those of the Church with some small talent in magic have reported that the magical energies in the world have been unpredictable."

Lerus Costanti, a large man with hair that was altogether too long for a man of his station, shook that very hair out of his eyes as he nodded. "Some say it is because the gods are returning to Dizhelim."

"Watch your tongue, Lerus," Ander Tosselnam, the third

of the high Itera and the most senior of the lot, said. His hair was short, and mostly grey. He looked as an Itera should. His robes were immaculate and he sat at the table with back straight and chin at the ideal angle, between haughty and too meek. Many who attained such rank were arrogant, but not Ander. He was a stickler for following the commandments, and even the Church guidelines, however. "There are no gods but Vanda. You know this."

Lerus swung his great shaggy head toward the other man. "Of course I know. I am merely stating what others believe. True or false, ideas such as these can cause unrest, riots, wars even."

The Patr Pruma sighed. "There is no disagreement. You two are merely stating the same ideas in a different way. The thoughts of the masses concern me. Magic changing, people believing the gods are returning, a resurgence in some of the old, false religions, those rumors of creatures roaming the land and killing people, all of these things are agitating the faithful and unfaithful alike."

"There is one more thing," Ander said. "According to information I have obtained, other facets of the prophecy are being fulfilled."

"Kaeso Hiberus's prophecy?" Raimund asked.

Ander glared at the other man. "Of course Kaeso's prophecy. The only true prophecy is that found in the Vandictae. We'll not waste our time talking about the one from the so-called prophet Tsosin Ruus. A pagan and a charlatan, that one was. There is but one true prophet, the one called by Vanda himself: Kaeso."

"But," Lerus said, "if the facets of the prophecy are being fulfilled..."

"Yes," Lucio said. "If the prophecy is truly being fulfilled, it means that the end of the age has come. It means there is only one thing that can save humankind, indeed, the world itself. There is only one power capable of preserving us: the Church of our one true god, Vanda.

"It is time, my brothers, that we mobilize the armies of the Church. It is time to bring all mankind together, even should it require us to kill any and all who will not submit. Outfit our troops for war and call up the reserves. The army of the Church of Vanda will march within a fortnight. Let darkness and any who try to impede our course be destroyed."

THANK YOU SO MUCH FOR READING HERO'S NATURE. **Please take just a moment to leave a review for the book.** It will not only help me to see what you thought and to improve the next story, but it will help tremendously in indicating to other readers how you feel about the book. As an indie author, there are few things better than word of mouth to spread the news to other readers. Thank you in advance. For your convenience, **here's the link** directly to Amazon's review box (for the electronic copy of this book).

HERO'S NATURE GLOSSARY

Following is a list of potentially unfamiliar terms. Included are brief descriptions of the words as well as pronunciation. For the most part, pronunciation is depicted using common words or sounds in English, not IPA phonetic characters. Please note that the diphthong *ai* has the sound like the English word *Aye*. The *zh* sound, very common in the language Alaqotim, is listed as being equivalent to *sh*, but in reality, it is spoken with more of a buzz, such as *szh*. Other pronunciations should be intuitive.

Abyssum (*a·BIS·um*) – the world of the dead, Percipius's realm.

Acolyte – a current Hero Academy student who has mastered at least one school, but not three or more.

Adept – a Hero Academy student who has mastered at least three schools and continues to study at the Academy.

Aeden Tannoch (AY·*den TAN·ahkh*) – a man born to and trained by a highland clan, raised by the Gypta, and able to utilize the magic of the ancient Song of Prophecy.

Aeid Hesson (*AY·id*) – former Master of the School of

prophecy at the Hero Academy. He was murdered in his office at the Academy.

Aesculus (*AY·skyoo·lus*) – the god of water and the seas.

Agypten (*a·GIP·ten*) – an ancient nation, no longer in existence. It was from this nation the Gypta originated.

Ahred Chimlain (*AH·red CHIM·lane*) – noted scholar of the first century of the third age

Aila Ven (*AI·la ven*) – a woman of small stature who joins the party and lends her skills in stealth and combat to their cause.

Ailgid (*ILE·jid*) – one of the five highland clans of the Cridheargla, the clan Greimich Tannoch's wife came from.

Ailred Kelzumin (*ILE·red kel·ZOO min*) – the Master of the School of Water Magic at the Hero Academy.

Ailuin Lufina (*EYE·loo·in loo·FEEN·ah*) – one of the adepts at the Hero Academy who volunteered to aid in the investigation of Master Aeid's murder.

Alain (*a·LAYN*) – the god of language. The ancient language of magic, Alaqotim, is named after him.

Alaqotim (*ah·la·KOTE·eem*) – the ancient language of magic. It is not spoken currently by any but those who practice magic.

Alaric Permaris (*AL·are·ic per·MAHR·iss*) – the thug who hired the guys who attacked Marla in Dartford.

Aletris Meslar (*ah·LET·ris MES·lar*) – the personal clerk and assistant to Headmaster Qydus Okvius, of the Hero Academy.

Aliten (*AL·it·ten*) – a type of animaru that is humanoid but has wings and can fly.

Alloria Yurgen (*ah·LORE·ee·ah YURE·gen*) – the leader (Vituma) of the Dark Council. She is the 102nd leader since the Council's creation.

Alvaspirtu (*al·vah·SPEER·too*) – a large river that runs from the Heaven's Teeth mountains to the Kanton Sea. The

Gwenore River splits from it and travels al the way down to the Aesculun Ocean.

Amatia (*ah·MAH·tee·ah*) – a member of the Dark Council, a seeress.

Ander Tosselnam – one of the three High Itera of the Church of Vanda.

Animaru (*ah·nee·MAR·oo*) – dark creatures from the world Aruzhelim. The name means "dark creatures" or "dark animals."

Arania (*ah·RAH·nee·ah*) – a kingdom in the western part of the continent of Promistala, south and east of Shinyan.

Arba – an essentially extinct race of magical people whose ancestors were directly created by Mellaine out of the stuff of the forest and her magical tears. They had a special connection to nature and could use magic directly from the natural world.

Arcus (*ARK·us*) – the god of blacksmithing and devices.

Arcusheim (*AHR·coo·shime*) – a large city on the southern shore of the Kanton Sea, the capital of the nation of Sutania and the home of Erent Caahs before he left to travel the world.

Arto Deniselo (*AHR·toe day·NEE·say·low*) – a dueling master in the Aranian city of Vis Bena who taught Erent Caahs how to drastically improve his combat abilities.

Aruna (pl. Arunai) (*ah·ROON·ah; ah·roo·NIE*) – a citizen of the tribal nation of Campastra. Originally, the name was pejorative, referring to the color of their skin, but they embraced it and it became the legitimate name for the people in Campastra.

Aruzhelim (*ah·ROO·shel·eem*) – the world from which the animaru come. The name means "dark world," "dark universe," or "dark dimension." Aruzhelim is a planet physically removed from Dizhelim.

Asfrid Finndottir (ASS·*frid fin*·DOT·*teer*) – the Master of the School of Cryptology at the Hero Academy.

Assector Pruma (*ah*·SEC *tor* PROO·*mah*) – roughly "first student" in Alaqotim. This is the student aid to a master in one of the schools at the Hero Academy. There can be only one per school and this person conducts research, helps to teach classes, and assists the master in any other necessary task.

Atwyn Iaphor (AT·*win* EE·*ah*·*fore*) – a student at the Hero Academy, a companion of Quentin Duzen when he was still on campus.

Aubron Benevise (AW·*brun ben*·*uh*·VEES) – the Master of History and Literature at the Hero Academy.

Auxein (*awk*·ZAY·*in*) – an aide to the master and the First Student (Assector Pruma) at the Hero Academy. For larger schools, there may be more than one. In some schools there may not be any.

Awresea (*aw*·*reh*·SAY·*uh*) – a kingdom that no longer exists, the home of Tazi Ermenko who taunted the god Fyorio and was destroyed. The fiery, desolate location where the kingdom was is now known as Fyrefall.

Ayize Fudu (*aye*·EEZ FOO·*doo*) – a Hero Academy adept, one of Quentin Duzen's associates.

Barda Sirusel (BAR·*duh seer*·*oo*·SELL) – the boy who tried to bully Marla when she was a child.

Batido (*bah* TEE·*doe*) – what Aeden's friends call their dormitory, from the Dantogyptain words for *second home*.

Beldroth Zinrora (BEL·*droth zin*·ROR *uh*) – the Master of the School of Dark Magic at the Hero Academy.

Bernhard Lindner – the owner of the inn in Ebenrau where the party stays. He was smitten with Fahtin.

Bhagant (*bog*·AHNT) – the shortened form of the name for the Song of Prophecy, in the language Dantogyptain.

Bhavisyaganant (*bah·VIS·ya·gahn·ahnt*) – The full name for the Song of Prophecy in Dantogyptain. It means "the song of foretelling of the end," loosely translated.

Biuri (*bee·OOR·ee*) – small, quick animaru that recall the appearance and movements of rodents. They are useful as spies because of their small size and quickness.

Blennus (*blen·oos*) – Dannel Powfrey's horse.

Brace – the term used by the Falxen for a group of assassins ("blades").

Braitharlan (*brah·EE·thar·lan*) – the buddy assigned in the clan training to become a warrior. It means "blade brother" in Chorain.

Brausprech (*BROW·sprekh*) – a small town on the northwest edge of the Grundenwald forest, in the nation of Rhaltzheim. It is the hometown of Urun Chinowa.

Brenain Kanda (*bren·AY·in KAHN·duh*) – a mythological heroine who stole magic from the god Migae.

Bridgeguard – the small community, barely more than a guardpost, on the mainland end of the northern bridge to Munsahtiz

Broken Reach – a rugged, unforgiving land to the southeast of the Grundenwald. There are ruins of old fortifications there.

Cularel Kelhorn (*CAL·ar·el KEL·horn*) – one of the adepts at the Hero Academy who volunteered to aid in the investigation of Master Aeid's murder.

Campastra (*cam·PAHS·trah*) – a tribal nation in the southwestern portion of the continent of Promistala

Cara Moore – a member of the Dark Council.

Catriona (Ailgid) Tannoch (*CAT·ree·own·ah ILE·jid*) – the wife of Greimich Tannoch. She is originally from the Ailgid clan, but now has taken the last name Tannoch.

Ceti (*SET·ee*) – a higher level animaru, appearing aquatic with small tentacles, even though there is no water in Aruzhelim. They are very intelligent and have magical aptitude. Some of them are accomplished with weapons as well.

Chorain (*KHAW·rin*) – the ancestral language of the highland clans of the Cridheargla.

Clavian Knights (*CLAY·vee·en*) – the fighting force of the Grand Enclave, the finest heavy cavalry in Dizhelim.

Codaghan (*COD·ah·ghan*) – the god of war.

Cogiscro (*coe·JEE·scroe*) – an ancient system of runic writing that was used in magic spells. The symbols are phonetic and are arranged in a circular pattern.

Colechna (*co·LECK·nah*) – one of the higher levels of animaru. Theyappear to be at least part snake, typically highly intelligent as well as skilled with weapons. They are usually in the upper ranks of the command structure. Their agility and flexibility makes them dangerous enemies in combat. A few can use magic, but most are strictly melee fighters.

Corcan – one of the five highland clans of the Cridheargla.

Cridheargla (*cree·ARG·la*) – the lands of the highland clans. The word is a contraction of Crionna Crodhearg Fiacla in Chorain.

Crionna Crodhearg Fiacla (*cree·OWN·na CROW·arg FEE·cla*)) – the land of the highland clans. It means "old blood-red teeth" in Chorain, referring to the hills and mountains that abound in the area and the warlike nature of its people. The term is typically shortened to Cridheargla.

Croagh Aet Brech (*CROWGH ET BREKH*) – the name of the highland clans in Chorain. It means, roughly, "blood warriors." The clans sometimes refer to themselves simply as Croagh, from which their nickname "crows" sprang, foreigners not pronouncing their language correctly.

Daana Vaskova (*DAHN·ah vas·COVE·ah*) – a prophetess

and author who lived at the end of the Age of Magic. She wrote many children's tales, the majority of which had hidden meanings and prophecies.

Daibhidh Trebhin (*DAY·vid TREH·vin*) – the clan chief of the Trebhin clan when Aeden went to meet with the other clans of Croagh.

Dannel Powfrey – a self-proclaimed scholar from the Hero Academy who meets Aeden on his journey.

Danta (*DAHN·ta*) – the goddess of music and song. The language Dantogyptain is named after her.

Dantogyptain (*DAHN·toe·gip·TAY·in*) – the ancestral language of the Gypta people.

Daodh Gnath (*DOWGH GHRAY*) – the Croagh Ritual of Death, the cutting off of someone from the clans. The name means simply "death ceremony."

Daphne – one of the tavern maids at the Wolfen's Rest inn in Dartford.

Dared Moran (*DAR·ed·mo·RAN*) – the "Mayor" of Praesturi. Essentially, he's a crime boss who controls the town.

Darkcaller – one of the Falxen sent to kill Khrazhti and her companions. A former student at Sitor-Kanda, her specialty is dark magic.

Dark Council – a mysterious group of thirteen people who are trying to manipulate events in Dizhelim.

Dartford – a small town on the mainland near the north bridge to the island of Munsahtiz.

Darun Achaya (*dah·ROON ah·CHAI·ah*) – father of Fahtin, head of the family of Gypta that adopts Aeden.

Denore Felas (*den·OR FEHL·ahss*) – a great mage in the Age of Magic, the best friend of Tsosin Ruus.

Desaru (*day·SAW·roo*) – an area in Aruzhelim, site of at least two historic battles, including the one where Khrazhti's victory granted her the position of high priestess for S'ru.

Desid (*DAY·sid*) – a type of animaru. They're nearly

mindless, only able to follow simple commands, but they are fairly strong and tireless. They are about five feet tall with thick, clawed fingers useful for digging. They have the mentality of a young child.

Dizhelim (*DEESH·ay·leem*) – the world in which the story happens. The name means "center universe" in the ancient magical language Alaqotim.

Dmirgan (*DMEER·gen*) – a town in Kruzekstan, where a young Erent Caahs killed a man he thought was a murderer

Drachvorden (*drakh·VOOR·den*) – a city in existence during the Age of Magic. Two rogue mages, called the Power Twins, attacked the city and were killed by the hero Zejo Troufal.

Dreigan (*DRAY·gun*) – a mythical beast, a reptile that resembles a monstrous snake with four legs attached to its sides like a lizard. The slightly smaller cousin to the mythical dragons.

Drugancairn (*DROO·gan·cayrn*) – a small town on the southwest edge of the Grundenwald Forest.

Dubhghall Trebhin (*DOO·gall TREH·vin*) – one of the representatives of the Trebhin clan who went to fetch Aeden to come back and talk to the clan chiefs. He is abrasive and impolite.

Ebenrau (*EBB·en·ra·oo*) – the capital city of Rhaltzheim, one of the seven great cities in Dizhelim

Encalo (pl. encali) (*en·CAW·lo*) – four-armed, squat, powerful humanoids. There are few in Dizhelim, mostly in the western portion of the continent Promistala.

Epradotirum (*EP·rah·doe·TEER um*) – an extremely powerful entity who lives in another plane of existence, touching the mortal plane when, every few centuries, he is hungry. Aeden and some of his friends met the Epra while running from assassins near Satta Sarak.

Erent Caahs (*AIR·ent CAWS*) – the most famous of the

contemporary heroes. He disappeared twenty years before the story takes place, and is suspected to be dead, though his body was never found.

Erfinchen (*air·FEEN·chen*) – animaru that are shapeshifters. Though not intelligent and powerful enough to be leaders among the animaru, they are often at higher levels, though not in command of others. They typically perform special missions and are truly the closest thing to assassins the animaru have. A very few can use some magic.

Erlan Brymis (*ER·lan BRAI·miss*) – one of the adepts at the Hero Academy who volunteered to aid in the investigation of Master Aeid's murder.

Esiyae Yellynn (*ess·SEE·yay YELL·in*) – the Master of the School of Air Magic at the Hero Academy.

Espirion (*es·PEER·ee·on*) – the god of plans and schemes. From his name comes the terms espionage and spy.

Eutychus Naevius (*YOO·tik·us NAY·vee·us*) – a renowned mathematician in ancient times. One of his principles, the third theorem of alternating magical series, was the key Marla used to decrypt Ren Kenata's letters.

Evindia Elkien (*eh·VIN·dee·ah EL·kee·en*) – a member of the Dark Council.

Evon Desconse – a graduate of the famed Hero Academy and best friend to Marla Shrike.

Exulmucri (*EX·ool·MOO·cree*) – an ancient game of strategy, thought to be the first of its kind. It was also the first game to use dice.

Fahtin Achaya (*FAH·teen ah·CHAI·ah*) – a young Gypta girl in the family that adopted Aeden. She and Aeden grew as close as brother and sister in the four years he spent with the family.

Falxen (*FAL·ksen*) – an assassin organization, twelve of whom go after Aeden and his friends. The members are commonly referred to as "Blades."

Featherblade – one of the Falxen sent to kill Khrazhti and her companions. He is the leader of the brace and his skill with a sword is supreme.

Fireshard – one of the Falxen sent to kill Khrazhti and her companions. She wields fire magic.

Forgren (*FORE·gren*) – a type of animaru that is tireless and single-minded. They are able to memorize long messages and repeat them exactly, so they make good messengers. They have no common sense and almost no problem-solving skills

Formivestu (*form·ee·VES·too*) – the insect creatures that attacked Tere's group when they were on their way to Sitor-Kanda. They look like giant ants with human faces and were thought to be extinct.

Fyorio (*fee·YORE·ee·oh*) – the god of fire and light, from whose name comes the word *fyre*, spelled *fire* in modern times.

Fyrefall – a desolate and dangerous land in the south central part of Promistala, full of hot pools, geysers, and other signs of volcanic activity.

Gamore Nabavian (*gah·MORE nah·BAHV·ee en*) – one of the Power Twins, rogue mages killed by the hero Zejo Troufal in the city of Drachvorden just after the War of Magic ended.

Gareth Briggs – a member of the Dark Council.

Gentason (*jen·TAY·sun*) – an ancient nation, enemy of Salamus. It no longer exists.

Gneisprumay (*gNAYS·proo·may*) – first (or most important) enemy. The name for the Malatirsay in the animaru dialect of Alaqotim.

Godan Chul (*GO·dahn CHOOL*) – an ancient mythological race of spirit beings, created accidentally from the magic of the God of Magic, Migae. The name means, roughly "spirit's whisper."

Goren Adnan – the Master of the School of Military Strategy at the Hero Academy.

Graduate (at the Hero Academy) – a student of the Hero Academy who is either an adept or a viro/vira. That is, anyone who has mastered at least three schools at the Academy and is either still studying there or has left the school.

Great Enclave – a nation to the west of the Kanton Sea and the Hero Academy.

Greimich Tannoch (*GREY·mikh TAN·ahkh*) – Aeden's close friend, his braitharlan, during his training with the clans.

Grundenwald Forest (*GROON·den·vahld*) – the enormous forest in the northeastern part of the main continent of Promistala. It is said to be the home of magic and beasts beyond belief.

Gulra (pl. gulrae) (*GUL·rah; GUL·ray*) – an animaru that walks on four legs and resembles a large, twisted dog. These are used for tracking, using their keen sense of smell like a hound.

Gwenore River – a large river that splits off from the Alvaspirtu and travels south, through Satta Sarak and all the way to the Aesculun Ocean

Gypta (*GIP·tah*) – the traveling people, a nomadic group that lives in wagons, homes on wheels, and move about, never settling down into towns or villages.

Hamrath – a small town on the coast of the eastern part of the Kanton Sea, just north of the bridge from the mainland to Munsahtiz Island.

Hane Bryce – a member of the Dark Council.

Harlen Sayla (*HAR·len SAY·lah*) – the leader of the homeless group of people living in the caves under the city of Ebenrau.

Heaven's Teeth – the range of mountains to the east of the Kanton sea, in between that body of water and the Grundenwald Forest.

Ianthra (*ee·ANTH·rah*) – the Goddess of Love and Beauty.

Ianthra's Breasts (*ee·ANTH·rah*) – a mountain range between Arcusheim in Sutania and Satta Sarak. Even though there are three peaks, the two that dominate were named for the physical attributes of the Goddess of Love and Beauty, Ianthra.

Inna Moroz (*EEN·ah MOE·roze*) – a Hero Academy adept, one of Quentin Duzen's associates.

Iowyn Selen (*EE·o·win SELL·en*) – a great mage in the Age of Magic, the love of Tsosin Ruus's life.

Iracundamel (*EER·ah·COON·dah·mel*) – the ancient name for the well of power at the center of the Mellafond swamp. The name means, roughly, *nature's wrath* or *Mellaine's wrath*.

Iryna Vorona (*ee·REEN·ah voe·rone·ah*) – Master of the School of Interrogation and Coercion at the Hero Academy.

Isbal Deyne (*ISS·bahl DANE*) – a member of the Dark Council.

Iscopsuru (*ee·SCOP·soo·roo*) – the name of Benzal's fortress outside of Nanris in Kruzekstan; it's over eight hundred years old. The name means Rock of Surus in Alaqotim.

Isegrith Palas (*ISS·eh·grith PAL·us*) – the Master of Fundamental Magic at the Hero Academy.

Itera (*ee·TARE·ah*) – high level functionaries in the Vandan Church. They are essentially the second level from the top, though the High Itera, the top three of their number, are above the rest, just below the Patr Pruma.

Izhrod Benzal (*EESH·rod ben·ZAHL*) – a powerful magic-user, one who has learned to make portals between Aruzhelim and Dizhelim. The dark god S'ru has an agreement with him so he is second to none in authority over the animaru on Dizhelim.

Jarnorun (*jar·NOR·un*) – an animaru lord, one of Kirraloth's two main commanders.

Jehira Sinde (*jay·HEER·ah SINDH*) – Raki's grandmother (nani) and soothsayer for the family of Gypta that adopts Aeden.

Jhanda Dalavi (*JON·dah dah·LAHV·ee*) – the Head Scrivener at the Hero Academy. He is in charge of the small army of scribes who make copies of books and who create many of the records necessary for the functioning of the school.

Jia Toun (*JEE·ah TOON*) – an expert thief and assassin who was formerly the Falxen named Shadeglide. She uses her real name now that she has joined Aeden's group of friends and allies.

Jintu Devexo (*JEEN·too day·VEX·oh*) – the high chieftain of the Arunai during the time of the false Malatirsay.

Josef – the owner of the Wolfen's Rest inn in Dartford, a friend of Marla Shrike.

Jusha Terlix (*JOO·shah TER·liks*) – the Master of the School of Mental Magic at the Hero Academy.

Kaeso Hiberus (*KAY·sew hi·BEER·us*) – the author of the holy book of the Church of Vanda, the Vindictae. He claims to be the prophet of Vanda and that he was given the information directly from the god at the end of the Age of Magic.

Kanton Sea (*KAN·tahn*) – an inland sea in which the island of Munsahtiz, home of the Hero Academy, sits.

Kebahn Faitar (Kebahn the Wise) (*kay·BAWN FYE·tahr*) – the advisor and friend to Thomasinus; the one who actually came up with the idea to gather all the scattered people and make a stand at the site of what is now the Great Enclave.

Khrazhti (*KHRASH·tee*) – the former High Priestess to the dark god S'ru and former leader of the animaru forces on

Dizhelim. At the discovery that her god was untrue, she has become an ally and friend to Aeden.

Kirraloth (*KEER·uh·loth*) – an animaru high lord, given the command of all animaru on Dizhelim after Suuksis failed to turn or destroy Khrazhti.

Kruzekstan (*KROO·zek·stahn*) – a small nation due south of the highland clan lands of Cridheargla.

Kryzt (*KRIZT*) – a type of animaru with spikes all over it, shaped roughly like a wolf but with a longer tail. It has sharp claws and teeth.

Leafburrow – a village in Rhaltzheim, north of Arcusheim off the River Road, the location of a bandit ambush where Erent Caahs demonstrated his special spinning arrow technique.

Leaf Talker – the historical name for an arba community's leader.

Lela Ganeva (*LEE·lah·gahn·AY·vah*) – the woman Erent Caahs fell in love with.

Lerus Costanti (*lehr·OOS coe·STAN·tee*) – one of the three High Itera of the Church of Vanda.

Lesnum (*LESS·num*) – large, hairy, beastlike animaru. These sometimes walk around on two feet, but more commonly use all four limbs. They are strong and fast and intelligent enough to be used as sergeants, commanding groups of seren and other low-level animaru.

Leul Abrete (*LOOL ah·BREET*) – a traveling merchant for whom Skril Tossin searches to get information in the murder investigation of Master Aeid.

Lilianor (Lili) Caahs (*LI·lee·ah·nore CAWS*) – Erent Cahhs's little sister; she was murdered when she was eleven years old.

Liluth Olaxidor (*LIL·uth oh·LAX·ih·door*) – the Master of the School of Firearms at the Hero Academy.

Lily Fisher – an archer of supreme skill who was

formerly the Falxen assassin named Phoenixarrow. She uses her real name now that she has joined Aeden's group of friends and allies.

Lis (*LEES*) – a minor deity who battled the sun, nearly killing it, and causing so much damage that to this day, it is weakened in the wintertime.

Lucas Stewart – a young student at the Hero Academy. He's often used by the masters as a messenger because of his strong work ethic and reliability.

Lucio Sanctus (*LOO·chee·oh SAHNK·toos*) – the Patr Pruma of the Vandan Church.

Lusnauqua (*loos·NOW·kwah*) – the rugged land surrounding Broken Reach, in the center of the eastern section of the continent of Promistala.

Malatirsay (*Mahl·ah·TEER·say*) – the hero who will defeat the animaru and save Dizhelim from the darkness, according to prophecy. The name means "chosen warrior" or "special warrior" in Alaqotim.

Manandantan (*mahn·ahn·DAHN·tahn*) – the festival to celebrate the goddess Danta, goddess of song.

Marla Shrike – a graduate of the famed Hero Academy, an experienced combatant in both martial and magical disciplines.

Marn Tiscomb – the new Master of Prophecy at the Hero Academy. He replaced Master Aeid, who was murdered.

Mellafond (*MEH·la·fond*) – a large swamp on the mainland to the east of Munsahtiz Island. The name *means pit of Mellaine.*

Mellaine (*meh·LAYN*) – goddess of nature and growing things.

Miera Tannoch (*MEERA TAN·ahkh*) – Aeden's mother, wife of Sartan.

Migae (*MEE·jay*) – the God of magic. The word "magic" comes from his name.

Mionn Bhais (*MYOON BAJH*) – the Death Oath, a tradition set forth at the beginning of the Croagh clans. It consists of a magical ritual that binds the clan chiefs to either submit to one leader or to challenge that leader in combat to the death.

Misun (*MEE·sun*) – the arba woman Urun's group encountered in the Mellafond who led them to the arba village.

Moroshi Katai (*mor·ROE·shee kah·TAI*) – a mythological hero who battled the Dragon of Eternity to found the nation of Teroshi.

Moschephis (*mose·CHE·feess*) – the trickster god, from whose name comes the word mischief.

Mudertis (*moo·DARE·teez*) – the god of thievery and assassination.

Munsahtiz (*moon·SAW·teez*) – the island in the Kanton sea on which the Hero Academy Sitor-Kanda resides.

Nanris – the unofficial capital of Kruzekstan, more important than the actual capital of Kruzeks because most of the wealth of the nation is centered in Nanris.

Nasir Kelqen (*nah·SEER KEL·ken*) – the Master of the School of Research and Investigation at the Hero Academy.

Omri – a fair sized city in northern Kruzekstan, one of the first of the cities to fall to the animaru.

Osulin (*AWE·soo·lin*) – goddess of nature. She is the daughter of Mellaine and the human hero Trikus Phen.

Pach (*PAHKH*) – in Dantogyptain, it means five. As a proper noun, it refers to the festival of Manandantan that occurs every fifth year, a special celebration in which the Song of Prophecy is sung in full.

Padraig Seachaid (*PAD·reg SHAW·chid*) – the clan chief of the Seachaid Croagh clan.

Patr Pruma (*POT·er PROO·mah*) – the leader of the Church of Vanda.

Pedras Shrike – Marla Shrike's adoptive father, the groundskeeper for the administrative area of the Hero Academy.

Percipius (*pare·CHIP·ee·us*) – god of the dead and of the underworld.

Phoenixarrow – one of the Falxen sent to kill Khrazhti and her companions. A statuesque red-haired archer who had a penchant for using fire arrows.

Pilae (*PEEL·lay*) – a type of animaru that looks like a ball of shadow.

Pofel Dessin (*POE·fell DESS·in*) – a traveling scholar who meets Marla and Evon on their journeys.

Pouran (*PORE·an*) – roundish, heavy humanoids with piggish faces and tusks like a boar

Praesturi (*prayz·TURE·ee*) – the town and former military outpost on the southeastern tip of the island of Munsahtiz. The south bridge from the mainland to the island ends within Praesturi.

Preshim (*PRAY·sheem*) – title of the leader of a family of Gypta

Promistala (*prome·ees·TAHL·ah*) – the main continent in Dizhelim. In Alaqotim, the name means "first (or most important) land."

Qozhel (*KOE·shell*) – the energy that pervades the universe and that is usable as magic.

Quentin Duzen – a Hero Academy graduate, the antagonist against Marla and Evon.

Qydus Okvius (*KIE·duss OCK·vee·us*) – the headmaster of the Hero Academy, Sitor-Kanda.

Raibrech (*RAI·brekh*) – the clan magic of the highland clans. In Chorain, it means "bloodfire."

Raimund Bainer (*RAY·mund BANE·er*) – one of the three High Itera of the Church of Vanda.

Raisor Tannoch (*RAI·sore TAN·ahkh*) – a famous warrior of Clan Tannoch, companion of the hero Erent Caahs.

Raki Sinde (*ROCK·ee SINDH*) – grandson of Jehira Sinde, friend and training partner of Aeden.

Ren Kenata (*REN ke·NAH·tah*) – a Hero Academy adept who was is not only one of Quentin Duzen's associates, but also a member of the Dark Council.

Rhaltzheim (*RALTZ·haim*) – the nation to the northeast of the Grundenwald Forest. The people of the land are called Rhaltzen or sometimes Rhaltza. The term Rhaltzheim is often used to refer to the rugged land within the national borders (e.g., "traverse the Rhaltzheim")

Ritma Achaya (*REET·mah ah·CHAI·ah*) – Fahtin's mother, wife of the Gypta family leader Darun.

Roneus Lomos (*ROE·nee·us LOE·mose*) – the Master of the School of Stealth at the Hero Academy.

Ruthrin (*ROOTH·rin*) – the common tongue of Dizhelim, the language virtually everyone in the world speaks in addition to their own national languages.

S'ru (*SROO*) – the dark god of the animaru, supreme power in Aruzhelim.

Saelihn Valdove (*SAY·lin VAHL·doe·vay*) – the Master of the School of Life Magic at the Hero Academy.

Saevel (*SAY·vell*) – the arba huntress who guided Urun's group through the Mellafond swamp.

Salamus (*sah·lah·MOOS*) – an ancient nation in which the legendary hero Trikus Phen resided. It no longer exists. Things of Salamus were called Salaman.

Sartan Tannoch (*SAR·tan TAN·ahkh*) – Aeden's father, clan chief of the Tannoch clan of Craogh.

Sastiroz (*SASS·teer·oz*) – an animaru lord, one of Kirraloth's two main commanders.

Satta Sarak (*SAH·tah SARE·ack*) – a city in the southeastern part of the continent of Promistala, part of the Saraki Principality.

Semhominus (*sem·HOM·in·us*) – one of the highest level of animaru. They are humanoid, larger than a typical human, and use weapons. Many of them can also use magic. Most animaru lords are of this type.

Seachaid (*SHAW·chid*) – one of the five highland clans of the Cridheargla.

Senna Shrike – Marla Shrike's adoptive mother.

Seoras Corcan (*SORE·us*) – the clan chief of the Corcan clan of Croagh.

Seren (*SARE·en*) – the most common type of animaru, with sharp teeth and claws. They are similar in shape and size to humans.

Shadeglide – one of the Falxen sent to kill Khrazhti and her companions. She is small of stature but extremely skilled as a thief and assassin.

Shadowed Pinnacles – the long mountain range essentially splitting the western part of Promistala into two parts. It was formerly known as the Wall of Salamus because it separated that kingdom from Gentason.

Shaku (*SHOCK·oo*) – a class of Teroshimi assassins.

Shanaera Eilren (*shah·NARE·ah ALE·ren*) – the Master of Unarmed Combat at the Hero Academy.

Shinyan (*SHEEN·yahn*) – a nation on the northern tip of the western part of Promistala, bordering the Kanton Sea and the Cattilan Sea. Things of Shinyan (such as people) are referred to as Shinyin.

Shu root/Shu's Bite (*SHOO*) – a root that only grows in Shinyan, the key ingredient to the poison Shu's Bite.

Sike (*SEEK·ay*) – a class of Shinyin assassins

Sintrovis (*seen·TROE·vees*) – an area of high magical power on which the Great Enclave was built. In Alaqotim, it means *center of strength*.

Sirak Isayu (*SEER·ack ee·SAI·yoo*) – a member of the Dark Council. He comes from the southern part of the continent of Promistala, near the Sittingham Desert.

Sitor-Kanda (*SEE·tor KAN·dah*) – the Hero Academy, the institution created by the great prophet Tsosin Ruus to train the Malatirsay. The name means roughly "home of magic" in Alaqotim.

Sittingham Desert – a large desert in the southwestern part of Promistala.

Skril Tossin – best friend of Marla Shrike and Evon Desconce, a Hero Academy adept.

Snowmane – the horse the Academy lent to Aeden, a chestnut stallion with a white mane

Solon (*SEW·lahn*) – one of the masters in Clan Tannoch, responsible for training young warriors how to use the clan magic, the Raibrech.

Souvenia (*soo·VEN·ee·ah*) – an empire that was one of the world powers before the War of Magic, and one of the major players in that war. It no longer exists.

Srantorna (*sran·TORN·ah*) – the abode of the gods, a place where humans cannot go.

Surefoot – Marla Shrike's horse.

Surus (*SOO·roos*) – king of the gods.

Sutania (*soo·TAN·ee·ah*) – the nation south of the Kanton Sea, the capital of which is the city of Arcusheim.

Suuksis (*SOOK·sis*) – an animaru lord; Khrazhti's father.

Tannoch (*TAN·ahkh*) – one of the five highland clans of the Cridheargla, the one to which Aeden was born into.

Taron Gennelis (*TARE·un jeh·NELL·iss*) – one of the adepts at the Hero Academy who volunteered to aid in the investigation of Master Aeid's murder.

Tarshuk (*TAR·shuk*) – a semi-desert-like area to the southwest of the Heaven's Teeth range that has stunted trees and scrub.

Tazi Ermengo (*TAH·zee air·MANE·go*) – the king of the doomed kingdom of Awresea. He taunted the god Fyorio and was destroyed along with his entire kingdom, which was renamed Fyrefall.

Tere Chizzit (*TEER CHIZ·it*) – a blind archer and tracker with the ability to see despite having no working eyes. He is Aeden's companion in the story.

Teroshi (*tare·OH·shee*) – an island nation in the northern part of Dizhelim. Things of Teroshi, including people, are referred to as Teroshimi.

Thalia Fendove (*THA·lee·uh FEN·doe·vay*) – a member of the Dark Council.

Thomasinus, son of Daven (*toe·mah·SINE·us*) – the hero who banded the remnants of the troops of Gentason together to create the Great Enclave. Once they elected him king, he changed his last name to Davenson.

Thomlin Byrch (*TOM·lin BIRCH*) – a member of the Dark Council.

Thritur Nyhus (*THRY·tur NY·hus*) – a member of the Dark Council.

Tildus Uworn (*TIL·duss YOO·worn*) – a Hero Academy adept, one of Quentin Duzen's associates.

Toan Broos (*TOE·aan*) – traveling companion of Erent Caahs and Raisor Tannoch.

Toras Geint (*TOR·ahs GAYNT*) – an old tracker and scout who befriended Erent Caahs when he was a boy and who mentored the young hero, training him to track and hunt, among other things.

Trebhin (*TREH·vin*) – one of the five highland clans of the Cridheargla.

Trikus Phen (*TRY·kus FEN*) – a legendary hero who battled Codaghan, the god of war, himself, and sired Osulin by the goddess Mellaine.

Tsosin Ruus (*TSO·sin ROOS*) – the Prophet, the seer and archmage who penned the Song of Prophecy and founded Sitor-Kanda, the Hero Academy.

Tuach (*TOO·akh*) – one of the masters in Clan Tannoch, responsible for teaching the young warriors the art of physical combat.

Tufa Shao (*TOO·fah SHA·oh*) – the Master of the School of Body Mechanics and Movement at the Hero Academy.

Tukra (*TOOK·rah*) – an ancient magical being whose responsibility was to guard a door in the tunnels of Valcordinae.

Ulfaris Triban (*ool·FARE·iss TRY·ban*) – a Hero Academy graduate, companion to Izhrod Benzal

Urtumbrus (*oor·TOOM·brus*) – a type of animaru that are essentially living shadows.

Urun Chinowa (*OO·run CHIN·oh·wah*) – the High Priest of the goddess Osulin, a nature priest.

Vadim Plesca (*VAH·deem PLES·kah*) – a mage during the Age of Magic, a close associate to Aquilius Gavros.

Vaeril Faequin (*VARE·ill FAY·kwin*) – the Master of the School of Mechanista Artifice at the Hero Academy.

Valcordinae (*val·COR·di·nay*) – a series of extremely ancient tunnels with a well of magical power at its core. The word is ancient Alaqotim for *strong minds*.

Vanda (*VAHN·dah*) – a modern god, claimed by his followers to be the only true god. It is said he is many gods in one, having different manifestations. The Church of Vanda is very large and very powerful in Dizhelim.

Vandictae (*vahn·DIC·tay*) – the book of holy writings of the Church of Vanda.

Vatheca (*VATH·ay·kuh*) – the headquarters and training center of the Falxen. It is a mixture of two Alaqotim words, both meaning "sheath."

Videric Dewitte (*VEE·dare·ic deh·VIT*) – the Master of the School of Magical Healing at the Hero Academy.

Vincus (pl. vinci) (*VEEN·cuss; VEEN·chee*) – Aila's chain blade weapons.

Viro/Vira (pl viri) (*VEER·oh / VEER·ah / VEER·ee*) – a former Hero Academy student who has graduated with a mastery in at least three schools and no longer lives at the Academy or participates in its function.

Vituma (*vi·TOO·mah*) – the leader of the Dark Council. The name derives from the ancient Alaqotim term for *prophet's shadow*.

Voordim (*VOOR·deem*) – the pantheon of gods in Dizhelim. It does not include the modern god Vanda.

Vora (*VORE·ah*) – the Leaf Talker of the tribe of arba in the Mellafond swamp

Vulmer Liadin (*VUL·mer LEE·uh·din*) – the first headmaster of the Hero Academy, appointed by Tsosin Ruus himself to run the school for the Prophet.

Wolfen – large intelligent wolves that roam desolate areas in the Rhaltzheim.

Wolfen's Rest – the inn in Dartford, on the mainland not too far east from the bridge to the island of Munsahtiz.

Xadorn Deleer (*ZAH·dorn de·LEER*) – one of the Power Twins, rogue mages killed by the hero Zejo Troufal in the city of Drachvorden just after the War of Magic ended.

Yezras Farlingian (*YEZ·rass far LIN·gee·an*) – the Master of the School of Conjuration and Invocation at the Hero Academy.

Yoniko Takesi (*YOE·nee·koe tah·KAY·see*) – a member of the Dark Council.

Yralissa Zinphinal (*eer·ah·LISS·ah ZIN·fin·all*) – the Master of the School of Illusion at the Hero Academy.

Yxna Hagenai (*IX·nah HAG·en·eye*) – the Master of Edged Weapons at the Hero Academy.

Zejo Troufal (*ZAY·joe TROO·fahl*) – a hero who lived at the end of the Age of Magic. He was Erent Cahhs's idol when he was a boy, before he himself became a hero.

Zhadril (*ZHAD·reel*) – an animaru mage—former high priest of S'ru—who was defeated in battle by Khrazhti to lose his position. In Dizhelim, he was given permission to study corrupted magic in a swamp area.

LETTER TO THE READER

Dear Reader,

What did you think of Urun's adventure? In most of my books, I try to give some insight into how several different characters think and feel about the events that happen, but with the Hero Academy series, I'm making an effort to delve deeper into the thoughts and feelings of the many fascinating characters. I still switch viewpoints at times, but in general one of the supporting characters in the entire saga is given a chance to shine in a story of their own for each book. I hope you're enjoying it because I find that I really like writing stories from the different characters' points of view.

As for the overall story of the Hero Academy (and Song of Prophecy) series, we're just getting started. The tension is building, the animaru are increasing, and things are afoot that we had no inkling of a book or two ago. Urun and his friends are going to need every ounce of courage, skill, and experience to make it through the gauntlet they'll have to face. Will you be there with them?

I appreciate you sharing in not only Urun's adventures, but those of the other heroes of Dizhelim. Believe me, there is a lot more to come, including the answers to some of the mysteries that are building as each new book is released.

If you'd like to learn more about some of the captivating characters in Dizhelim, aside from those who are highlighted in the main series books, I have other novels set in the world that I give out for free to my newsletter subscribers. Besides being kept up to date on what's coming out and where the different series are going, there are plenty of freebie reads that might interest you. If that sounds interesting to you, you can join by going to my website at https://pepadilla.com. I hope to see you there.

P.E. Padilla

AUTHOR NOTES

This year (2020) was an interesting one. Not only was the world afflicted with the Coronavirus and all the resultant issues, but my writing took on a life of its own. I had the idea in the early part of the year to rapid-release six or seven books about a month apart and got everything in place in July of 2020. From that month until this one (I'm writing this in late December 2020), I got six books prepared for launch. The sixth, this one, launches on December 31st.

There is another book that is completely written and has cover art, but won't be edited until the beginning of the year so my editor can have some time off for the holidays. It'll be the seventh book, though it will launch a bit more than a month after this one.

I learned a lot from the experience, but mostly that I won't be putting out a book a month again in the near future. I still plan on writing and launching several books a year, but coordinating editing and cover art, self-editing, working with my editor, formatting, and of course writing all the books at that pace is a bit too much right now. I'm sure I'll do a string of one-per-month books again in the future, but for now, I need to catch up on everything else and take a breather.

Have no fear, though. I have the entire Hero Academy series planned out and have plotted out the next several books specifically. I have a lot of work to do on timelines, maps, and how exactly I'll handle the things I know will happen but haven't drilled down to the fine details yet. It's going to be a fun ride.

ABOUT THE AUTHOR

A chemical engineer by degree and at various times an air quality engineer, a process control engineer, and a regulatory specialist by vocation, USA Today bestselling author P.E. Padilla learned long ago that crunching numbers and designing solutions was not enough to satisfy his creative urges. Weaned on classic science fiction and fantasy stories from authors as diverse as Heinlein, Tolkien, and Jordan, and affected by his love of role playing games such as Dungeons and Dragons (analog) and Final Fantasy (digital), he sometimes has trouble distinguishing reality from fantasy. While not ideal for a person who needs to function in modern society, it's the perfect state of mind for a writer. He is a recent transplant from Southern California to Northern Washington, where he lives surrounded by trees.

pepadilla.com/
pep@pepadilla.com

ALSO BY P.E. PADILLA

Adventures in Gythe:

Vibrations: Harmonic Magic Book 1 (audiobook also)

Harmonics: Harmonic Magic Book 2 (audiobook also)

Resonance: Harmonic Magic Book 3

Tales of Gythe: Gray Man Rising (audiobook also available)

Harmonic Magic Series Boxed Set

The Unlikely Hero Series (under pen name Eric Padilla):

Unfurled: Heroing is a Tough Gig (Unlikely Hero Series Book 1) (also available as an audiobook)

Unmasked (Unlikely Hero Series Book 2)

Undaunted (Unlikely Hero Series Book 3)

The Shadowling Chronicles (under pen name Eric Padilla):

Shadowling (Book 1)

Witches of the Elements Series :

Water & Flame (Book 1)

Song of Prophecy Series :

Wanderer's Song

Warrior's Song

Heroes' Song

Hero Academy Series :

Hero Dawning

Hero's Mind

Hero's Nature (this book)

Tales of Dizhelim (companion stories to the SoP and HA Series):

Arrow's Flight

Song's Prophet

Order of the Fire Series:

Call of Fire

Hero of Fire

Legacy of Fire

Order of the Fire Boxed Set